Love At 11

MARI MANCUSI

ISBN-13: 978-1-48405-154-2

PRAISE FOR LOVE AT 11

"Sassy, clever, and surprisingly heartwarming."
—Gemma Halliday, *NY Times* bestselling author

"What a great read by Mari Mancusi! Heart warming, funny, sweet and a page turner from start to finish!"
—Tara Sivec, bestselling author of *Seduction and Snacks*

"Zany, humorously flippant and surprisingly emotionally moving amidst the chaos of modern life!"
—*Merrimon Book Reviews*

"Mari Mancusi has a great sense of humor and isn't afraid to use it."
—*Once Upon a Romance*

"Hilarious and enjoyable."
—*The Romance Readers Connection*

"So much fun to read...Love At 11 is one book you won't be sorry you picked up."
—*Single Titles*

"Another winner from Mari Mancusi."
—*Joyfully Reviewed*

PROLOGUE

I still couldn't believe I was actually doing this.

Clutching the videotape in one Clutching the videotape in one trembling hand, I strode down the hallway, heading for what in the TV news world we called Receive. The place where my story could broadcast to the world. Well, at least the world of San Diego. Receive was the gateway to the airwaves, and its guardians had no idea what they were about to let loose.

In just minutes, my career at News 9 would be over forever. Heck, they'd probably blacklist me from ever setting foot in a TV station again. My dream of working at *Newsline* would never come true. But it didn't matter. I didn't want to work in a business that was as corrupt as I'd recently determined it to be.

The truth was more important. My sister and the others like her were more important.

My heart slammed against my rib cage as I pushed open the door. The Receive coordinator gave me a stressed smile before going back to organizing the videotapes for tonight's broadcast. I smiled back, knowing from her look that no one had time to check to see what was on the tape I delivered.

I took a deep breath. This was it.

"This is for you, Lulu," I whispered to myself, then handed the coordinator the tape. "Here's tonight's feature story. 'Cosmetics That Kill.'"

I held my breath as she took the tape and examined the label. *Please don't check, please don't check.*

"Great," she smiled, filing the tape in its appropriate slot for the five o'clock news. "Thanks, Maddy."

It was done.

CHAPTER ONE

TWO MONTHS EARLIER…

FROM: "Laura Smith" <lsmith@news9.com>

TO: "Madeline Madison" <mmadison@news9.com>

SUBJECT: re: story idea

Hi Maddy,

Thank you for your story idea about how dangerous blind spots behind SUVs have caused parents to inadvertently back over their own children--striking them down in their very driveway. It's distressing to hear that more than 72 kids died last year alone in this horrific manner.

But after talking it over with the promotions department, we think it'd be better if you could just stick with the "Cosmetics That Kill" story we assigned you last week.

```
Thanks!

Laura
Executive Producer
News 9 —San Diego, CA
```

I pressed "delete" and leaned back in my squeaky cubicle chair, suppressing a long sigh of frustration.

Why was I even surprised?

After two years of working as an assistant producer at "if it bleeds, it leads" News 9, I knew I should have been used to the rejection of thought-provoking, legitimate stories in exchange for sensationalistic trash. I should have been content pitching the plastic surgery, the diet, the who-is-Paris-Hilton-sleeping-with-now stories.

I was a glutton for punishment.

I should have known that my boss Laura didn't want to do a story about SUVs with dangerous blind spots. News 9 aired advertisements for those same SUVs during its commercial breaks. Paid advertisements. It was simple as that.

"Hey, Maddy, why the long face, girl?"

The voice of my coworker and best friend Jodi brought me back from my job-induced doom and gloom. Spinning around in my chair, I watched the five-ten blonde plop herself down at my cubicle-mate's vacant desk and look at me with concerned eyes.

"Oh, nothing. Just the usual," I said with a shrug. "Typical day at News Nine, San Diego."

"Uh-oh." Jodi grinned. "I know that look. What is it this time? Deadly Dishwashers? Perilous Pets? Killer Clay?" she mocked in her best TV newsman voice.

"Killer Clay was last month," I reminded her. "This episode of the fabulous *Household Products That Kill* series features murderous makeup."

"Oh dear," Jodi said, feigning shock. "I'm going to have to rethink my whole morning routine."

I swatted at her with the back of my hand.

"I mean, don't get me wrong," I said. "It's not that I'm against informing the public against the hidden dangers of Mary Kay and the rest. It's just that as far as I can tell cosmetics simply don't kill. Ever. Like, in the history of cosmetics there hasn't been a single fatality."

"Did you look up ancient Egypt? I read once that they wore makeup. Maybe someone crushed up a poison berry or something."

I rolled my eyes, not even dignifying that with a response.

The problem was, the powers-that-be at News 9 didn't care that cosmetics didn't actually kill; it sounded good in the promo and that was all that mattered. If the station could convince the twenty-four- to fifty-five-year-old woman who planned to go to bed after she saw who got fired, kicked off the island, or brutally humiliated by an arrogant Brit named Simon, to stay up and watch the evening news, that was enough. And they believed scaring her half to death was the best way to accomplish this goal.

Two years ago, I, Maddy Madison, graduated from the ivory tower of journalistic ethics, Columbia University, ready to save the world. Expose the bad guys. Right society's wrongs. Be the voice of truth in a sea of lies.

Boy, was I an idiot.

Anyone who thinks TV news has anything—and I mean *anything*—to do with journalism should take a major reality pill. Our business is entertainment. Period.

Except on those network TV magazine shows. Like *60 Minutes*, *20/20*, *48 Hours* or my favorite—*Newsline*. *Newsline* did important stories. They uncovered scandals and weren't afraid to name the bad guys. It'd been my dream to become a producer for *Newsline* ever since their star investigative reporter Diane Dickson came to speak at my high school ten years ago. She'd been so cool. So smart. So polished and important. I'd hero-worshiped her ever since.

So, I continued to toil away at local news producing, honing my résumé videotape and hoping that someday I'd have enough experience to be worthy of walking the same halls as

Diane and the gang.

Hey, a girl could dream.

"I've got some news that may cheer you up," Jodi announced.

"Oh?" I asked, crossing my fingers for jelly donuts at the assignment desk.

"They hired a new photographer. And he's to *die* for!"

"Perfect." I grinned. "I'd been thinking of pitching 'Fatal Photographers' at the next story meeting. Do you think he'll agree to be interviewed?"

"Hah!" Jodi laughed appreciatively. "But seriously, Maddy. He's really hot."

"Easy, tiger," I warned. "You're taken, remember?" Jodi, a dog freak, met the man of her dreams a couple years back on Dog Beach, a pet friendly patch of sand on the northern border of San Diego's Ocean Beach. Her three male Great Danes came bounding over to sniff the butt of his delicate female Italian greyhound, and the rest, as they say, was history. The two got married a year ago and live happily ever after, squashed into a hair-infested, Great Dane/Italian greyhound-filled bungalow on the shores of Ocean Beach. Luckily, neither could afford much furniture.

"But you're still single," Jodi reminded me with a sly smile, brushing dog hair from her otherwise adorable black sweater.

Typical. She was *always* trying to set me up, so I'd have a fourth wheel to balance things when we all went out. In fact, she was so desperate for me to get a boyfriend she'd been less than selective with her set-ups than I might have desired.

I mean, sure there's probably a woman out there for the guy who thought a replica Captain Kirk uniform was proper attire for a first date. And I imagine it'll be quite simple for that man with a penchant for farting at dinner to find the woman who better appreciates his bodily functions. And the guy who was so cheap he made me write an IOU when I needed a quarter for the bubblegum machine? I bet his Mrs. Right's just around the corner.

So when Jodi got that excited matchmaking gleam in her

blue eyes, my guard immediately went up.

"What's he look like?"

"Go see for yourself. He's in the newsroom."

"I don't know. I've got to go work on 'Cosmetics That Kill.' It edits Tuesday and I've yet to find a single person who will agree to be interviewed on the topic."

Jodi put on a mock pout. "Fine. Go ahead and work. But when Christine in sales snatches this one, you'll be sorry you didn't get to him first."

I was saved by the bell—my phone rang. I hesitated before picking up the receiver: It was an inside ring, which meant someone somewhere in the building wanted something from me. This could be as simple as "Where's the tease for last night's story?" or as bad as "You're fired, pack up your desk and leave." That's how it worked at News 9.

Curiosity won out over common sense and I put the receiver to my ear. "This is Maddy."

"Madeline, this is Richard. Can you come down to my office for a moment?"

It was the news director. While Laura was the executive producer of our department, Richard was the big boss of the entire newsroom. He wasn't a tyrant or anything, but no one wanted to be called down to his office. It was like being sent to the principal—and never turned out well. My hand shook a little as I set the receiver back in its cradle.

What could he want from me? Were the ratings for "Killer Clay" bad? Had he decided to replace me with a twenty-two-year-old natural blonde? (As a twenty-four-year-old bottled blonde at News 9, I was already getting over the hill.) Or, maybe he was promoting me. Maybe for some incomprehensible reason he'd thought "Killer Clay" was Emmy-worthy and he wanted me to take Laura's job.

Yeah, right. And maybe they'd raised the *Titanic*, too. The only way to find out was to go down to the newsroom. I rose from my chair, told Jodi I had to leave, and headed from our Special Projects alcove to the massive Newsplex below.

The Newsplex looked like something out of Future World

at Disney World: very sci-fi, with neon lights zooming everywhere, a billion TV sets, strategically placed, and furniture that looked like something out of *The Jetsons*. It was a bit overwhelming, and I was sometimes glad to be stuck in tiny, overcrowded Cubicle Land on the fourth floor.

I scanned the room from the balcony before walking downstairs. The place was alive, as usual. Worker ants scurrying around to serve their queen, News 9's main anchor Terrance Toller. (Yes, a guy, but very queen like, trust me!) Now in his sixties, the clinically narcissistic anchor defined the stereotype of male diva, and struck fear into the hearts of the young production assistants and writers who lived to serve him. One of his favorite tortures? Asking random questions moments before going live.

Example: Story is about a soldier's death in Uzbekistan. Seconds before the commercial ends and Terrance is supposed to read the twenty-second blurb on the event, he turns from his camera-facing position and demands, "What's the capital of Uzbekistan?" to the hapless writer who sits behind him.

It doesn't matter that the death didn't take place in the capital of Uzbekistan. It doesn't matter that Terrance will never mention the name of the capital on air even if it did. (He'd never be able to pronounce it anyway.) If the poor writer doesn't instantly have the answer to his trivial pursuit, she's going to get it after the show. Needless to say, whenever Terrance took the anchor desk, all the writers had Google fired up and were ready to search.

I carefully made my way down the steep steps into the Newsplex. My pitiful salary didn't afford me good shoes and I was forced to run around in ill-fitting irregulars from a factory outlet. They looked pretty cool, but the tops were already detaching from the soles. One wrong step and I'd stumble down into televised embarrassment.

That was the thing about the Newsplex. As it was the backdrop of the newscast, anything that happened behind the scenes was broadcast on live TV. I remember one time the overnight engineers set the house channel to some porn station and forgot to change it back. Let me tell you, the FCC wasn't so happy when morning viewers got their daily breakfast news with a side of Ron Jeremy.

Richard's door was closed when I arrived and I wondered if I should come back later. The idea was more than tempting, but I decided to brave it out with a timid knock.

"Come in."

I slid my hand around the knob and opened the door. The news director sat behind his great mahogany desk, leaning back in an ultra-comfy executive chair. I duly noted his smile. So, this wasn't bad news. Okay. I let out the breath I hadn't realized I'd been holding.

"Hi. You wanted to see me?" I asked, hovering in the doorway like a vampire waiting for my invitation to come in.

"Sit down, Madeline," Richard said, gesturing to an empty seat—an empty seat beside the hottest guy in the known universe, I suddenly realized.

Oh. My. God.

Was this the new photographer Jodi had been talking about? "To die for" had been the understatement of the century. More like to die for, be raised from the dead for, and live an entirely new existence based on worshiping him.

He had shiny light brown hair, clipped short in the back, hanging a bit longish over his green eyes. Well built, but not huge, he wore Diesel dark-rinse jeans and a tight black T-shirt stretched across his chest, delightfully hugging his pecs and flat stomach. He gave me a smile that nearly made me melt into a soppy puddle on Richard's floor.

Stop staring, Maddy!

I forced my eyes away and back to Richard, concentrated on Richard's bulgy paunch of a stomach—a definite buzz-kill—and sat down next to Adonis.

"Thanks for coming down, Madeline," Richard said. He never could come to terms with the fact that everyone called me Maddy since birth. "I'd like you to meet Jamie Hayes. He's our new photographer and today's his first day."

I turned slowly to face Adonis/Jamie and attempted a

friendly—but not too friendly—smile. He flashed his white teeth again and held out his hand.

"Hi, Madeline, nice to meet you."

"M-Maddy," I corrected before I could stop myself. I bit my lower lip. One did not correct men who looked that good. That was, like, Adonis 101.

"I'm sorry?"

I swallowed. Hard. Twenty-something years mastering the English language and I could barely spit out a sentence. "You can call me Maddy."

He grinned again. "Maddy. I had a dog named Maddy once."

I reminded him of a dog. Ugh. Did I look that bad? I tried to surreptitiously check my reflection in the glassed trophy cabinet behind him. My ridiculously expensive Hillcrest hairdresser had assured me my flippy do was artfully messy, but all I saw in my reflection was a blond Cousin It. And why hadn't I worn something cute? Hip? What had possessed my bleary-eyed six a.m. self to choose the ugly green sweater that was currently draped over my body? And my three-year-old faded Express pants screamed last day before laundry.

After giving up on the reflection—I was never winning Fairest of Them All at this point—I realized Jamie was still holding out his hand. Doh. I was really making a great impression on the guy. I shook his hand and focused all my energy on ignoring the romance novel–like sparks that shot down to my toes when our palms came into contact with one another. I accidentally looked up and my eyes slammed into his sparkly kryptonite green ones. Like Superman, I was instantly rendered powerless.

"Madeline." Richard's voice brought me back to reality. Happy for the interruption, I dropped Jamie's hand like a hot potato. "How long have you been with us now?"

I stared at him, horrified to realize my mind was completely blank. Come on, this wasn't the capital of Uzbekistan. How long had I worked here? Jamie's proximity was doing bad things to my brain.

"Um, two years, sir."

"Right." Richard noted something on a legal pad. "How would you like a change?"

"What kind of change?" I cocked my head in interest. I mean, he'd have to be more specific before I could answer that one. Like, if it were a flipping-burgers-at-McDonald's kind of change, I'd pass. Big raise with exciting new responsibilities? I'm your gal.

"I'm starting a new franchise. An investigative kind of thing. It'll be a vehicle for Terrance—that's our main anchor," he told Jamie, "to get his face out there more, though it'll be completely producer driven. He'll just read your scripts. What do you think?"

What did I think? I thought that sounded great! Who wouldn't? It was a dream come true. My own segment—and an investigative one at that. A chance to help right the wrongs viewers faced each day. Sure, it would involve working with Terrance, but I could do it. How hard could it be? After all, he wouldn't be that involved. He'd simply be reading what I wrote. Besides, I'd make any sacrifice to have my own segment.

"I'm honored you thought of me," I replied in my most respectful voice. "I'd love to produce the new segment." Maybe *Newsline* would notice me now. My idol Diane Dickson would call me personally. Ask me why I hadn't yet applied. They'd send me a first-class plane ticket to New York. Wine me. Dine me. Beg me to work for them. And then I'd …

"Since you'll be doing a lot of shooting, I figured it'd be good to assign you your own photographer," Richard was saying. I immediately woke up from *Newsline* dreamland to even more delicious reality. He was assigning me my own photog? No more fighting with the other producers for five minutes of camera time, squeezed in between their supposedly more important shoots? This got better and better.

"Great," I managed to spit out. "Thanks."

"I'd like you and Jamie to start immediately. Why don't you give him a tour of the station now?"

And immediate face time with Adonis? This day got better and better. Whatever I did in a past life to deserve this luck, I'm glad I got around to it.

"Sure," I said, now teeming with self-confidence. I gestured to Jamie. "Shall we?"

He grinned, rising from his seat. "We shall." Together we walked out of Richard's office and into the Newsplex. I pointed out all the major sites—anchor desk, assignment desk, editing, etc. Introduced him to a few nosy coworkers (mostly women) who made their way over to pretend to ask me something and then casually question, "Oh, who's your friend?" As if I'd be fooled by that old ruse.

I considered showing him the broom closets, just in case the mood happened to strike him in a closed-in, private area like what might happen on a soap opera, but then forced myself to stay professional. After all, I'd be working with the guy every single day. I didn't have to rush things.

"And this is Special Projects," I said as I led him into our upstairs alcove. "Tucked away from the hustle and bustle of the Newsplex." I brought him over to my cubicle. "You can hang here for a moment." I gestured to the empty desk across from mine. "I have to check my e-mail real quick."

The desk's owner, a political producer named David, was currently on the campaign trail with Senator Gorman, the incumbent Republican Senator from San Diego. Seeing as Gorman was the most conservative guy on the planet and David probably the most openly gay, I greatly regretted missing witnessing the two of them hanging out on the same tour bus.

I signed in and scanned for new e-mail. I had eleven unread messages: five on enlarging my member, three offering to overnight me Valium, two in Chinese that might have been really interesting if I could read the language, and one which, were I considering buying a house, I'd be offered a super interest rate.

No reply from any doctors eagerly awaiting fifteen minutes of fame garnered by ousting those secret cosmetics that killed.

Darn.

"So, do you like working at News Nine?" Jamie asked, interrupting my systematic deletions.

I tried to keep my face expressionless. I hated this question from newbies. They'd just started and, for them, this job was a dream come true. A chance to work in TV news in "America's Finest City." They might have slaved years to get to this place. I didn't want to be the one to burst their bubbles, tell them the newsroom was a shithole with terrible managers and even worse journalistic ethics. That it was the bane of my existence, and I had only stayed so long out of an overwhelming fear of the unemployment line. I was pretty sure that a degree in TV wouldn't elicit very many good job offers.

"Yeah, it's cool," I said nonchalantly. He'd find out soon enough. "Like any newsroom, it's got its idiosyncrasies."

He laughed, seeming to catch my meaning. "I see."

"Where did you work before this?" I asked. I wondered if his newsroom was as bad as News 9.

"Actually, this is my first TV news job," he admitted, leaning back in his chair, his hands behind his head. "I worked in LA before this. Doing movies. Documentaries. That kind of thing."

"Really?" I asked, too enthusiastic before I could help myself. *Come on, Maddy. At least a shred of dignity would be nice.* "What movies?"

He listed off several very cool independent films. Wow, this guy got better and better. Not only was he good-looking, but he was talented, too. Total boyfriend material. Though way out of my league. He probably dated models.

"So, why are you here?" I couldn't help but ask.

He sighed and stared at the ground. Oh, good one. I'd asked him something that made him uncomfortable.

"You don't have to go into it," I added.

"No, it's okay." He shrugged. "Basically, the projects dried up. The economy's so bad now. I figured I'd get a 'real job,'"—he made finger quotation marks—"until a new project started. Get some money saved up."

I nodded. That made sense. Poor guy, though. He was going to hate working at News 9. I, on the other hand, was very, very happy about his arrival. I wondered how I could make my first move. Would it be too forward to shove him against the desk and have my way with him?

As I was pondering possible photog molestation, his cell rang. "Hello?" he said, after pulling an iPhone from his pocket and putting it to his ear.

He was so cool. So, so cool. And he was all mine for at least eight hours every day. How did I get so lucky? I casually gave him another once-over as I waited for him to finish his conversation. God, he was cute. Long eyelashes, high cheekbones, a full mouth that was perfectly kissable. Just a hint of five o'clock shadow scruffiness to keep him from looking too pretty.

He glanced over at me and I felt my face heat with embarrassment. Did he know I was checking him out? He gave a brief smile, then made a gun out of his forefinger and thumb and mimed shooting himself in the head. Whoever was on the other line, he didn't want to talk to. Maybe it was his mother. Or maybe it was his psycho ex-girlfriend. Or …

"Yes, dear. I know our wedding's in three months. That's plenty of time," he said, blowing out a deep sigh of frustration.

Or, dammit, maybe it was his fiancée.

CHAPTER TWO

FROM: "Laura Smith" <lsmith@news9.com>

TO: "Madeline Madison" <mmadison@news9.com>

SUBJECT: re: story idea

Maddy,

Thanks for your story idea on pharmaceutical companies fixing prices to drain Medicare and make more money. It's great that an ex—employee sent you all the documentations on this scandal.

However, seeing as this story would only affect under-insured old people on a lot of drugs (so not our demo!) I would prefer you work on the following. Gather ten purses from around the newsroom and have them tested for E-Coli and Staph bacteria and other such grossness. We'll call it "Handbag Horror." Perfect for that 24-55—year-old woman viewer we're targeting, don't you think?

Thanks!

Laura

Executive Producer

News 9 —San Diego

P.S. In order to avoid a repeat of "Icky Ice"—which unfortunately tested pure as the driven snow and had to be canceled as a sweeps story—please take each purse into the bathroom and drag it across a toilet seat a few times before testing. This should ensure we don't waste a ton of money again at the testing labs for a story that doesn't pan out.

The sun had set moments before, painting the Tijuana sky with a rosy glow. Jodi and I sat in our plastic outdoor chairs at the little Mexican café, soaking up the colorful atmosphere and our even more colorful margaritas. Coming down to TJ, just across the border, was one of our favorite after-work activities. We stayed away from the noisy, tourist-packed Avenida Revolucion, however, in favor of a smaller, quieter market square just before the canal bridge.

Of course, "quieter" was a relative term in Tijuana. The square still boasted loud '80's music, blasting from the karaoke bar next door and little Mexican children still pulled at our sleeves, wondering if we'd like some *Chiclets.* The first time I came here, I thought they meant those pink-colored books about girls in the city. But no, they were talking about gum.

Still, there was something serene about sitting back and watching the shopkeepers harass tourists into buying their cheesy wares. Or spying on the druggies browsing the plethora of pharmacies for their Percocets and Valiums. (And the shy, old, balding men who slunk in and whispered their Viagra orders to a Mexican pharmacist who didn't give two *cajones* about whether or not they could get it up.) Okay, so it was a bit sketchy. But also a much cheaper night out than hitting any of the San Diego bars. There, even the dive places charged like ten bucks a margarita.

We'd started coming here about a year ago, after Jodi produced the "Tijuana Tacos" story. That was one of the few occasions we could name names on News 9, basically because they had absolutely no chance of becoming potential advertisers. So we bankrupted ten taco stands by getting a food inspector to test the temperature at which they kept their meat. A proud day, even though it turned out in the end that the so-called food inspector Laura dug up wasn't even licensed to test food and most likely made up all the results. But hey, the story looked good and got killer ratings—all that mattered to the News 9 Gestapo.

Anyway, when working on the story, Jodi came across the most amazing find. Fake purses! You name it, this Mexican shop had it. Prada, Gucci, Fendi, Kate Spade. All 100 percent counterfeit and all 100 percent cheap. So of course she'd wanted to return when she had more time to shop and brought me with her. At first I was a little skeeved out by all the poverty and dirt and puking eighteen-year-old drunk San Diegan kids, but once I saw the purses and the price of margaritas, I realized TJ could very well be the Promised Land.

"So, what's up with the photog?" Jodi asked, paying the waiter for our third round of drinks. It was going to be one of those nights, I could tell already. And it was only a Wednesday!

"Well, you were right about him being cute. And he's so cool, too. He used to work on movies," I related, trying to mask the dreaminess in my voice. He was so perfect. So, so my type. It was really too bad that he wasn't available.

"Sounds amazing. When's the wedding?"

"Rather soon, actually. Problem is, it's not mine." I gloomily sucked down a huge portion of my frozen raspberry margarita.

"Girlfriend?"

"Worse. Fiancée. And not a 'we'll get married someday, but we haven't picked the date' type, either. He's getting married in three months. There are invitations. Caterers. Probably a Vera Wang white dress."

"Yeah, at three months, you've pretty much lost your chance at getting your deposits back," said Jodi, knower of all things wedding. "Might as well go through with it at that point."

"Just further evidence that all the good guys are gay or taken."

"Oh, Maddy," my optimistic friend cooed. "There's someone out there for everyone."

I snorted. "Thanks, Pollyanna." I took another sip. "I suppose now you're going to tell me there are lots of fish in the sea, too."

"Clichés become clichés 'cause they're true."

"Yeah, yeah. Anyway, it doesn't matter. Tonight I'm celebrating my promotion at News Nine. That's what's important. I'm one step closer to *Newsline*."

Jodi raised her margarita. "To *Newsline*!"

We clinked glasses, somehow managing not to spill any alcohol, and took deep sips.

"So. Um. Want to go check out the fake purses?" Jodi asked casually. Too casually.

I grinned. "Look at you, jonesing over there for your fake-purse fix. You're completely addicted!"

We didn't need any new purses at this point, but it was still fun to look at the latest knockoffs. At last count, I owned four Gucci, two Christian Dior, and nine Kate Spades. I was a sucker for Kate's iconic bags. I only wished I could afford a genuine one with a sewn-on label to replace the oh-so-obvious fakes whose labels were sloppily glued.

"I'm not addicted," Jodi protested, a bit defensively.

"Ah, denial. The first sign of a fake-purse addict."

She swatted at me, managing to tip over my margarita. I jumped up to avoid getting drenched. Oh dear, she was more wasted than I thought.

"Nice one, drunk girl."

Jodi, as much as I loved her, defined the word *lightweight*. Three margaritas was way over her limit. If I didn't watch out, she'd be dancing on tables or stripping for the immigration officers at the border. Not that either of those actions would have anyone batting an eye in TJ.

"I'm so not drunk. The table was wobbly," Jodi said, not yet willing to own up to her current state of inebriation. Problem was, to prove her point about the wobbly table, she wrapped her hands around it and wobbled it some more, succeeding in knocking over her own margarita in the process.

"Yeah, yeah. Definitely the table's fault." I fished in my purse for a ten and threw it down on the table as a sympathy tip for the guy who'd have to clean up the mess. "Come on, let's get the hell out of here before the waiter comes back."

Giggling, we got up and scampered away from the scene. Like a bug to light, Jodi was hopelessly drawn to the fake-purse store.

"Ah, my girls are back." The short, skinny shopkeeper behind the counter greeted us with a big toothless grin. Sad to say, but we'd been there so many times that at this point he had a right to be named Godfather of Jodi's firstborn.

"Hi, Miguel," Jodi said with a hungry smile. "Got any new ones?"

"For you? My special customer? *Si*, of course." Miguel reached under the counter, where sellers typically stored all the premiere fakes, and placed various purses purporting to be from top designers on the counter. Jodi immediately started grabbing at them and checking for obvious signs of counterfeit.

"Do you have any Kate Spades with a sewn-on label?" I asked, hopeful. I so didn't need another purse, but a good knockoff was a good knockoff.

He shook his head. "Sorry my pretty one. Not today." He paused for a moment, as if thinking, then added, "If you want to leave me your phone number, I can call you if one comes in."

Did I really want to leave Miguel my phone number? What if he was some stalker? Sure, he looked pretty innocent, but still. You never knew these days.

I decided to give him my business card. At least at work I was protected by security guards and a barbed wire fence.

"Ah, you work for News Nine?" Miguel asked, taking the card and stuffing it in the pocket of his faded blue jeans.

"Yup. And she just got promoted to investigative producer," Jodi informed him, not able to withhold a single personal-life detail from my potential stalker. "How much is this one?"

"For you? Because you are so *bella*, I give it to you for five hundred pesos." He turned back to me. "Investigative producer?" he asked, grinning again. "Senorita, do I have a story for you."

"Oh?"

"Five hundred pesos? How about two hundred?" Jodi interrupted, her voice slurring a bit as she bartered. I needed to get her home soon. But first, I wanted to hear the story idea Miguel had. If Jodi's addiction was fake purses, mine was story ideas. All it took was one really, really good one and I'd be clocking in at *Newsline.* Miguel glanced around the square before leaning into me and lowering his voice to a hoarse whisper. "A cartel in San Diego. *Mucho* drugs being imported every day. Cocaine. Ecstasy. Meth."

"I only have three hundred pesos. How about three hundred?"

"Really?" I asked, intrigued. Exposing a drug cartel sounded exactly like the type of story *Newsline* would like. And it was a perfect News 9 story, too, because it didn't burn any potential advertisers. "How do you know about this? There'd have to be some kind of facts. Proof."

"Come on, it's got a real cheapo lining. It's not worth over three hundred fifty pesos."

Miguel nodded. "The man who runs the cartel, he is a bad man and he killed my brother. I would like to see him brought to justice."

"Couldn't you go to the police?"

"Ah, senorita, you do not understand how the law works in Mexico. You get pulled over in a car and you pay the policeman not to write you a ticket. It is the same with all things."

"Police on the payroll. Right." That made sense.

"Okay, fine. Four hundred. But I'll have to borrow money from Maddy. Maddy, can I borrow fifty pesos? I think that's like five bucks, right?"

"They have dug a long tunnel out in the desert. They use it

to transport the drugs from Mexico to America. My brother, he used to work for them as a driver before he was killed. Before he died, he told me where the tunnel is."

Jodi waved the purse in Miguel's face. "Four-fifty? Come on, dude. I really want this purse."

"Wow." I tried to sound casual, as my insides did the Snoopy dance. I'd found a whistle-blower. Someone actually wanted to blow a whistle at me. Give me information no one else knew. This was something that happened to *Newsline* producers, not little old local news me. "That's such a great story. I'd love to hear more about it. Seriously. Can you call me with all the details?"

"*Si.*" Miguel nodded. "I will call you tomorrow."

"Okay, fine. Five hundred pesos. And that's my final offer."

"Sold. You are a shrewd barterer, *chica.*" Miguel winked at me as he took Jodi's money and wrapped up her purse. I smiled back. "If all Americans were like you, my nine children would starve."

Jodi grinned stupidly, pleased by her bargaining prowess. She was going to be so pissed tomorrow when she woke up and realized she'd spent fifty bucks on a cheesy Louis Vuitton knockoff that had Xs instead of LVs on the pattern. As her best friend, I should have dragged her away a long time ago. But at this point it was easier to let her have her simple purse-buying happiness. Besides, she could live with the loss of fifty bucks.

I, however, had a feeling this story was going to change my life forever.

CHAPTER THREE

FROM: "Victor Charles, MD" <tvdoc@ermedicalhosp.com>

TO: "Madeline Madison" <mmadison@news9.com>

SUBJECT: re: cosmetics that kill?

Dear Maddy,

Thank you for writing to me regarding your story on "Cosmetics That Kill." However, in all my forty years as a doctor at this major medical institution, I have never once come across a single case where cosmetics were responsible for someone's death.

Perhaps you'd be better serving the community by doing a story on a new over-the-counter diet drug that uses herbs hand ground by Aboriginal tribe members. As the company's paid spokesman I'd be happy to extol its virtues to your viewing audience and I'm sure it'd be a great ratings booster. I could even provide you with a patient who lost over fifty pounds in one week by taking this pill.

Your favorite TV doc,

Victor

```
P.S. The FDA has not yet approved this drug
(you know how they are!) So I would suggest
you don't bother contacting them to ask them
if it is safe and effective, but rather take
my word for it. After all, I am a doctor.
```

Bing!

Bmadison231@usermail.com: hi!

I squinted in puzzlement as an instant message popped up on my computer the next day at work. We weren't really supposed to be IMing on the job. The IT department had even put a block on our computers so it'd be impossible to download an IM program. Luckily, AOL's service had a Java Express version, which meant it could run online and there was nothing to download. Let's just say the brilliance of such a concept wasn't lost on our department.

In fact, in News 9 Cubicle Land all you ever heard was *bing, bing, bing* all day long with a sole *bong* thrown in from Jodi's computer. She had gotten sick of thinking other people's *bings* were hers and changed the sound settings.

So, while the appearance of an IM wasn't unusual in and of itself, I couldn't help but notice this particular IM came from my father, the most un–computer savvy, low-tech guy on the planet. The man didn't know how to program his DVR. Didn't own a cell phone. And now he was IMing me? I had no idea he even knew IMing existed. I would have been willing to make a bet before this very minute, in fact, that he would have happily gone through his whole life never knowing or caring that communication with his oldest daughter was simply a bing away.

Bing!

Bmadison231@usermail.com: Are you there, sweet pea?

mmadison@news9.com: Yes. Hi Dad. What's up?

Bmadison231@usermail.com: Wow! This instant messaging thing is very tight, huh?

Oh-kay. Now I'm officially freaked out. Not only was my dad using IMing technology, but he was using expressions like "tight."

Bmadison231@usermail.com: Listen, hon. I was wondering if you would like to come over for dinner tonight.

mmadison@news9.com: Well, it is a work night ...

Bmadison231@usermail.com: Your mother and I have some news we'd like to share with you.

mmadison@news9.com: Is it bad news??????

Bmadison231@usermail.com: Oh no. It's nothing bad.

mmadison@news9.com: Okay, phew. For a moment it sounded like you guys were going to get a divorce or something. :)So what is it? Did you win the lottery? If you did, can you buy me a condo?

Bmadison231@usermail.com: My hands are getting tired from typing. Just come by for seven, okay?

mmadison@news9.com: Ok. Bye dad. :)

Bmadison231@usermail.com: :)

Oh. My. God. My dad used an emoticon! Another twenty-first centuryism that I figured he'd never work out. Something was definitely up.

"So, what are we doing today?" Adonis—sorry, that would be Jamie—slid into David's seat and smiled at me. I tried not to cringe as my insides instantly turned to mush.

That smile of his had to be outlawed in at least thirty-three states. He shouldn't be allowed to spring it on me like that. But what could I say? Excuse me, gorgeous photog, could you please not smile at me? Ever? Then he'd want to know why, and I'd have to admit I had the total hots for him, which he'd think was "really cute" and say I was a "nice kid" but he had a real woman back at home. One with caterers, swan napkins, and a sparkling diamond ring that he'd placed on her delicate finger. She probably had perfect nails and went to the manicurist seven days a week.

Stop it, Maddy. Imagination running wild. She could be an ugly troll for all you know.

I realized Jamie was still waiting for the response one would typically receive after asking a simple question of one's coworker—if one's coworker didn't belong in a drooling mental ward due to raging female hormones.

"Well, I don't know if I have anything for you to shoot," I said with a sigh. "I'm desperately researching a story on 'Cosmetics That Kill' and unfortunately keep coming up a bit short on interview subjects."

He raised an eyebrow. "Cosmetics can kill? I had no idea."

"It's okay, neither does the rest of the world. But promos decided it'd sound like a good ad to run during that *Extreme Makeover* reality show we air on Tuesday nights."

"You know, now that you mention it, I think I received some chain e-mail with something about deadly lipstick," Jamie said thoughtfully. "Though I probably deleted it."

"Really? Do you think it's still in your trash folder?" I asked, trying not to get my hopes up. Wow. First day on the job and my photographer was helping me produce! He was actually interested in my story and wanted to contribute.

You got to understand. Most of our photographers at News 9 were die-hard union guys. They did exactly what you told them, with no thoughts or creative suggestions. It was not a team effort. Ever. They might as well have been robots, though I was pretty sure robots didn't bitch and whine every time they were asked to do something. And heaven forbid you break a union rule. One time, I hit the "eject" button on the camera to get my tape. I thought the photographer was going to have a heart attack. I had to sit through this half-hour lecture about how my hitting "eject" could lead to photographer layoffs because there wasn't enough work for them to do. Evidently I'd personally be responsible for hundreds of starving children whose photog daddies and mommies stood in the unemployment line.

Jamie turned around in his chair and logged into my cubemate's computer. I watched eagerly as he pulled up his Internet e-mail account and selected his trash folder. "Here it is." He clicked on the little envelope icon and the e-mail popped up. Because I was blind and refused to wear glasses or get contacts, I had to come up pretty close behind him to read over his shoulder. And this close proximity made me realize he was wearing spicy cologne that sparked a direct tingling effect you know where. Man, this guy could turn me on without even touching me.

To: Jamie Hayes <superphotog53@email.com>

From: Jennifer Quigley <sweetbaby23@email.com>

Subject: FWD: LIPSTICK —Please Read

Lead is a chemical that causes cancer. The higher the lead content, the greater the chance of it causing cancer. Watch out for those lipsticks, which are supposed to stay longer. If your lipstick stays longer, it is because of the higher content of lead. This is how to test lipstick for lead.

1) Put some lipstick on your hand.

2) Use a 24k -14k gold ring to scratch on the lipstick.

3) If the lipstick color changes to black then you know the lipstick contains lead.

NOTE: Please pass this along to all your friends. In addition to saving their lives, you will also receive good luck in three days. If you do not pass this along and simply delete it, something really bad will probably happen to you. There was this one guy in Cuba who deleted it and he died in a fiery car crash five minutes later. Doctors said it was because he was checking his e-mail and driving at the same time, but we know better! You have been warned!

"So, what do you think?" Jamie asked, turning around to look at me. Since I had been leaning over so close, the sudden movement caused us to bump noses and an electric shock zapped through my entire body. It was like accidental Eskimo kissing!

"Sorry," I said, even though I wasn't. I sat back down in my chair. "Can you forward me that e-mail? I'm pretty sure it's an urban myth, but it's definitely worth checking out."

"Sure, no prob." After getting my e-mail address, Jamie forwarded the message. Then he turned back to face me.

"That's a cute skirt," he remarked casually, his eyes roaming my brand-new black swishy skirt I'd run out and bought last night before going to Tijuana. After learning I'd be working side by side with a sex god, I'd decided money needed to be spent on clothes. And evidently, I thought with delight, the investment was paying off.

"This old thing?" I brushed off. "Thanks. I suppose it's cute."

"Um, I think you forgot to take off the price tag though," he added, gesturing to the hem. *Oh shit.* My face flamed as I looked down to see that he was right. There was definitely a price tag hanging from a plastic loop on the right side of the skirt. I thought I'd removed them all. He must have thought I was the biggest geek loser in the known universe. Who would put a tag there anyway? One so easy to miss. Was there some disgruntled Nordstrom's employee out there who thought it'd be amusing to embarrass poor innocent people who bought clothes from her?

Now, there was a story. "Clothes That Kill." You *could* die from humiliation, right?

"Actually, it's a new thing," I said, recovering just in time. "Keeping the price tags on is very hip these days." *Please believe me*, I begged silently. *Or, if you don't, please don't call me on it.*

"Oh. Sorry." He smiled sheepishly. "My fiancée Jennifer always tells me I'm perpetually unhip."

Ew, there he went, spouting the F-word like it was no big deal. I couldn't stand it.

"Listen," he added, rising from his chair. "Why don't you research the lipstick thing and in the meantime, I'll go around the station and get some people to let me videotape them putting on makeup. That way you'll have some video for the piece in case it pans out."

I wanted to hug him. Or fall over in shock. I'd never, ever had a photographer volunteer to do something without me having to beg and plead and listen to him whine. This guy was unbelievable.

And during the eight hours of the workday, he was all mine!

*

I arrived at my parents' house at about quarter to seven. They lived in an adorable Craftsman-type house in Normal Heights, one of the older neighborhoods in San Diego. The houses there were small and quaint. And now, with the backlash against the extravagant monster houses with no yards being thrown up in urban sprawl subdivisions all over the county, the old-school houses were extremely desirable and super pricey. My parents' house had tripled in value since they bought it when I was a kid.

The door opened at my knock and my little sister Lulu answered it with typical Lulu exuberance. At sixteen years old, she was a bundle of unrepressed energy and while I loved her, sometimes she was a bit on the exhausting side. A total wild child, every time I saw her she had different-colored hair. It was currently bleach blond and shorn to a boyish cut. She wore tight, distressed jeans and a tiny, belly-baring pink tank top that declared one could evidently get "Lucky in Kentucky."

"Hi, Maddy!" she cried, throwing her arms around me and almost knocking me over with a huge hug. "How are you? What are you doing here?"

"Um, Dad instant messaged me. Said he needed to see me."

"He did?" Lulu raised her eyebrows. "I didn't know he knew how to IM."

"Yeah. Neither did I." I shrugged.

"Well, come on in." Lulu gestured widely. "We've just finished dinner."

Uh, that was weird, since the whole reason I was supposed to be coming here was for dinner. What the hell was going on?

We walked into the foyer and then headed for the living room. My parents were seated in the same seats they always sat in after dinner since I was a toddler. Dad in his ultra-comfy, well-worn leather armchair and my mom knitting on the far end of the couch.

Except, my mother wasn't knitting. And as I sat down next to her, I realized she looked like she'd been crying. A swelling of fear fluttered through my stomach. I thought this wasn't supposed to be bad news.

"Hi, Maddy," my father said with a wide smile. He didn't seem upset at all. "Thanks for coming over. How was work?"

"So, what's your news?" I wanted to cut to the chase at this point; the suspense was killing me.

Please be that you won the lottery, I begged silently, suddenly realizing the chances of that being the news was slim to none. I sat down on the sofa and held my breath, waiting for the inevitable bomb to drop.

"Lulu, sit down," my father reprimanded the bouncy sixteen-year-old. With a huff, Lulu complied, squashing herself between Mom and me.

"Your mother and I have some news," my father said, leaning forward in his armchair. Even in his fifties, he was a good-looking man with a sprinkling of distinguished salt-and-pepper hair and a trim waistline. "We've decided to live apart."

"What? What?" Lulu screeched, jumping up from the couch, hands on her low-rise jeans. "You can't get a divorce! That's, like, so not fair!"

My heart fell into my stomach. For a moment I thought I would be physically ill. My parents were splitting up. It seemed so wrong somehow. I mean, I knew almost everyone's parents got divorced. But usually it was when they were kids. No one's parents lived happily ever after for thirty years and then decided one day it wasn't working out and they were moving on. It just didn't happen like that. There was a point where you were safe. You could relax and know that your family was one of the rare ones that beat the odds.

And now they were going along with the rest of the crazy world and getting divorced.

"Why are you getting a divorce? Who am I supposed to live with?" Lulu demanded. Poor girl. While it was devastating news for me, at least I'd moved out of the house. This would impact my sister's entire existence.

"You can stay with your father and his little whore," my mother said in an odd, cheery voice.

I whirled my head around, jaw hitting the floor. What? What did she just say? I'd never, ever heard my mother use bad language in all my existence. She was the sunshine and oatmeal-raisin cookies stay-at-home mom who used to read us Bible stories. She didn't say things like "his little whore."

Which brought me to my next question. I turned to look at my evidently philandering father. Had he really cheated on my poor, sweet, innocent mother? How dare he? Anger replaced my sadness and I rose from my chair.

"Dad. What the hell is going on here?" I demanded, hoping he could hear me over Lulu's wailing sobs.

My dad squirmed in his chair. For a chair he'd sat in for the last thirty years of his life, he suddenly seemed to find it mighty uncomfortable.

"I'm seeing someone else," he said at last.

"Someone else?" My mother raised a carefully plucked eyebrow. Since when did she pluck her eyebrows? "Aren't you going to tell them who?"

He took a deep breath. "Someone from my office."

"Who happens to be twenty-three years old and pregnant with your child!" my mother added helpfully, if not a bit bitterly.

Nausea overcame me at that point, and I ran to the bathroom to retch. This couldn't be happening. This could NOT be happening. It had to be some ridiculous dream. I'd wake up any minute now and realize the whole crazy scene was just a dream. My family was still together. My dad didn't have a pregnant girlfriend who was younger than me by a year.

I started to retch again and bowed to the porcelain god in front of me. As I puked my guts out, I felt someone come up behind me and hold my hair back. After I was done sacrificing a good portion of my lunch, I turned around to see who it was.

My father.

I wanted to hit him. To strangle him. To kill him for his betrayal. How could he be so selfish? How could he put himself before his family?

"Can we take a walk?" he asked with a sad smile.

I nodded wordlessly, hating him and loving him more than anything at that very moment. We walked out the door into our backyard. The flowers my mother had planted, bright cheerful sunflowers, seemed mocking.

"I'm sorry if you feel I've let you down, Maddy," Dad said as he settled down onto the backyard swings. The same swings he had pushed me on so many times growing up.

Higher! I'd scream. *I want to touch the sky!*

I joined him, scuffing the toe of my shoe against the dirt. Swaying back and forth, but not swinging.

I turned to face him. "Why?" I asked.

He reached over and brushed a tear from my cheek. "Every relationship is different," he said. "And no one who's not in the relationship can see what goes on behind closed doors. Your mother and I have been together in name only for years. We don't talk. We don't make love. We simply cohabitate. We tried marriage counseling. It didn't help."

I could feel my heart slamming against my rib cage and had to struggle to catch my breath. I had no idea. I thought my parents loved each other. But as memories of the last few years flooded my brain, I realized suddenly that I might have been looking at their marriage through rose-colored kid glasses. I tried to remember the last time I'd seen them kiss. Hug. I couldn't. But I had simply chalked it up to it being an older, more mature marriage.

"But you didn't have to cheat on Mom," I reminded him

with a frown. Falling out of love was one thing. Cheating was another.

He sighed. "Your mother is a very special person," he said, swaying from side to side on his swing. "I tried to tell her I was unhappy for years. She begged me to stay. Said I could go out and do what I had to do as long as I didn't leave her."

This was surely a shocking day to end all shocking days. My mother had told my father he could go out and have affairs? I couldn't even fathom the idea.

"So you've been fucking other women this whole time? While pretending to be a family man?" I demanded, not caring at my father's cringe at the F-word.

"That's kind of a harsh way to put it," he said in a sad voice. "I simply opened myself up to new opportunities. I guess you could call them affairs. But there was no deception involved."

"Oh, right," I said sarcastically. "Because you had permission."

"Yes."

"You're a bastard."

"I know. I soon realized the situation wasn't fair to anyone—your mother or the woman I fell in love with."

Oh, now he was in love, was he? Anger burned through my stomach, and I rose from the swing. "I don't want to hear this!"

"I know, honey. I'm sorry. This is a lot to take in."

"So who is she?" I may not have wanted to hear this, but at the same time I couldn't stop my overwhelming masochistic curiosity. "And is she really carrying your child?"

My dad looked old. Drained. "Her named is Cindi. With an 'i'," he added, as if that made everything okay. Cindi with an "i"? My whole world was turning into a bad made-for-TV movie. "And yes, she's pregnant. You're going to have a new brother or sister," he added, as if that were a good thing.

That was it.

"You know what? Fuck you! You've ruined my life. You've ruined Mom and Lulu's lives. Now you're going to go start a whole new family and probably ruin their lives, too! You're such a selfish asshole. I never want to see you again!" I stormed off into the house, slamming the back screen door with as much force as I could muster.

I wanted to throw things. I wanted to beat someone senseless. I wanted to drink myself to oblivion.

I took a deep breath. I had to talk to my mother. My poor, long-suffering, abused mother. If only I had known what she was going through all these years, I could have been there for her.

"Where's Mom?" I asked Lulu as I entered the living room. No answer. My little sister was catatonic, crunched up on the floor, hugging her knees and rocking back and forth. Shit. I'd need to comfort her, too. How did I get stuck in the sane-person-who-picks-up-the-pieces role? I wanted to be the fall-apart-and-do-stupid-things one.

"Lulu, are you okay?" I knelt down and gave her a warm hug. Her body was cold. She looked like she'd gone into shock. But then she reached out her arms and hugged me back.

"I don't want them to get a divorce," she wailed, sobbing into my shoulder. I could feel nasty snot from her nose, dripping onto my new shirt, but I didn't care. "I know. Neither do I." I stroked her bleached-blond hair. "But it will be okay. Things will work out."

"That's easy for you to say. You don't have to figure out an entirely new living situation."

She had a point. As much as this sucked for me, it was much worse for her.

"Why don't we go talk to Mom?" I suggested. "We'll figure out what's what."

"Mom left."

"What?"

"Right after you and Dad went outside, she grabbed her car keys and said she was going shopping."

"Shopping?" I repeated, like a dumbfounded parrot. "She went shopping?"

"Yup," Lulu said glumly. She pulled from the embrace and

slunk over to the couch. Plopping down, she pulled her knees to her chest. I was about to big sister her about grimy sneakers on the couch, but bit my tongue. What did it really matter?

"I can't believe she went shopping." I scrambled up from the floor. Could this day get any weirder? "Should we go after her?"

Lulu shrugged her shoulders. "Maybe she needs time alone."

Maybe. I didn't know. Was it a cry for help or a cry for new shoes? How could I be expected to know these things? I wasn't some shrink. I had no experience dealing with the parents-divorcing scenario.

Lulu used her forearm to wipe the tears from her eyes. "I'm going upstairs to my room to call Dora. If Dad comes back in the house, tell him I'm not to be disturbed." She got up from the couch and headed for the stairs. Then she turned around. "If things are really bad, can I come live with you?" she asked, her eyes wide and pleading.

"Of course," I said, even though I didn't really mean it. I lived in a cramped one-bedroom apartment in Pacific Beach. I had no room for another person and no time to parent my wild-child sister. Still, I was pretty sure Lulu would never take me up on the offer. Mom would come back from shopping. (Shopping!) And she would convince Lulu that the two of them would get along just fine here in the Normal Heights house. Dad was the betrayer so he'd have to move. That was how it worked: I'd seen it with all my friends' parents.

Lulu went upstairs, and I was left alone. Out the window, I saw my dad getting up from the swing and heading into the house. I had no desire to talk to him anymore. In fact, all I wanted to do was be sick again. My stomach had knotted like I had severe indigestion. Not surprising since "Dad's got a pregnant twenty-three-year-old girlfriend and is leaving Mom" news is a bit tough to digest in one sitting.

So I did the cowardly thing. I left. I opened the front door, sucked in a huge breath of fresh air, and headed to my car. There was only one thing left to do.

I was going out drinking.

CHAPTER FOUR

FROM: "Terrance Toller" <superanchor@aol.com>

TO: "Madeline Madison" <mmadison@news9.com>

SUBJECT: ME!!!!!

Dear Madeline,

I am writing to say how delighted I am that we will be working together on my new investigative feature, "Terrance Tells All." I just wanted to go over a few teensy weensy things that I need, to make sure our time together is productive. After all, as the anchor most San Diegans trust to bring them all the day's events, I have a certain image to project. I'm SURE you understand.

1) I require three hours advance notice before any shoot that will involve my participation. I need to put on my makeup and get my hair professionally set and dried and, as you know, beauty takes time! Also, I am not available for shoots on Monday, Wednesday, Thursday, or Friday so please plan accordingly.

2) I would prefer not to go on location—I have better things to do than spend my day driving to some viewer's dog hair-infested, beanie

baby-decorated house and make idle chitchat while the photographer takes forever setting up the lights. Besides, I might get mobbed by the paparazzi on the way over and this could mess up my hair. Therefore, I'd like to be shot in the studio (give my lighting director approximately two hours to set up—after all, I must look good!) and ask the questions there. Then you can intercut my questions with the interview subject's answers. Don't worry if the background doesn't look the same. Or if my questions don't exactly match up with his answers. The ignorant Wal-Mart shoppers who watch our news will never know the difference.

3) I enjoy triple venti nonfat sugar-free vanilla dry soy lattes from Starbucks. Please insist the lazy employees HAND GRIND my espresso beans. (They may grumble a bit, but they *will* do it if you insist, take my word for it.) My last producer brought me lattes every morning and I found this quite a lovely gesture. Of course, if you are "too busy" you can feel free to let me succumb to caffeine depravation, but don't expect a stellar performance. Personally, I wouldn't want to be the one to let the whole show sink because I was "too busy" to run to the coffee shop, which happens to be only four blocks from the station, but that's completely up to you.

Great to be working with you, Madeline!
Terrance

Back from the parents' fiasco, I showered, changed, and checked my e-mail. Deleted the lovely note Terrance had sent me, detailing exactly how he was going to make my life miserable. As if I needed any help in that department. It was definitely going to be a pleasure working for him, I could tell already.

But work problems were the last thing on my mind that night. My biggest challenge? How to get as drunk as humanly possible in the least amount of time.

After shutting down my computer, I called Jodi. She was always good for a night of sorrow drowning. Unfortunately, she wasn't home. Probably off with her husband as people with husbands (who weren't cheating on them with people half their age) tended to do. The thought made me even more depressed.

I called a few other friends, but for some reason, no one was around. Since when did everyone have important Thursday-night plans? I was evidently destined to spend my night alone.

Being alone, however, did not preclude me from wanting a drink. But I decided against the alcoholic wallowing-in-my-misery-home-alone route. I would go out. There was no shame in going to a bar alone. Who knew, maybe I'd meet some uber-sexy guy who wanted nothing more than to distract me from my hideous situation with wild and crazy sex. Not that I'd necessarily give it up on the first date, mind you. Well, unless he was uber, UBER sexy, that was.

Since I didn't have to consult with others on bar choices that evening, I chose to hit my favorite: Moondoggies, a real chill bar just a block from the beach. It had great drinks, a large outdoor patio area with a fireplace and drew a fun, non-stuck-up crowd. Plus it was within walking distance of my apartment so I could crawl home without worrying about a DUI.

I arrived, showed my ID to the doorman, and took a seat by the sidewalk (to people-watch), and ordered one of Moondoggies' special K9 Kosmos—a cosmopolitan made with Absolut Mandarin.

Unfortunately, after only a few sips, instead of feeling liberated, I got the damn alcohol blues. What was I doing, sitting at a bar all by myself? Why wasn't I home comforting my sister? Looking for my mother? My family had fallen apart that evening and what did I choose to do? Go to a bar.

I was a loser. A total loser. Probably an alcoholic, too. I'd soon be hiding vodka in the bathroom. Not that I had anyone to hide it from. I could drink it with my morning Cocoa Puffs and no one would know. In fact, if I died in my apartment from a bad vodka/Cocoa Puffs overdose, no one would come looking for me for at least three days. Until the smell started getting really bad. After all, it was blatantly obvious my family was too busy messing up their own lives to care about mine.

Why did my father decide to leave my mother? At what point did the marriage fall apart? Was it in any way my fault? Did I say or do something to convince him that my mother wasn't worth staying with? I know there had been times when my mom had said something idiotic and I'd rolled my eyes to my dad. Did I diminish her worth in his eyes and make him go elsewhere? Find someone smarter? Cooler? Oh, this was probably all my fault. I'd broken up my entire family with my callous eye rolling.

Yup. Here came the tears. Perfect. I could feel several people staring at me as I swiped at my eyes. Of course. Why wouldn't they stare? I was a loser sitting in a packed bar, by myself, drinking a Cosmo (sorry, Kosmo) and crying my eyes out.

Loser with a capital "L," that was me. "Are you okay, Maddy?"

Oh no, I'd been spotted by someone who knew me! How embarrassing. I looked up to see who had discovered me in my less than desirable, probably raccoon-eyed state.

It was Jamie. What was he doing here?

"Oh. Hi," I said, grabbing a napkin and blotting my eyes. "Yes, I'm fine. Bad allergies this time a year."

Man, I was such a terrible liar. I wondered if it was something you could take classes for at the Learning Annex. They had everything else under the sun—why not Lying 101?

"Can I sit down?"

"Um, sure." Man, he probably thought I was the biggest dork on the planet. First there was that whole price tag on the skirt thing earlier. I was pretty positive he didn't buy the idea that it was cool to leave price tags on. Now he'd found me sitting at a bar by myself, crying into my drink. Great.

He took the chair across from me and propped his elbows on the table. He looked good. He'd added a well-worn leather jacket over the black T-shirt he had on earlier. It gave him a slightly rebellious look. Just bad boy enough to look cool, but not skanky.

"I was riding by on my motorcycle, on my way to check out the beach, and I saw you sitting here. Are you sure you're okay?"

Why yes, I'm fine. Like I said, allergies …

Oh, what the hell.

"Not exactly," I blurted, against my better judgment. I barely knew this guy, but suddenly I couldn't help the flow of words spewing from my lips. Alcohol did that to me. Jodi even had a nickname for me in this state—Loose Lips Lola.

And so I spilled the whole sordid tale to a guy I barely knew. To his credit, Jamie listened to the whole 411 on my family situation without interrupting once.

"Wow," he said as I finished the tale. "You've had a tough day, huh?" He reached over and squeezed my hand. In any other circumstance, the move might have seemed a bold come-on. But at that moment, it was simply a gesture of comfort. One I definitely appreciated.

"Yup. You could say that."

Before he could respond, the waiter appeared to take his drink order.

"Do you have Mojitos?" he asked, picking up a drinks menu and paging through it.

After the waiter nodded, he added, "And get the lady another one of those pink drinks."

"Thanks." I smiled as the waiter left, sucking down my beverage so I'd be ready for round two. "What's a Mojito?"

"It's this Cuban drink. Rum and mint. I got addicted to them when I spent three months working on a documentary in Miami last year. Most bars in So-Cal have yet to catch on." He grinned. "But hey, here we can choose from twenty varieties of Margaritas so I guess we should count our blessings."

I laughed. The tequila snobbery in San Diego had always amused me. Napa had wine tasting; we had tequila. Some bottles cost over a hundred dollars. There was this one bar down the street that boasted a tequila club. If you could drink shots of their fifty different brands, (not all in the same sitting, mind you!) they'd buy you a plane ticket to Cabo.

"I'd like to try a Mojito," I said. "So if you find a San Diego bar that serves them, let me know."

"You know, they were one of Hemingway's drinks of choice," Jamie informed me.

I was impressed. "Really? Now I definitely want to try them. Hemingway was kick-ass. I loved his books."

"Me, too. Especially the *Sun Also Rises.*"

"Ooh, yes." I nodded enthusiastically. "That's my fave, too. I used to imagine how cool it'd be to be a writer like Jake in gay Paris, loafing around all day and hitting the bars all night. The unrequited love with him and Brett. It's so romantic. Tragic and romantic."

"It's definitely given me inspiration."

I cocked my head in curiosity. "Are you a writer or something?"

"Aspiring. Well, I did publish one small-press book. A sci-fi action-adventure. Not exactly Hemingway," he clarified, his cheeks coloring a bit.

"Really?" I'd never met a real author before. "Can I read it?"

His blush deepened. "I guess. If you really wanted to. And you're not just being polite."

"No way." I shook my head. "I'm never polite. Bring it in tomorrow."

"It's a deal."

The waiter returned with our drinks. I was having so much fun talking to Jamie, I suddenly realized I hadn't thought about my tragic life in ten minutes. Amazing. The alcohol helped, too, warming my insides and making my troubles seem inconsequential.

"Where's your fiancée?" I asked, remembering for a moment that the attractive man charming me from across the table belonged to someone else. Not that it mattered. We weren't on a date. We weren't even flirting.

"In LA," Jamie told me between sips. "She has about a month left at her job before she moves down here."

"Ah, I see. So you're down here all by your lonesome," I couldn't help but coo in mock sympathy.

"Not really. You're here, aren't you?" The corners of his mouth quirked up in a grin.

Now it was my turn to feel my face heat with embarrassed pleasure. Oh, how I wished he wasn't half of a committed couple. How serious was the engagement anyway? The woman didn't even move down with her man? She left him alone in a strange city? Didn't seem very loving to me! Maybe he was looking for a way out of the relationship. That was why he moved down to San Diego. Hey, you never knew.

Before I could ask him more about this fiancée character, a scantily dressed waitress approached our table. She held out a tray full of florescent-colored shot glasses.

"Care for a shot?" she asked. "We have Scooby Snacks, Ding Dong Dogs, and Oatmeal Biscuits."

I had no idea what any of those were, but they looked delicious. And this *was* supposed to be my night for getting trashed. I raised my eyebrows at Jamie, wondering what he thought of the idea.

"We'll take two Scooby Snacks," Jamie said, answering my question by handing the woman a twenty and a five. "Actually make that four."

The woman placed four shots on our table and headed for her next round of victims.

"What do you think they are?" I asked.

"Only one way to find out!" He took a shot in his hand. I grabbed another. "To new beginnings," he toasted.

"New beginnings!" I chorused before I downed the shot. It was delicious. Tasted like whipped cream and pineapple. I grabbed the other one and proceeded to suck that down as well.

"Hey, wait for me!" Jamie cried, grabbing his other shot. "I'm not having a pretty girl drink me under the table!"

I beamed, licking the whipped cream off my lips. He

thought I was pretty. This sexy, cool, motorcycle-riding, ex-film photographer thought I was pretty.

We talked. We laughed. We drank a few more rounds. And by the time midnight rolled around and the DJ came on to start spinning some tunes, I was feeling pretty darn good.

"I love this song!" I cried, as The Cure's "Just Like Heaven" started playing. "I'm a total sucker for eighties new wave."

"Yeah. Me, too. Especially the British stuff."

"Really?" He was too good to be true. Way, way too good to be true. He was so cool and nice and he liked '80s Brit Pop? I sucked down the rest of my fourth (or was it my fifth?) K9 Kosmo. "We should go dancing."

"You think?" he asked with a twinkle in his eye.

"Definitely. And there's a club right down the street." Suddenly I had a bundle of energy. "It's way cheesy, but they do play eighties."

"Cool. Sounds like a plan."

We finished our drinks and left the bar. While trying to coordinate my feet for the walking thing one had to do when one bar-hopped, I realized I was drunker than I'd thought. Jamie propped me up a bit to make sure we traveled in a straight line. We laughed and giggled the whole way down the street.

When we got to the club, I tripped. Damn platform shoes. The bouncer took my lack of coordination as alcohol related and told Jamie I was too drunk to enter.

"But I want to hear eighties music!" I protested as Jamie led me away. I liked the feeling of his strong arms possessively wrapped around my waist. If he were my boyfriend I'd want him to always walk with me this way.

"We can come back another time," he comforted. "Unless you know another club around here."

"I know! I have eighties music at home. It's only a block away. We could have a dance party in my living room."

"Hmm, I don't know," Jamie said with a teasing look. "Do you have Depeche Mode?"

"I do!" I cried triumphantly. "I have lots of Depeche Mode. Even some of the early bootleg singles."

"Then lead the way."

*

Argh, my head.

My head really, really hurt. And I was dying of thirst.

I pulled the blankets over my head to block the rays of strong San Diego sun from blasting my sensitive morning eyes. What time was it? Why was I naked?

Uh-oh.

A flashback of memory—a snapshot of my body on autopilot—hit me like a rock dropped from ten stories up.

The last thing I remembered clearly was leaving Moondoggies. With Jamie. Getting refused at the next club. With Jamie. Going back to my apartment.

With Jamie.

The rest was blurry. But what I did remember was truly horrifying. Blasting '80s music from my stereo. Mixing up margaritas (like I needed more alcohol!) in my blender. Jumping on my bed, singing and dancing like an idiot to Simple Minds.

Making out with Jamie like there was no tomorrow.

I slowly rolled over to face the other side of the bed. To confirm my worst fear. Was there another body in my bed?

There was.

Not just any body, either. But a sexy, rumpled, naked, sound asleep, Jamie body in my bed.

Again. Uh-oh.

I groaned. How could I have been such an idiot? Gotten so drunk I didn't even remember having sex with the guy? That was so bad. So alcoholically bad. On about a million and three levels:

a) Having sex and not remembering it.

b) Having sex and not remembering it with a guy I barely knew.

c) Having sex and not remembering it with a guy I barely knew who happened to have a fiancée he was going to marry in three months.

d) Having sex and not remembering it with a guy I barely knew who happened to have a fiancée he was going to marry in three months and that I had to work with day in and day out for the foreseeable future.

Now what should I do? Did I snuggle up next to him and pretend I had planned the seduction? Get the hell out of bed and pretend I'd slept on the couch, hoping he didn't remember, either? Make breakfast? Leave the country and open up shop as a WWJD bracelet maker in Tijuana?

Hmm. Speaking of, what *would* Jesus do in a case like this? No, bad question. He wouldn't have gotten himself in this mess to begin with.

I noticed with some relief a ripped open condom package on my nightstand. One of the ones Jodi had stuffed in a drawer one time "just in case." Thank god, even in my drunken blackout I'd still had the wherewithal to be safe.

I tried to crawl out of bed, but at that moment the sleeping Jamie rolled over, tossing a heavy arm over my body and pulling me closer so I was spooned against him. I was stuck. Extremely comfortable, but stuck.

I felt his hot breath warm my skin and tried to think back to the night before. Damn it, why couldn't I remember the hot sex I'm sure we must have had? I bet it was incredible. He was incredible. Not that I should be thinking about that. After all, he was taken. And not just kind-of taken, but wedding-invitations-and-white-dress taken.

Oh my god, I was the other woman.

How ironic that I'd been out mourning the fact that my father had cheated on my mother and had inadvertently helped some other guy cheat on his fiancée. And not just any other guy, but my new coworker! How was I supposed to work with him now? Would I have to go into Richard's office and beg for a new photographer to combat the awkward morning-after syndrome?

Jamie grunted contentedly and snuggled in a bit closer. Was he conscious? Could he possibly know whom he was holding in his arms? Maybe he had been completely aware of his actions this whole time. Had he been as drunk as I? I couldn't remember. Was he a good guy who made a mistake or a jerk who liked to cheat on his fiancée by taking stupid, drunk girls home and screwing them?

I suddenly felt disgustingly dirty. Why had I been so easy? Slut girl: give her a drink and watch her spread her legs. Except, that wasn't me at all. Hell, I could count the guys I'd slept with on one hand and still have a thumb left over. What in the world had possessed me to drunkenly hook up with a guy I barely knew who was getting married in a few months?

I thought of Jen, sound asleep in LA, trusting that her fiancé was alone in his bed too and not curled up, buck naked, in another woman's arms. She trusted him, and I'd helped him betray that trust. My stomach rolled, and not just from the hangover. I needed to get up. Now.

I squirmed out from under Jamie and vacated the bed. Scanning the room, I found a pair of boxer shorts and an old t-shirt strewn on the floor. After donning the ensemble, I walked to the bathroom.

Staring in the mirror wasn't pretty. I looked like hell on toast. Black circles under my puffy eyes. Makeup smeared. Bleh.

I brushed my teeth and washed my face and then hit the kitchen to make eggs. What the hell, right? Even the "other woman" needed to eat a balanced Atkins breakfast, and maybe it would get my mind off things at the very least. I tried to swallow down the guilt, but it determinedly rose like bile to my throat. The smell of the scrambled eggs only served to nauseate me further.

"Maddy?" a sleepy voice behind me said a few minutes later. I whirled around. Jamie stood in the doorway, deliciously rumpled. He'd donned his blue jeans but no shirt. I scolded my eyes for straying a second too long on his perfectly sculpted chest. After all, I'd already done more than my share of sampling the forbidden goods. Time to get my mind out of the gutter and behave like a responsible human being. I realized my heart was pounding in my chest as I waited for what he'd say next. Then I remembered my manners.

"Do you want some eggs?"

"Maddy, I've got to ask you …" He raked a hand through his mussed hair in a way that made me pretty sure his question wasn't whether the eggs came from cage-free chickens.

"Yes?" Cool, calm, collected. Whatever he wanted to ask me, I'd be okay with it.

"I had a lot to drink last night and I wasn't sure … Well I woke up and …" He looked around the apartment. "Are we at your place?"

"Yeah," I said quietly. He didn't even remember agreeing to come here. Guess that answered my question about his level of sobriety.

"Oh. Right. And I woke up in …" He pointed vaguely toward the bedroom. "… and I didn't know …"

"You want to know if we had sex." I spelled it out, shocked at how clear and cold my voice sounded.

"Y-yeah." His face reddened at my bluntness. He hadn't been so shy last night.

"I don't know, Jamie. I don't remember either. But I woke up in my bed naked. And you were naked next to me. So I'd say chances are pretty darn good." I realized I sounded angry. Hurt. *Don't let him see that you care.*

"Oh God," he cried, sinking down onto the sofa, head in

his hands. "Oh God."

I stared down at him, not sure what to do or say. This was so outside of my expertise it wasn't even funny. I'd never had a one-night stand before. And I certainly had never hooked up with someone who had a fiancée. What would Miss Manners suggest in a case like this?

"Don't worry," I said harshly. "It's no big deal. Just forget it ever happened." I actually had reservations about letting the jerk off the hook like that, but it took two to tango and so really, I was as guilty as he was, right? Best to just move on and forget it ever happened.

He looked up. "God, I'm so sorry, Maddy. I don't know what I was thinking. I'm such an idiot." His face was white as a ghost and it appeared he couldn't meet my eyes. "I swear to you, I didn't mean for this to happen. I'm not that guy. I'm really not."

"I said it's *fine*," I cried, my voice breaking on the word. *Don't cry, Maddy! Don't you fucking cry!* But I couldn't help it. It was all just too horrible. I felt sick and confused inside. What was wrong with me? I should be screaming at him and telling him to get the hell out of my house. Instead, I was feeling sorry for the jerk. Like, I hated him for what happened, but at the same time, his distraught face tugged at my heart.

Jamie rose from the couch and approached me. He took my trembling body in his arms and pulled me close. Unable to stop myself, I buried my face in his chest and started sobbing like a baby. He smoothed my hair and kissed the top of my head.

"Shh," he whispered soothingly. "I'm sorry."

"I said it was fine," I repeated, bawling. He led me over to the couch and sat me down. "The eggs will burn," I protested.

He nodded and walked back into the kitchen, switching off the stove. So much for breakfast,

I guess. Then he returned to the couch, sitting down beside me. "I'm sorry, too," I said, staring down at my lap. "I never should have—"

He pressed a finger to my lips, stopping my words. "No,"

he said. "You did nothing wrong. It was completely my fault. Here I am trying to comfort you over your family situation, and I end up making it that much worse. I'm the only one here who needs to fucking apologize."

He pulled me into another hug, holding me close. I could feel his heart beating fast in his chest. He held me there for a moment, not saying anything. It should have been suffocating, but the closeness was strangely calming.

Finally, he pulled away, meeting my eyes with his own sad green ones. God, he was good-looking, I couldn't help thinking. Jennifer was one lucky girl.

"What do you want me to do?" he asked, his expression earnest. "Is it going to be too hard to work together now? Do you want me to ask them to reassign me to news?"

I swallowed hard. What did I want? Was I going to be able to move on from this? Or would it be eternally awful and embarrassing and weird between us?

"I don't know," I said truthfully. "I've never had to deal with anything like this before."

He gave me a wry smile. "Yeah, me neither," he said. "I guess if you think we can work through it … and be mature adults and all that," I mused. "I guess then it'd be okay to try working together still."

"Are you sure? I mean, I'm totally fine with that. But I don't want to make things hard for you. I feel so awful as it is."

I shook my head. "I'm a big girl," I said, though I didn't completely feel it at the moment. "I'll be fine. We'll just have to keep it professional from now on. Stay away from the Scooby Snacks."

Jamie laughed. "If I never have another Scooby Snack it will be too soon." He paused, then held out a tentative hand. "So, still friends?" he asked.

I shook it, hoping he didn't notice my fingers were still trembling. "Friends," I agreed.

But inside I wondered if it'd really be that easy.

CHAPTER FIVE

FROM: "Dr. Barbara Wilens" <bwilens@boston hospital.com>

TO: "Madeline Madison" <mmadison@news9.com>

SUBJECT: re: Leaded Lipstick

Dear Maddy,

Thank you for your inquiry about whether or not lipstick contains dangerous levels of lead. The chain e-mail you forwarded me is incorrect in saying that lead in lipstick causes cancer. Exposure to lead does not cause cancer. However, lipstick pigments can contain some amount of lead and while the levels are not sufficient to harm a grown woman, a pregnant woman might be inadvertently poisoning her unborn child, which could possibly lead to brain damage. It's a pretty big stretch to say cosmetics can kill, but we would certainly advise pregnant women to stay away from lipstick, just in case.

Sincerely,

Barbara Wilens, MD

P.S. To avoid bad luck, I did pass the e-mail on to five of my friends. Sure, it's probably

> completely unethical to forward incorrect medical information to the public, but I'm in surgery today and I couldn't really risk dropping the knife or leaving a sponge inside the patient's body!!! That would be a good story, huh? <vbg!>

I was never going out on a Thursday night again. I was way too old to handle such hangover potential.

I peeked around the corner of my cubicle to make sure the Special Projects department remained vacant, then plopped my head in my hands on my desk. So tired. Just needed a minute of shut-eye.

Jamie had offered to drive me to work that morning (on his motorcycle, no less!), but I decided it would look a little strange to anyone who saw us pull into the News 9 parking lot. Like why were we together in the a.m.? Didn't need those kinds of rumors on top of everything else.

I closed my eyes, attempting to block out the world. I felt terrible—both physically and emotionally—and couldn't stop beating myself up over all that had happened. How could I have been so stupid? How could I have let things get so out of control?

Deep in my heart, I knew the answer was simple. I had a massive, out of control, raging crush on the guy. And it didn't seem to be fading very fast, even with the awkward morning-after syndrome.

I was in such trouble.

"Sleeping on the job, are we, darling?"

I looked up, bleary-eyed. In my hangover stupor, I'd failed to realize David, my very gay political producer cubicle mate, had sat down across from me. Guess he was back from Senator Gorman's reelection tour. He grinned nastily, enjoying my pain a bit too much. I flipped him the bird and returned my head to its resting position.

"Girlfriend, you so *cannot* sleep! I have big gossip." He reached over to shake me by the shoulder. "Big!"

"I'm listening." Didn't have to raise my head for my ears to work.

"I slept with Brock."

Okay, that was news enough to warrant a head lift. "Brock?" I asked, incredulous. "As in Senator Gorman's son, Brock? As in Ivy League, Preppy Crew Captain Brock?"

"There's only one Brock, sweetheart," David said in his flamingest voice. "And let me tell you, he is prime grade-A beefcake."

"I didn't know he was gay." Senator Gorman was the most conservative Republican on the planet. Hell, he'd spearheaded the committee to make gay marriage illegal and had tried for years to stop gays from adopting children. "Does his father know?"

"Nope!" David looked pleased as punch. "He'd totally kill him if he did. And I'm sworn to secrecy. Of course, I was like: 'You know, Brock, I could ruin your daddy's career with this.' And he's like: 'Yeah, I guess I'd better be nice to you.'" David giggled. "And then he sucked my dick, which let me tell you, was very, very nice."

"Oh-kay then. Too much information alert."

David grinned wickedly. "Oh grow up, Maddy Pants. You're just jealous 'cause you aren't getting any."

"Yes I—" … was stopping right there. I would not say *anything* about sleeping with *anyone*. "You're right, David. I'm completely and utterly jealous. Cause I am getting nothing. Nada. Zip, zilch. I'm practically a born again virgin. And I am *so* jealous of all your gay action."

"Hmm. Methinks my cubemate doth protest too much." David studied me closely. "Me also thinks she has an I-just-got-fucked look in her eyes."

"No, I don't."

"You do."

"I DON'T!"

"You do. You do. You just got fucked. Who's the lucky guy?"

Unfortunately, the "lucky guy" picked that moment to walk over to my cubicle. I must have turned beet red, 'cause David's eyebrows shot up in recognition.

"So what's on the agenda today?" Jamie asked innocently. He must have gone home to shower and change. His hair was still slightly damp and he wore a button-down surfer shirt and a pair of khaki shorts. Delicious. Not that I was tasting. I'd already done too much of that the night before.

"Um, we, um, got a lead on the lipstick e-mail you sent me. I have an, um, interview with a doctor who can talk about it." Why could I barely form a sentence? I shot a glare at David who had turned around to check his Gmail, still giggling to himself. "Want to meet me in the parking lot in fifteen minutes?"

"Okay. I'll go get a coffee while I'm waiting. You want one?"

"No, I'm okay. Thanks." I'd already drunk about ten and my hands had the shakes.

After Jamie disappeared, David, as I knew he would, whirled around and started screeching. "Who was THAT? I go away for four days and we get THAT as a new photog? He is sooo cute. But I guess you already know that." He looked at me with a mischievous smile. "So, what was he like?"

"Like?" I asked innocently.

"Oh, come on, sistah soul. I totally gave you the scoop on Brock, and that's way more of a secret than you shagging the new photog."

"Yeah, but …" I lowered my voice. "He's engaged."

"Oh puh-leeze. Does he have a wedding band on his finger yet? No? Well, then, he's still fair game in my book." David clapped his hands together in glee. "So, I will repeat my question. What was he like? Divine with a capital 'D'?"

"Honestly, I don't remember." I told David the whole story, starting with my family falling apart and ending with Jamie comforting me the morning after.

"Awh, so sweet. Honey, he sounds like a keeper to me."

Was he on crack? "Did you listen to a thing I just said? I can't keep him. I don't even have him to begin with. He belongs to someone else."

"For now."

"Look, I'm not the type of girl who goes and steals other women's fiancés. The whole thing was just a stupid, lousy, drunken mistake that I will never, ever repeat again."

"Smart. Next time I'd do him sober. So you can remember how divine he is."

I groaned. "There's obviously no talking to you. Anyway, I have to go on my shoot. Do *not* under any circumstances tell anyone about this, okay?"

"Please. As if I knew anyone who would care about your little vanilla sexcapades."

"Good. Keep it that way. I'll see you later." I printed out the directions to the doctor's office and grabbed them off the printer.

"Peace out. Don't let the man get you down."

I rolled my eyes at him and gave him a wave goodbye, then headed out to the parking lot. I found Jamie loading his camera into the Ford Expedition news truck. Without saying anything, I hopped into the passenger side and took a deep breath. He joined me moments later.

"We off?"

"Off." I passed over the directions, looking straight out the window. What did I say to him? This was so awkward.

To make matters worse, my memory decided to treat me with a fleeting flashback of the night before. Namely, us collapsing on the bed after a particularly rowdy rendition of bedroom karaoke to Duran Duran's "Save a Prayer." (A song about a one-night stand—how appropriate!) Him, kissing me senseless. Me, weak in the knees. Him, pulling my tank top over my head. Me, well, still weak in the knees. Pretty pathetic, considering I wasn't even standing up. Hopefully he didn't regain any memories of the night in question, as I was becoming quite certain I hadn't exactly been up to par in the bedroom department. Not that I necessarily wanted him to have fond memories of my prowess there, either. "So, got any fun plans for the weekend?" Jamie asked, interrupting my musings.

Well, I had planned on painting my bedroom forest green, but suddenly that sounded overwhelmingly lame. After all, he was a filmmaker. He probably spent his weekends going to trendy parties with movie stars and complicated cocktails. I couldn't possibly tell him I had no plans and was going to stay home and paint.

"Actually, I've got a hot date."

Oh, Maddy? Why did you say that? Once again, my mouth had blurted before my brain could rationalize that the impulsive idea to tell Jamie I had a hot date was an extremely bad one on many, many levels. The most basic being because it was a complete and utter lie.

"Oh yeah?" Jamie turned to look at me. "Who's the lucky guy?"

He said it so casually it made my stomach ache. Not a hint of jealousy in his voice. He'd obviously moved on from last night's encounter already. Couldn't care less that I had a potential new lover. And why would he? He had his fiancée, after all. I was nothing to him.

Get a grip, Maddy. Forget about last night. Or you're in for a world of hurt.

I realized Jamie was waiting for me to describe imaginary-date man. "Um, well, he's this surfer guy." Yeah, surfers were cool. "With blond hair, blue eyes. About six foot." If I were going to have an imaginary date, he might as well be a hottie. "He's sponsored, actually. Does all these competitions."

"Really? What's his name? I did a documentary on surfing in So-Cal. I know most of the guys."

Argh. Maddy, why? Why not just say he was some normal guy Jamie would have never heard of?

"Oh, you probably wouldn't have heard of him …"

"Try me."

"… because he's from, um, Czechoslovakia," I said, naming the country farthest away from So-Cal that I could think of. "Just moved here last month."

"A Czech surfer?" Jamie asked, sounding intrigued. "Interesting, since the country's so far inland. How'd he become so good at surfing?"

Oh yeah, I'd conveniently forgotten the Czech Republic wasn't exactly beachfront property. Duh.

"His father sent him to, um, Ibiza every summer as a kid. He learned there." Ibiza was an island, right? I was saved.

"The Spanish Island with all the nightclubs? I didn't realize it was a kid-friendly place."

Darn. "Um, no, no. Ibiza, *Florida.* It's near, um, Fort Lauderdale." I laughed nervously.

"Hmm. Never heard of it." Jamie shrugged. "I spent a few months in Miami last year, too. Must be a small town."

"Yeah. Real tiny, evidently." *Please don't press me on it,* I begged silently. I was running out of lies.

Luckily at that moment, we turned in to the doctor's office. I breathed a sigh of relief. Jamie parked the SUV and turned to me. "Well, I hope you have fun on your date. You just let me know if this blond-haired, blue-eyed Czech surfer who grew up in a tiny town in Florida gives you a hard time, okay?"

I felt my face heat. Was he teasing me? Did he know I made the whole thing up? I narrowed my eyes. I wanted to protest, tell him I did have a real date. But problem was, I didn't.

I know! I'll find one!

Jodi had been trying to get me to sign up for that online dating service for months. She said it had tons of cute guys. From all over. I was sure out of the thousands available I could find a blond-haired, blue-eyed Czech surfer who summered in Florida, right?

Yup, that's what I'd do. I'd go home from the shoot, find myself a surfer and go out on a date. Then I'd take pictures with my phone and casually show them to Jamie on Monday to prove that I wasn't some pathetic lying girl who made up a whole person because she was too embarrassed to admit she planned to stay home and paint her bedroom.

"What are you up to this weekend?" I asked as I waited for him to unload his gear from the back of the Expedition.

He groaned. "Nothing as exciting as your weekend. I've got

to paint the bedroom of my new place."

Oh.

"I have to do some major yard work, too. I want to have the place all ready for when Jennifer comes down next month."

Argh.

I tried to squash the jealous feeling that bubbled deep inside, but no luck. All I could think of was what a nice guy Jamie was. Why couldn't I find someone who would sacrifice his weekend just so his fiancée could waltz down from LA and have a great place to live?

"What does Jennifer do?" I asked, trying to sound casual. After all, we were supposed to be friends, right? "She's an actress," Jamie said as he closed the SUV's back door.

Of course.

"Has she been in anything I might have seen?"

He shook his head. "She's done cameos in some low-budget movies. She's also a model."

"And a waitress?" It was cruel, but I suddenly realized her type.

He grinned sheepishly. "How'd you guess?" Easy. Though he already knew how. Actress/model/waitress types were par for the course in So-Cal. Just most people sort of tried to hide the waitress part.

"So, what does she think of relocating to San Diego?" I couldn't imagine if she was trying to have a career in Hollywood she would think this a very good move.

Jamie sighed. Deeply. "She realizes it's necessary for us at this time."

In other words she was pissed off about it. Poor Jamie. Here he was, sacrificing his moviemaking career to work in local TV news, so his loser waitress fiancée could continue to live in the lifestyle she was accustomed. And did she thank him for his dedication? No. She bitched about moving from LA where she would compete with two thousand other blond bimbos for lousy movie roles in even lousier movies that were destined to tank on opening day.

Okay, maybe I was projecting a bit here, but I bet I wasn't too far from the truth.

"When she comes down, you'll have to meet her," Jamie added as we walked into the hospital. "You'd like her, I think."

Men were so clueless. Didn't he know that I could never like her? You could never like the fiancée of a guy you slept with. It just didn't happen.

"Sure. We'll do lunch," I said, trying to sound amiable.

Jamie looked at me funny, but didn't reply. We took the elevator up to the correct floor and entered the doctor's office.

The interview went well. The doctor talked about the dangers of lead to a fetus and gave us examples of lipsticks that had tested positive. Evidently it wasn't an exact science. When the lipstick goo was being stirred at the factory, the lead levels didn't mix in evenly. So each tube from the same batch could have completely different levels of lead. And while nine times out of ten you were probably pretty safe, she did advise pregnant women not to use lipstick during their pregnancy just in case. And that was all I needed for my story.

It would have been better if we had a victim. I knew the station would have loved to get video of a brain-damaged baby, forced to live out a miserable existence all because his mother vainly applied lipstick every morning. But I could work around it.

I had to get this piece done and on the air so I could start working on that Mexican drug cartel one. Miguel had left a voice mail for me this morning before I got in and I couldn't wait to call him back and get the scoop.

I just had a feeling that was going to be the story that changed my life.

*

"How about that guy? He's cute." Jodi pressed a well-manicured finger up to the computer screen. Back at the station, she and I had holed up in her office and opened the Match.com dating site.

"He's not a blond, blue-eyed surfer from Czechoslovakia."

She rolled her eyes. "Tell me again why he has to be that?"

"That's my type." I shrugged. I didn't want to admit my embarrassing lie if I didn't have to. Plus, Jodi might get suspicious about Jamie. I wasn't ready for the lecture she'd be sure to give if she heard of my overnight adventure. As much as I loved Jodi, let's just say she once had a cheating fiancé of her own and wasn't too keen on encouraging her friends to engage in such activities.

"Since when is your type a blond? You're always dating brunettes. You hate blonds."

"Tastes change. Besides, I like Jamie Campbell Bower. He's a blond."

"Right." Jodi gave me a weird look and went back to searching. Unfortunately, there were fewer blond-haired Czechs who lived in Southern California and surfed than one might have imagined.

"Click on him." I pointed to a cute blond guy. Jodi complied and a profile popped up.

Ah-ha! He was perfect.

Blond, blue-eyed surfer. Lived in Czechoslovakia for several years as a child though he was originally from Germany. Under hobbies he listed surfing. I couldn't believe my luck. My imaginary guy actually existed. I should try this Match.com thing more often.

According to his profile, Ted liked long walks on the beach, cuddling up to a roaring fire. Thunderstorms. (Why did everyone always put that in their "likes" category? Was it supposed to be romantic or something?)

I pushed Jodi out of the way and jotted off a quick e-mail to Ted, asking him to check out my profile and whether or not he wanted to go out tomorrow night. I normally would have been a bit more coy, but these were desperate times.

Then I went in and changed my profile so my likes agreed with his likes. Sure, I didn't really enjoy foreign films or follow European football all that closely, but the likelihood was that these topics wouldn't come up on a first date anyway and I only needed that one date to prove to Jamie I hadn't lied.

I clicked back to his profile to see what he put under family. Ten kids?! He wanted ten kids? Wow, I felt bad for the woman he'd make his broodmare. But okay. I typed "ten" under my desire for kids. Why not? I wouldn't know him long enough for it to matter.

Satisfied that I had created a profile that would intrigue him, I clicked off the site. Tomorrow night at this time, I was sure to be on a date.

*

Ding, dong!

Why did the doorbell always ring the second I stepped in the shower? I could be conditioning my hair at four a.m. and someone would be sure to stop by. It'd better not be a vacuum salesman, I thought as I turned off the water and grabbed a towel. Or some Girl Scout. Actually, that wouldn't be so bad on account of getting some cookies out of the deal. Thin Mints. Mmmmm.

Ding, dong!

"I'm coming!" Whoever it was, they sure were impatient. I scurried down the hallway, clad only in my towel, and opened the door.

Lulu. And she had a big backpack, stuffed to the brim. "Hey, sis, what's up?" I asked, already kind of getting the gist.

"You said I could stay with you, right? Well, here I am." She pushed by me and dumped her grimy backpack on my beige IKEA couch.

Oh, great. Just what I needed. My crazy sister living in my tiny apartment. She stayed with me for a weekend once when my parents went to Vegas, and she trashed the place in two days. It was not for nothing her childhood nickname had been Pigpen.

"Did something happen, Lu?"

Lulu slumped down on the couch, putting her combat-booted feet on the coffee table. "Dad took off to go be with what's-her-face. And Mom hasn't been back from shopping."

"What?" I asked, alarmed. "She never came back?"

"Nope. I stayed up 'til like one a.m. last night and there was no sign of her. When I woke up, I was still alone. I decided to skip school and wait for her. But she's not back yet."

Fear raced through my heart. This was not good. Not at all. Mom could be lying in a ditch. She could have rented a hotel room and committed suicide. She could be dead. My mother could be dead!

"Omigod. Omigod. What are we going to do?" I asked, not really addressing my sister, since I knew she would have no solution. I grabbed the telephone and dialed Dad's cell.

"Hi honey," he answered. "I'm so pleased to hear from you."

"I'm not calling for a friendly chat, Dad," I said testily. I was still very angry at him and wanted to make sure he knew it. "It's Mom. She never came home."

"I'm sure she's fine, Maddy."

I white-knuckled the phone. "She's not fine. She's missing. Do you have any idea where she might have gone?"

"Well, according to my online banking register, it appears to be Hawaii. Oh, no. Wait." I hear clicking in the background. "She flew to Fiji this afternoon."

"What? Why would Mom be in Fiji? Or Hawaii for that matter?" I screamed into the phone. This was unbelievable.

"Well, from what I can see by looking at the charges, it appears she's shopping."

"And we are not to be concerned that our cookie-baking, stay-at-home, never-been-outside-the-continental-United States mother is suddenly on a globe-trotting shopping spree?"

"Honey, I'm sure she's fine. She's free for the first time in her life and she's enjoying herself."

"Fine. Whatever, Dad." Furious, I threw the phone across the room. Unfortunately, phone throwing only hurts the phone itself, not the person on the other line.

"So can I live with you?" Lulu asked.

I sank down into the armchair, head in my hands. What did

I do in a previous life to make my karma so screwed up?

CHAPTER SIX

FROM: "Diane Madison" <knitting_mom@email2.com>

TO: "Madeline Madison" <mmadison@news9.com>

SUBJECT: Hello from Japan!

Hi Sweetie!

Sorry this comes by e-mail, but you know those foreign phone charges can really add up! I'm at a Tokyo Internet café having a grand old time and I thought I might drop you a line. So, how are you? How's Lulu? Hope you are all doing well.

Not sure when I'll be home—having way too much fun! I can't believe all these years I sat around wasting time raising children (no offense, Sweetie), when I could have been traveling the world!!!! Now your father will soon be stuck changing diapers again and I'm free to do whatever I want—all on his dime!!! I may NEVER come home.

Make sure Lulu is doing her homework. And remind her that skipping school just ain't cool.

```
Love you to pieces,
MOM
```

I couldn't believe my mom was traveling the world and I was stuck taking care of my crazy sister. You had to understand, my mother was the most non-travel-the-world type you'd ever meet in your life. And she never, ever shirked from the smallest parental duty, never mind getting up one day and abandoning her teenage child. It didn't make any sense.

I couldn't mother Lulu. I could barely take care of myself. Like tonight. I had a date with the surfing Czech. Did I have to now make dinner first? Get home in time to check if she made curfew? I didn't want that kind of responsibility. I didn't even own a goldfish for this very reason.

Still, what could I do? She *was* my sister, after all. And despite what a pain in the butt she could be, at the end of the day, I loved her dearly. What was I supposed to do, kick her out on the street? Sure, her being here would cramp my style a little, but we were sisters. And sisters stuck together when their parents went off the deep end as ours had.

Besides, it wasn't as if Lulu was in diapers and needed constant surveillance. She was sixteen. Mary from *Little House on the Prairie* got married at sixteen. And she was blind! Lulu had perfect twenty-twenty vision—surely she could figure out how to use a stove or call for takeout.

So after laying out a few ground rules, I headed to my bedroom to find an outfit to wear on my date. Ted, the surfing Czech had called me yesterday, soon after I sent my e-mail. We talked for about three minutes—he said he was impressed by my profile—and ended the conversation by making dinner and movie plans for tonight. To avoid potential future stalker issues when I inevitably dumped him, I said I'd meet him at the Old Town Mexican Cafe, a fun restaurant in San Diego's historic Old Town. We'd have dinner. We'd have drinks. (Though not too many. I was so not having a repeat of Thursday with Jamie.) Then, we'd go to the movies in Fashion Valley and at some point I'd take a photo for proof. This way, I could prove to Jamie that I wasn't: a) lying to him and b) pining over our one-night stand. He'd know that I, Maddy Madison, had a full, active social life with cute surfer boys.

Then I could tell Ted it wasn't working out and move on. Hopefully the surfing Czech wouldn't be too broken up about losing me, poor desperate online-dating-service guy.

The only problem now was what the heck I was going to wear on the date. After a brief closet assessment, I resigned myself to the fact that everything I owned was hopelessly worn and/or ugly. Not that it mattered. After all, I was only using Ted for a quick photo op. But what if he turned out to be really cool? What if by some rare stroke of luck, he was The One and I had worn such an awful outfit that he ran away screaming and I ended up living out the rest of my life as the crazy cat lady because I didn't dress appropriately for the date? It was a risk I wasn't willing to take.

Finally, I decided on a swishy black DKNY skirt, a red strappy tank top, and cute little flip-flops I'd gotten from Urban Outfitters. The outfit said fun and flirty, but not to expect too much. A quick brush of eyeliner and a dab of lip-gloss and I was ready.

At first, Lulu wasn't too happy to learn that I was ditching her on our first night as roommates, but she seemed somewhat appeased after I handed her twenty dollars, a pizza menu, and the telephone. I promised myself that I'd spend some quality time with her the next day. See how she was doing. After all, this divorce was a major life change for her and I wanted to make sure she was okay with everything.

Thanks to traffic and zero parking, I arrived at the restaurant fashionably late and scanned the place for a blond-haired surfer-looking guy. No one in sight.

Maybe he decided to be fashionably late as well and was simply a bit more fashionable than me. As long as he didn't stand me up. That would be unbearable. To be stood up by a guy you were just using to prove to the guy you just slept with that you weren't a loser. Ugh.

Calm down, Maddy. Go get a drink.

After checking in with the hostess, who told me there'd be

a half-hour wait for a table anyway, I hit the bar and ordered myself a nice glass of Chardonnay. I would have much rather had one of their delicious margaritas (they had *eighty* different types of tequila here), but this was a first date which meant I had to behave myself. I had to seem grown-up and sophisticated.

I took a sip and then (in a very un-grown-up fashion) managed to spill half the glass of wine down the front of my tank top. Great. Thank goodness I didn't order a Merlot.

"Are you Maddy?" a male voice asked as I frantically tried to dab my soaking breasts with a napkin. I looked up.

"Yes, hi," I said brightly, pleased to see the Czech surfer (okay, I was going to have to start referring to him as Ted from here on out) was actually pretty cute in real life. Had the total surfer look going on. Tanned, in good shape. And of course blond hair and really intense blue eyes. Why the heck was he on an Internet dating service? I mean, he could surely get real life women. Then again, I was on it, too. Though that was sort of for a different reason.

I realized he was staring at my chest and was about to be of ended when I remembered I was still holding a napkin over my right boob. Oh yes. Great way to make a first impression. I lowered the napkin, painfully aware that the combination of cold wine and napkin rubbing had made my nipples stand at attention. He probably thought he turned me on or something. Bleh.

"Nice to meet you, I'm Ted." He held out his hand. He had nice hands. Not too callused, but not too femininely smooth either.

"There's like a half hour wait for a table," I informed him, after we shook. "I put our name in."

"Cool." He had an American accent and didn't seem Czech or German at all. But that was okay. I just needed a photo, not a voice memo, to prove our date. Though that brought me to my next question. How the heck was I going to snap a photo without him thinking I was a freak of nature?

He ordered a Corona and paid with a Platinum card. Ooh,

that meant he had money. Not that I was some gold digger, but still … very interesting. Maybe this date wouldn't be such a wash after all. Then again, he failed to ask me if I wanted a refill, which wasn't exactly a good sign.

"So," he said after getting his beer, "do you use Match dot com often?"

I felt my face heat. Did he think I was some pathetic creature who couldn't get a date? Then I remembered he was on it, too, so he probably wasn't trying to insinuate anything.

"Nope. I'm a Match dot com virgin." I chuckled. He didn't.

"My brother signed me up as a joke a couple weeks ago," he said. "We had a good laugh over some of the photos."

Or maybe he *was* trying to insinuate something. I withheld a grimace. Who did this jerk think he was? He wasn't *that* good-looking. In fact, if you lined him up side by side with say, Brad Pitt, he'd seem downright ugly.

"So, then, why did you decide to go out with me?" I asked, realizing my voice sounded a little huffy. "If it was all, you know, a joke."

"Well, duh. You're a major babe. Not like some of the other women on there."

Okay, he was redeeming himself a bit. A lot, actually. I smiled and flipped my hair back behind my ears in what I hoped was a "major babe" manner.

"Also, you said you loved European football on your profile. Do you know how hard it is to find an American girl who likes football?"

Uh-oh.

"So, what team do you support?" he asked.

Was it too late to run screaming from the restaurant? "Um, team?"

"Yeah, you know. Football team."

"Oh, right."

Think, Maddy! Think! My brain went completely blank. Actually "went" was probably the wrong term since it wasn't exactly full of European football team names to begin with. In fact, I wasn't even positive if European football was football at all. Something told me it might be soccer.

"England?" I said as half a question, praying that since England was a country in Europe they'd have a football team.

"Ah, you follow the national teams, eh? Should have known. Probably were a Man-U fan, too, before Becks crossed the pond, right?"

"Um, yes?"

"Can't say I blame you. I'd much rather see the old skipper in his natural habitat, too—rather than playing for the frogs."

What the hell was he talking about? I took a big gulp of my wine. I knew he was speaking English, but I had no idea what anything coming out of his mouth meant. Oh, why had I written that I followed football on my profile? This was going to be a long date.

Definitely time for a subject change. "So, um, you surf?"

"No." He laughed. "Sorry. My brother put that on my profile 'cause he said girls dug surfers."

Of course. The football thing (which I had no clue about) was real and the surfing thing (which I could at least hold my own in a conversation) was fake. I didn't want to even broach the topic of the ten kids. So now what did we talk about?

Luckily at that moment the waitress announced our names and we were ushered past other diners to our table in the back of the restaurant. Unluckier, when we got there, The Date From Hell turned the conversation back to football. He was like a mad dog with a bone. Who cared how many goals this player scored last night? Or how so-and-so was probably going to get traded because he screwed up royally in the midfield? Or how this other guy was always diving? I mean, diving? Was there a pool or something?

He paused only for a moment, as the waitress took our orders and then launched back into his incomprehensible spiel.

I desperately wanted him to shut up. But what could I say? I mean, I was the liar who initiated the date under false pretenses, not him. Now I simply had to sit back, enjoy my food and get through the night. Then I'd never have to see this football bore again.

Oh, and I had to get a photo. Might as well get that over with now. Then maybe after dinner I could feign a headache and get the hell out of Dodge.

"I have to make a quick phone call," I lied, reaching into my handbag for my cell.

"Is that a fake Kate Spade?" he asked. "The label looks funny."

Oh, nice. My counterfeit bag was evidently so counterfeit-looking that even a macho guy who had been delivering a sports monologue stopped long enough to notice it. I sort of gave him a half laugh which he could interpret as he would, ditched the bag back by my feet, and grabbed my phone. Needed to get this over with ASAP.

Pretending to dial a number, I turned on the camera and framed him up. I felt like a secret spy. A double agent. I was on a stealth mission to get photographic evidence of an international conspiracy.

I clicked.

SNAP!

Oh, shit. I forgot to turn the fake camera snapping sound off. I would definitely be fired from James Bond duty. Maybe Ted wouldn't notice.

"Is that a camera phone?" he demanded, looking a little pissed off. You know, between the handbag and the cell phone, he'd become suddenly become quite observant.

"Oh, ha, yeah," I said quickly closing the phone and stuffing it in my bag. "I guess so."

"Did you just take a photo of me?"

My face flamed. "Uh, I think maybe? It went off? By accident?"

"Did you delete it?"

"What?"

"Did. You. Delete. The photo. That you 'accidentally' took?" Now Ted looked seriously angry.

"Um, yeah. I did. It's gone."

"Let me see."

I was in hell. Seriously in hell.

"What? Why? It's fine. It's gone," I said. "Give. Me. The. Phone. Now!"

Reluctantly, I pulled the phone from my bag, hoping to delete the photo before he could see.

Unfortunately, he grabbed it out of my hands before I could manage to open the app. And when he did his own app opening, of course he saw his own mug staring back at him.

He pressed "delete" and threw the phone back at me. It landed with a loud clatter when it hit my bread plate and several diners turned their heads in interest.

"You're psycho," he said. "Completely and utterly psycho. Who does that?" He rose from the table. "No wonder you need a fucking service to find a date! You're pathetic!"

Before I could protest, he stormed out of the restaurant, leaving me to face the stares from the other patrons. "She took a picture of him," whispered an elderly woman at the next table. "On a first date?"

"Those camera phones should be illegal. I heard once that some people take them into locker rooms and then post naked photos on the Internet."

I had never been so humiliated in all my life. I wanted to stand up and scream and inform the whole restaurant that I wasn't a camera phone pervert, that I just needed a picture to prove to my engaged coworker with whom I'd had sex that I wasn't a loser with no life. But unfortunately, as willing as I was to make that speech, I didn't think it would change any diner's opinion of me. In fact, it might sway the few holdouts in the opposite direction.

Now what did I do? We'd already ordered dinner. Did I sit in my seat, suck up my pride and eat my meal? Would I have to pay for his? Did I even have enough cash on me for that? My credit cards were maxed and I hadn't deposited my paycheck yet. I'd come prepared to pay for my own meal, if it'd come to that, but not someone else's. What if they made me wash dishes? Let's see, I had sixteen dollars probably left on my MasterCard. Maybe seven fifty on my Visa. If I combined those two cards with the cash I had …

I felt tears prick at the corners of my eyes. Why did I always end up crying? It was my body's first reaction to upset, anger, fury, whatever. So embarrassing. Especially when it happened in public places. I angrily swiped at my eyes with my arm.

"Maddy?"

I looked up at the voice addressing me. Into the eyes of an angel. Jamie stood at my table. How did he find me yet again? It was like we were two soul mates, destined to keep running into each other.

"Jamie!" I cried, overjoyed to see him. I didn't care if he had a fiancée. I didn't care if our relationship stayed platonic forever. At that moment I simply needed a friend. "I'm so glad to see you."

"Are you on your date?" he asked, his eyes sparkling. "Do I get to meet the famous blond-haired, blue-eyed Czech surfer in the flesh?"

Shit. I was hoping he'd forget about that.

"He, uh, had to leave early." I grimaced. "I did have a picture, but …"

I waited for him to tease me, but he didn't.

"Didn't go as planned, huh?" he asked sympathetically.

"Not exactly." I sighed. "But he ordered before he took off, so if you're in the mood for a chicken fiesta burrito, you're in luck."

A ray of hope peeked through my dark evening clouds. This would be great. Jamie and I could have a nice meal. We could become friends. Other diners would see that I wasn't a loser who got walked out on by her date.

Jamie smiled. "I would but …"

"Jamie! Our table's over here. Did you get lost?" A tall, anorexic-looking blonde came up behind Jamie and slipped her arm around his waist. Protectively.

Oh. Jamie wasn't alone.

Of course he's not alone, a jeering voice in my head taunted. *Who eats at a restaurant alone? Well, except for you, you loser.* I suddenly realized this was the second time in a week Jamie caught me drinking by myself.

"Uh, Maddy. I'd like you to meet Jennifer. My fiancée." Jamie said, succeeding to unintentionally rub salt on my wounds. "Jennifer, this is Maddy. My new coworker at News Nine." He introduced us so casually, as if I weren't the other woman. The one who, just days ago, he'd accidentally had sex with.

"Nice to meet you, Jennifer," I said in my best new-coworker voice. If he could be cool and grown up, so could I. "I didn't realize you had moved to San Diego yet."

"She came down from LA for the weekend to surprise me," Jamie explained. I studied his face. Was he even the least bit bothered by the introduction?

"To check up on him, more like," Jennifer said with a saucy grin. She poked him in the ribs. "Make sure he isn't succumbing to the charms of some San Diego beach babe."

Ah-ha! There was the uncomfortable look!

"Well, it's great to meet you." I held out my hand. "I'm looking forward to working with your fiancé."

"Nice to meet you." Jennifer's hand reminded me of a dead fish. Bony and cold. "Jamie, they're going to give away our table if we don't get over there. And I'm *not* going to wait another forty five minutes."

"Maddy, would you like to join us for dinner?" Jamie asked, ignoring or not picking up on her tone.

Would I what? No way. No way was I going to torture myself by going to dinner with Jamie and Jennifer. I would be a third wheel. I'd have to hear about their wedding plans. I'd be nauseated when they called each other pet names.

Then again, I realized, this was exactly the kind of thing I *should* be doing if I wanted to get over my silly crush and develop a good working relationship with Jamie. After all, I'd agreed to be friends with him, and friends had dinner together. Simple as that.

"Sure," I said with a big, overly cheerful smile. "I'd love to!" I rose from my seat to join them at their table.

It wasn't really that bad actually, having dinner with Jamie and Jennifer. Not half as bad as eating alone would have been anyway. Jamie insisted he had planned to order the same chicken fiesta burrito Ted had (even as Jennifer questioned him about suddenly preferring chicken over steak) and proceeded to tell the waiter he'd eat my dearly departed date's meal so it wouldn't go to waste.

"So, what's it like to be a TV producer?" Jennifer asked after we had gotten our meals. She stabbed her salad with a fork. A plain garden salad. That was all she ordered, making me feel like a heifer for having gotten the fried chicken quesadilla. But screw it. After the embarrassment I'd suffered, I needed major carbage.

"It's okay, I guess." I shrugged. What else could I say? That it was a hideous job with hideous people? That it proved on a daily basis that journalism was truly dead? No. People didn't want to hear that. They only wanted to know what anchor X was like off the air and where reporter Y got her hair done.

"I'm actually trying out for this role of a TV reporter in a new Katherine Bigelow film," Jennifer told me. "Maybe if I get it, I can interview you. Kind of get into character. I love method acting, don't you?"

I had no idea what method acting was, though I was pretty sure it had something to do with Marlon Brando and James Dean.

"Uh, yeah. Method acting's cool," I agreed, a little hesitantly.

"Method acting's for freaks," Jamie interjected, taking a sip of his Corona. Damn. I so wanted to change my answer.

"Oh, I suppose you're going to tell me that the great Lee Strasberg was a freak, too, huh?" Jennifer demanded, dropping her fork with a clatter. "And that we actors are simply empty vessels, on set to illustrate an illustrious director's vision and not artists in our own rights."

"You said it, not me." Jamie said with an easy grin. "To me, method acting is nothing but mental masturbation. Feels good, but it doesn't get you anywhere. Why don't you use your imagination instead? You don't have to experience something to act it."

"Tell that to Mr. Robert DeNiro. Dennis Hopper. Some of the greatest actors of all time have been method actors."

I forked a piece of quesadilla into my mouth, trying to follow the conversation without much luck. It was suddenly painfully obvious that I knew nothing about Jamie and Jennifer's Hollywood world. They seemed so glamorous, sitting there, dressed to the nines, chatting about filmmaking, acting, and the rest. What did I have to contribute to this kind of intellectual discussion? I was a fool to have thought Jamie would ever like me or relate in any way to my pathetic common existence. I couldn't have conversations about who directed this or what 1939 film dealt with that. I didn't even go to foreign films 'cause of the subtitles. I always said that if I wanted to read something, I'd hit the bookstore.

I watched as Jennifer pressed her point, hands gesturing, eyes flashing with passion. She had a dream. A goal. She studied her craft. She'd probably be a famous actress someday. She certainly looked the part. Real pretty, with watery blue eyes, pale skin and straw-colored hair. Kind of Paris Hiltonesque. No wonder Jamie was in love with her.

And Jamie—I glanced over at him—how his eyes were alight as he bantered back, easily countering her statements with intelligent ideas of his own. I felt bad for him, being stuck at News 9 until the economy cleared up. He must feel so stifled, shooting brainless news video. He had this whole world. This whole life that he had to leave behind.

"Uh, Jen? I think we've put Maddy to sleep," Jamie's voice brought me back to the present.

"I'm sorry, Maddy," Jennifer said. "It must be so boring for you to have to listen to us drone on and on about filmmaking." She didn't sound too sorry, actually, but I let it slide. After all, I was the one barging in on her date.

"No, it's fine. I'm fine." I straightened up in my chair, suddenly realizing I'd almost been asleep.

Jennifer excused herself to go to the bathroom. Once alone, Jamie turned to me and smiled.

"Sorry about that. Ever since she took Acting one-oh-one

at Hollywood Community College she thinks she's Cecil DeMille."

Argh. I didn't know who that was. I mean, of course I'd heard the name but I couldn't place it to an occupation. I was so subscribing to *Variety* when I got home.

"It's okay. It was interesting." I tried to sound convincing.

Jamie laughed. "Yeah, right. You're a good sport. But Jennifer's like a pit bull when she gets on a rampage like this. She loves to argue. And I can't help egging her on, she gets so pissed." He took a bite of his burrito and chewed. "It's how all these Hollywood types act. They memorize a few directors' names, throw in a couple obscure film references and they think it makes them sound all intellectual. And then at parties they sit around and argue points that don't even make sense with one another. Each has no idea what the other is talking about, yet out of fear that they'll be labeled wannabes, they pretend to." He took a sip of Corona. "I can't stand when Jen acts like them, so I always call her on it. If she's going to spout of filmmaking nonsense around me, she's got to at least know what she's talking about. I don't like being around pretentious fakes."

"Well, you don't have to worry about me. I admittedly know zilch about Hollywood," I said, making a zero out of my fingers and thumb. "In fact, I don't even like artsy movies."

"You know, most of these snobs don't like art films, either. They simply pretend to so they'll seem cool, intellectual." He grinned. "If they knew my secret love of cheesy eighties movies I'd probably be banned from LA."

My eyes widened with interest. "You like eighties movies?"

He looked sheepish. "Not very manly, huh? Combine that with my love for eighties music and I might as well go around wearing a skirt."

"Actually, I think it's very manly to admit you like something unmanly. Shows you're sexually confident. So what's your favorite eighties movie?"

He thought for a moment. "Probably *The Breakfast Club*."

"I love *The Breakfast Club*." I tapped a finger to my chin, thinking. "But my favorite would have to be *Some Kind of Wonderful.*"

"*Some Kind of Wonderful,*" he repeated. "Yeah. I never got that one. I mean, why would Eric Stoltz spend the whole movie drooling over the boring, popular girl, even though he had that smoking best friend all along? I mean, he made poor Watts actually sit through their date."

"Right," I said, suddenly realizing the movie's parallels to our present situation and hoped he didn't think I'd brought it up on purpose. Time to change the subject. "And then there's *Pretty in Pink.*"

"That's worse." Jamie groaned. "At least in *Some Kind of Wonderful* he ends up with the right girl at the end. Molly Ringwald screws poor, faithful Ducky in favor of that sissy Andrew McCarthy."

"Hey, watch what you say about my boyfriend!" I laughed.

Who would have thought I'd ever end up at a Mexican café debating the endings of John Hughes movies with a hot guy? Now if only the hot guy in question wasn't on a date with another girl, I'd be all set.

"What are you guys talking about?" Jennifer asked, returning to interrupt our debate.

"Eighties movies," Jamie said. "What's your favorite, Jen?"

She rolled her eyes and turned to me. "Oh Maddy, don't get him started. He's like a girl with that stuff. You'd think he was gay."

I laughed. "It's okay. I like them, too."

Jennifer shot me a sympathetic smile, as if to say she understood I was just humoring her deluded fiancé and then launched into another tirade about acting in independent films.

At the end of the meal, Jamie insisted on paying for everyone. I protested, of course. But he laughingly forced my money back in my pocket. Then we headed out into the balmy San Diego night air and for a moment everything seemed all right with the world. The two of them walked me to my car and both hugged me good night.

I got into my car and waved to them as they walked away.

What a weird night! Definitely not how I planned it. But somehow it all seemed okay.

Still, I was exhausted. Trying to be ultra-charming through a whole meal proved more than a bit tiring. I couldn't wait to go home, crawl into my cozy IKEA platform bed, and go to sleep.

I pulled into my neighborhood about ten minutes later. Unfortunately, there was no street parking to be found. Sometimes this happened on Saturday nights in Pacific Beach (known to the party-loving locals as PB). One resident would invite fifty of their closest friends over for a little get-together and there'd be no place to park for the poor slobs who actually lived there. I didn't mind walking ten blocks back to my house as much as I minded the noise, and prayed that the party was on the other end of the street.

Unfortunately, this time around the party noise seemed to be coming from my apartment building. Worse, as I got closer, I realized it seemed to be coming from my actual apartment.

"What the hell?" I muttered as I fit the key in the lock. The door swung open. There was a rave going on in my house.

Techno music blared from my stereo. Kids in bright-colored T-shirts and even brighter-colored hair packed the place to the brim. People were dancing on my beige sofa. They were smoking and flicking ash on my carpet. There was even, I realized in horror, a smoke machine puffing out billowing clouds. The neighbors were going to think the place was on fire!

"Lulu!" I screamed, slamming the door. Like one of those '80s movies we'd just been discussing, someone turned down the music. Everyone stopped dancing. And stared. At me. The evil adult, come home to ruin the party. As I fielded their disgusted glares I suddenly felt very, very old.

"What?" demanded my sister, coming out from the kitchen. She had a bottle of beer in one hand and a lollipop in the other.

"Outside. Now," I said, pointing to the front door. She grudgingly complied.

"Who are these people?" I asked as I shut the door behind us. I could hear someone inside requesting the music get turned back on, now that the "wicked witch has left the building."

"Just some friends," Lulu said sulkily. She popped the lollipop in her mouth and sucked. "We were at this party and, like, the cops came and busted it up. So I figured you wouldn't mind if I had some people come by for a little after-hours …"

"I wouldn't mind?" I asked. "Since when did you think I wouldn't mind?"

"Well, you had a date. I figured maybe you'd get lucky and not come home." Her rationality was truly amazing. "What's the big deal anyway?"

"The big deal is that I've had a long night and all I want to do is go to sleep, but there are fifty freaks sprawled around my living room."

Oh, man, I sounded like my father. I, Maddy Madison, was officially a party pooper.

"They're not freaks. They're my friends."

"And you're drinking! Is anyone here even of age?" Lulu shrugged.

"I think Bill is. He bought the beer. Though I guess he could have a fake ID…."

I couldn't believe this. I had to stop the party. Now. The cops could come and bust me for allowing underage kids to drink in my home. And they probably wouldn't believe me when I told them I had absolutely nothing to do with it.

"What's your problem?" Lulu whined. "I always thought you were cool."

Oh, man. She was actually pulling out the "cool" card? Her words hit me hard. *I am cool*, I wanted to protest. *Really!*

I swallowed hard. I didn't want Lulu to hate me, but at the same time I couldn't allow this type of thing to go on. It was for her own good, after all. I had to be the adult, as much as it pained me. She'd thank me someday. Maybe.

"Lulu, if you're going to live in my house, you need to follow some rules. You can't walk all over me, trash my house and completely disrespect me and then tell me I shouldn't mind because of some warped sense of coolness you think I have. It's not acceptable."

"Fine. What-EVER. I'll stop the party. Geez!" Lulu opened the front door, then turned back to shoot me an evil glare. "You know, I was *totally* wrong about you."

"Sucks to be you then, doesn't it?" I snarled back. As soon as the words came out, I regretted them. As a rule, responsible adult types should not say phrases like "sucks to be you." But hey, I was parenting on the fly here.

To her credit, it took her less than ten minutes to clear everyone out. Of course, she wanted to go with them to the next party, but I, the loser adult, told her to go to bed. Actually, I told her if she went to bed I wouldn't tell Dad about the party, but hey, whatever worked.

After giving her a blanket and pillow and settling her on the couch, I headed to my bedroom, which unfortunately hadn't been spared from the party mess. Worried about potential teenage hormone-induced action between the sheets, I stripped the bed and made it again.

When had my life spun so out of control? It used to be so deliciously boring. Not that I was uncool as Lulu said or anything. Was I? I mean, coolness shouldn't be judged by one's acceptance of an underage rave at her apartment, should it?

I crawled into my newly made bed and blocked the troubling thoughts from my mind. A good night's sleep and everything would be okay.

I hoped.

CHAPTER SEVEN

FROM: "Laura Smith" <lsmith@news9.com>

TO: "Special Projects Group" <specialprojects@news9.com>

SUBJECT: Sweeps Story List

Hi Guys!

After much planning, Richard and I have finally finalized the story list for May. I think we've got some good ones this time! Please review the following stories:

- **Spray-on Nylons** —A new spray makes wearing pantyhose passé.
- **Cellulite Sneakers** —Special sneakers help you lose weight while you walk.
- **Pudgy Pets** —Now it's Fido and Fifi's turn to go low-carb.
- **The Fast Food Diet** —Big Mac can mean BIG weight loss.
- **Nocturnal Positions** —The positions you sleep in can predict the future of your marriage.
- **Nail Salon Nightmare** —How acrylic nails can lead to amputated fingers.

We will also be kicking off our latest *Household Products That Kill* series. Maddy has been working on our first segment—"Cosmetics That Kill" which edits tomorrow. We'll also be assigning Deadly Doorknobs, Kitty Killer, Bad Beanie Babies, and Suspicious Sinks. And we're looking for additional ideas, so if you come across something that can kill, please pitch it to me ASAP.

When working on these stories, please keep in mind that we are not to name any brand names unless we are saying something GOOD about the product. And please make sure if you're writing about an experimental new diet product that may or may not work, you add a quick sound bite at the end from some grumpy, old physician who doesn't believe anything but old-fashioned diet and exercise will lose weight. (As if people have time for that! :))

Your Boss,
Laura

Monday morning. Back at work. I had to write the "Cosmetics That Kill" story and get Terrance to record it. It amazed me sometimes to think how little I got paid to shoot, write, and edit a story and how much he got paid to read it. When I first started, my family always harassed me about when *I'd* be on air. Uh, that would be never.

It bugged me that most non-news people thought producers were all wannabe reporters. That we were all just sitting back, waiting for our big break. I had no interest in going live on the air. I liked working behind the scenes and never having to worry about getting fired because the latest surveys found that viewers trusted five-foot-two brunettes more than five-foot-six blondes. As a producer you got to do all the fun stuff and never had to worry about your hair and makeup or getting old and fired. The only downside was the pay. But I'd heard top *Newsline* producers made a good six figures, so at least I had a goal.

The mail icon popped up on my computer screen. I knew I should have closed the program before starting my script; it was too tempting to click over to see who had written, even though usually it was either spam, e-mail forwards, or pesky viewers who wanted to complain about a story I'd produced. Not that I minded viewer feedback, but nine times out of ten the viewer in question hadn't actually viewed my story—just the promo—and were condemning me on the fifteen-second tease I didn't even write.

This time there were two e-mails in my box. One from my dad and one from the promotions department. Both were bound to be equally upsetting.

I clicked open my dad's first.

Hi Maddy,

How's my little girl? How's work? When are they going to let you on TV?

Anyway, Cindi and I were wondering if you'd like to come to her ultrasound appointment tomorrow at noon. I bet you're just DYING to see your little unborn sister or brother. (Don't tell anyone, but I'm hoping for a boy!)

Let me know if you want to come. It'd mean a lot to Cindi. She really wants to meet you! Oh, and she wanted me to ask you if you knew her older brother. She thinks he might have went to high school with you. Does the name Tad ring a bell?

Love,

Dad

P.S. Is Lulu eating right? The girl is too skinny.

Ewh. All I could say was *ewh.*

Why on earth would I want to go see photographic evidence of Dad cheating on Mom? To me, the ultrasound would be a live video starring the evil seed that broke up my parents' marriage. Sure, technically the fetus would be my half brother or sister, but just because we shared a sperm donor didn't mean I had to have anything to do with this unborn creature.

And how dare he ask about Lulu as if it were no big thing? He should be the one making sure she ate, not me! He or Mom, who was now equally pissing me off with her globe-trotting adventures. One of them needed to climb the hell back on the parental wagon and start acting like the adults they were supposed to be.

Lulu still wasn't talking to me after Saturday night's incident. She'd left the house before I woke up Sunday morning and for part of the day I'd sustained the hope that she'd gone back home. But late Sunday night she showed up again, drunk off her ass, and passed out on my couch. Like a good sister, I left her a glass of water and some Advil on the coffee table. I wanted to lecture her about underage drinking but didn't want to set her off again. Besides, it wasn't that big of a deal, was it? I mean, I drank when I was sixteen. Maybe not on Sunday afternoons, but still …

I guess I didn't blame her for wanting to check out of reality. My parents' marriage had broken up, and besides passing P.S. e-mails inquiring about her weight and school attendance, neither seemed interested in how she felt about the matter. I'd probably react the same way if I were her. Poor kid.

I closed Dad's e-mail without responding and turned to the one from the promotions department. I knew from experience this one ought to be good.

> Hi Maddy,
>
> It's Ron, your favorite Promo Boy! Here's what we decided on for the promo for "Cosmetics That Kill."
>
> LURKING IN YOUR MEDICINE CABINET THEY SEEM INNOCENT …
>
> HARMLESS.

BUT YOUR COSMETICS … CAN ACTUALLY KILL YOU!

TERRANCE TELLS ALL, TONIGHT AT ELEVEN.

What do you think? Awesome, huh?
Ron

"Ugh" seemed the appropriate response. Nothing like a bad promo to ruin your day. Now I had to go argue with the promotions producer and beg him to change the promo to something that remotely resembled the story itself.

I picked up the phone. It'd take way too long to respond by e-mail.

"Ron speaking."

"Yeah, hi Ron. It's Maddy down in Special Projects. About that promo you e-mailed me …"

"Isn't it great? I showed everyone up here and we all agree it's one of our best promos ever."

"Um, yeah. Very catchy. But you see, the thing is, it's not exactly true."

"True?"

Of course. The word was a foreign phrase to the promos department. Actually, to the whole newsroom if it came to that.

"Yeah. As in, cosmetics don't actually kill you."

"Of course they don't actually kill *me*. I'm a guy. I don't wear cosmetics. By 'you,' we mean the viewer. The twenty-four- to fifty-five-year-old soccer mom we call Abby who has two point four kids, a white picket fence and a ton of disposable income."

I took a deep breath. "Right. But they don't actually kill Abby either."

"Hmm. Do they kill people who watch other stations besides News Nine? We might be able to work that in."

"Uh, no. Sorry. The story is basically how certain lipsticks that contain lead may lead to brain damage to unborn babies."

"Unborn babies can be considered viewers," Ron said defensively.

I grimaced. "They can't view. They're blocked by a wall of mommy flesh."

I could hear Ron's annoyed sigh on the other end of the phone line. "Since when did you get so technical? I showed the promo to my boss Chris and he loved it."

"There's nothing wrong with the promo. Except that what it says is not true." I couldn't believe I had to argue this point.

"Yeah, well, it took a day and a half to come up with this. We're editing tomorrow and I have no time to rewrite my entire promo just because of some technicality," he said in a huff.

It took him a day and a half to come up with five lines? It took me about an hour to write a four-page script. Promo producers had the best jobs in the world. I envisioned them having wild parties in their fourth-floor offices, laughing at the rest of the newsroom, who actually had to work. When an order came up for a promo they scribbled something out that took five minutes and then resumed the party.

"Look," Ron said. "How about this? We change the line 'your cosmetics can actually kill you!' to 'can your cosmetics actually kill you?' with a question mark. That way if anyone says anything you can say it was a question not a statement and that the answer to the question happens to be no."

I wondered if *Newsline* producers had to put up with this kind of bullshit.

"Fine. Whatever. Thanks, Ron." I got off the phone quickly, my heart no longer into fighting the good fight. Why did I even care? In the grand scheme of things it didn't matter one bit. So a few viewers might stay up a half hour later, worrying a bit about their killer cosmetics. When they saw the story they'd be relieved, right? It wasn't like an incorrect promo would destroy the world.

After squashing all my noble journalistic ethics, I went back to writing my script. All I could do was be responsible for my own work. And my script was good. It contained facts, figures, and useful information. People would learn something. Unborn babies would be saved from possible brain damage.

I'd have to tell Dad to make sure Cindi didn't wear any lipstick during her pregnancy. Not that I cared about her, but the baby's brain itself shouldn't be damaged simply because its mother was a home wrecker.

I finished the script and sent the file to the printer. I was actually pleased at how it had come out. A fair, well-balanced story that aimed to scare the viewer a little, but then brought back reason in the end so as not to keep them up at night. Sure, it wasn't the ideal piece to kick off the new *Terrance Tells All* franchise. Not big and sexy and undercover. But it was better than half the drivel that ended up on TV, and hopefully after I got this one on the air I could turn my focus to bigger investigations and really make my mark at the station and pad the résumé videotape I'd eventually send to *Newsline.*

I grabbed the script off the printer and headed down to the Newsplex to give it to Terrance to voice. That's one thing I definitely liked about my job. I had all the creative input and followed the story from beginning to end. The anchors and reporters simply read my words. I was the news world's Cyrano de Bergerac.

"Hi, Terrance," I greeted my own Christian de Neuvillette, approaching his desk.

He looked up, an annoyed expression on his face. I glanced at my watch. I didn't catch him right before a show, did I? No. He wasn't on for hours.

"What?"

"Um, I'm Maddy. Your new producer? I have a script for you to voice."

"You think I'm going to voice something I haven't even read?" Terrance reached out and yanked the script from my hand.

"No. Of course not," I said, a bit taken aback. "I want you to read it. If you want to tweak it that's fine, too."

I stood there, hovering like an idiot, while Terrance grabbed a black sharpie from his desk and started making corrections to the script. Actually, corrections might be an understatement. I watched in horror as he made sweeping Xs through almost every line of text, mumbling as he did.

"No! No! NO!" The last no was almost a scream. Several other employees looked over, and I felt my face heat.

"Is something wrong?" I asked, a bit freaked out.

He looked up, a brilliant newsman smile on his face. "Oh, no. Nothing. I'm just making a few tweaks, like you said."

A few tweaks, my ass. There wouldn't be a word left on the page after he was done with it. But what could I do? He was the million-dollar anchor; I was the lowly producer. Even though Richard had said that this was a producer-driven segment—that Terrance should simply read what I wrote—if Terrance wouldn't do it, I didn't have a leg to stand on. I couldn't force him to read it, could I?

This sucked. My beautiful, thought-provoking, factual, and fair script now looked like a two-year-old had gone mad with a marker. How was *Newsline* going to see my work if it never got on the air the way I'd written it? I mean, I could see tweaking. Editing. Questioning But not ripping to shreds. There was simply no reason. It was a good script.

"Retype this with my corrections," Terrance said after he finished his Texas Chainsaw Script Massacre. He handed me the paper's mutilated corpse. "*Then* I'll voice it."

I stared at him. "Was there something wrong with the script?" I asked, trying to bite back my tears. Maybe we could work together. I could learn to write in his style and then in the future we could avoid this embarrassment.

"Besides the fact that it was the most shoddy, badly written piece of drivel that I've ever had the misfortune of reading?" he asked, picking up a hand mirror and teasing his anchorman hair.

"But—"

"Look." He set the mirror down and turned to face me. "You obviously only spent about five minutes on that piece of garbage. If you're going to be writing for me, you need to work a lot harder. My viewers have certain expectations. I cannot, in good conscience, let them down."

I swallowed hard, crossing my arms under my breasts. "I

worked hard on that script. I didn't whip it out in five minutes."

He shook his head, a disgusted look on his face. "Well, if that's your best work, darling, we have a major problem."

I opened my mouth to defend myself again, but the phone rang. Terrance grabbed the receiver.

"Hello?" he said. "Oh, hi Susan … Oh really? The new Armani ties are in? Okay, pick me up one red and one blue … Oh, you think blue's too much? Okay, okay. Well, of course. You're my personal shopper after all. I simply must trust you."

He looked over at me, still hovering like an idiot. He frowned and waved his hand in a you-are-dismissed-insignificant-one kind of way. I backed off, humiliated beyond belief, while he continued to argue the pros and cons of Prada footwear.

I ran upstairs into the safe haven of Special Projects. David was out on a shoot so I had our cube to myself. I put my head on my desk and started to cry. I knew it was a babyish thing to do, but I couldn't help it. All the events of the past week—my parents' divorce, Lulu's party, Jamie and the one-night stand, and now being told I was no good at the one thing I knew I was good at—came crashing together. I couldn't take any more. I wanted to die. I knew that sounded overly dramatic, but I was in an overly dramatic state of mind.

"Maddy? Are you okay?"

I felt a hand on my shoulder and looked up, my face probably disgustingly bloated and red from my cry. For the third time that week, it seemed Jamie would be my guardian angel. He must have thought I was a pathetic blob of a human being, always crying about this or that.

"Yeah. I'm fine." I sniffed, my nose running like crazy. Jamie reached into his pocket and pulled out a napkin. He handed it to me and I blew my nose. "S-sorry."

He sat down across from me in David's chair. "What happened?" he asked in a voice that sounded like he really cared.

I related the Terrance story. "But it's not only that. It's

everything. That was the straw that broke the camel's back, really. I'm so sick of everything in my life falling apart in one week."

Jamie nodded. Then he smiled. "You know what cures life-falling-apart syndrome?"

"What?"

"Starbucks venti white chocolate frappuccinos with extra whipped cream."

"They do?" I said, trying to smile through my tears.

"My mom swears by them. Says they're a magic cure for all of life's ills," Jamie assured me with a serious expression. He rose from his chair. "Though, personally, I like a more manly-man drink myself." He beat on his chest for mock emphasis.

I laughed, despite myself. "Yeah, right. You're totally a closet whipped-cream junkie, I know."

"Hey! Quiet. You'll ruin my rep." He winked at me. "Come on, let's go."

Minutes later we sank into the plush purple velvet Starbucks chairs and sipped our decadent coffee beverages. Jamie with his triple Americano and me with my delicious girlie frappuccino.

"You're going to get sick of being my knight in shining armor," I said, feeling much better already.

"Never," he declared. "We're partners. That's what partners do."

"But it's so one-sided. You're always rescuing me and never needing your own rescuing."

"Oh, please."

"I'm serious."

"So am I." He set his beverage down and leaned forward in his chair. "You rescue me from boredom."

I giggled. "Are you bored?"

"Of course. And I'm a bit embarrassed to admit it, but you're my first—and at the moment—only San Diego friend."

"Really?"

"Really." He smiled. "We are friends, right?"

"Definitely." I smiled back and lifted my almost empty

drink. "To friendship."

He picked up his cup and touched mine, then took a sip. I watched him, feeling a bit warm and fuzzy inside. It was odd. You'd think that because we'd slept together things would have been completely awkward. But they weren't. And I did feel like I was his friend in a weird way.

Of course I also still wanted to jump his bones, but I wouldn't act on it. After meeting Jennifer she had become a real person in my mind instead of a vague idea. And I realized that no matter how much I lusted after her fiancé I had to rein in my desire. It wouldn't be right—and not because I was some saint, either. Rather, because I knew how these stories always ended: He and Jennifer would get married and live happily ever after and I would be the one left with a broken heart.

Much better to stay friends, keep the heart intact.

"Oh, I almost forgot." Setting down his cup, Jamie reached into his bag and pulled out a worn paperback. "That night at Moondoggies you said you wanted to read it."

I took the book and turned it over so I could check out the cover. The artwork depicted a dashing man dressed in black leather, carrying a futuristic-looking gun. In the background hovered a spaceship and a scantily dressed woman with big breasts. The gold embossed title declared the man was *Trapped on Mars*. Underneath in smaller letters it said, "A Novel, by Jamie Hayes."

"Your book!" I exclaimed, fascinated. I turned the novel over to read the back blurb.

AN INTERGALACTIC PRISONER WITHOUT A CAUSE

All Kayne wanted was a simple life. He and his wife lived comfortably in one of the few remaining Earth cities. But then he was accused of a crime he didn't commit and forced to leave everything behind—to serve out a life sentence on the Royal Mars Penal Colony.

There he meets Marla—the brave, independent rebel

> who would change his life forever. But could the two lovers hatch a daring plan of escape? Or would they forever be: Trapped on Mars?

"I know it's not Hemingway," Jamie said, a bit sheepishly, as I looked up from my reading. "But it's mine."

"Are you kidding? This is better than Hemingway. He just wrote about old guys fishing. This sounds really exciting." I looked down at the cover again. "When was this published?"

"Five years ago," he said with a sigh. "And I haven't been able to get anything published since."

"Why? Didn't it do well?"

"No. It did great, actually. I mean, not best-seller great or anything, but good for a sci-fi book."

"So what happened?"

He shrugged. "I must be the literary equivalent of a one-hit-wonder. I've started several books since and haven't been able to finish any of them. Two years ago my agent dumped me. After that, I kind of gave up on the whole dream."

"But you can't give up on a dream," I protested. "That's against the rules. I mean, look at me. My dream is to be a *Newsline* producer. Sure, it's a long shot—especially with what I'm stuck producing at News Nine—but I'm not going to give up on it."

"You're cute," Jamie said with a smile. "You know that?"

Oh, man. I knew I was blushing a deep purple. "Yeah, yeah." I brushed him off. "But I'm right, too. Do you think Hemingway never got rejected? In fact, I read somewhere that before he became a successful writer someone stole his suitcase and it had almost everything he'd ever written in it. And you know in the 1920s they didn't have any of it backed up on a hard drive."

"Man. That would have sucked."

"Yes. I'm sure it sucked royally. And imagine if Mr. Hemingway, greatest author of our time said, 'Okay screw this, I'm just going to be a lame-ass journalist for the rest of my life and never write shit ever again.'"

"I'm willing to bet money that Hemingway never once used

the term 'lame ass' in a sentence. Or 'screw this' for that matter."

I rolled my eyes. "Exactly. And he didn't quit, either."

"Fine. I get your point."

"So you're going to start writing again?"

"Just for you."

"Good." I nodded firmly, ignoring the chills of pleasure running up and down my spine. *Just for me.* I shouldn't like the sound of that as much as I did. "And I expect to see this work in progress on a regular basis."

"Yes, ma'am."

"And in the meantime I'm going to read this."

"If you want to. But don't feel obligated."

"Are you kidding? I'm dying to read it!" I stuffed the book in my purse before he could change his mind. "Thanks for bringing it in."

"No prob," he said. "On one condition."

I cocked my head. "Which is?"

"You're not allowed to let those losers at News Nine get you down, either. That bastard with a superiority complex, Terrance Toller, or anyone else."

I grinned. "Fine. It's a deal."

"And no matter how many exposés you have to do on killer household products, you are hereby not allowed to give up your *Newsline* dreams."

"Roger that." I lifted my hand in mock salute.

"Good. As long as we understand each other."

We did, I thought as Jamie stood to throw his cup away in preparation to go back to work. In fact, we understood each other too well. And that was becoming a problem. At least for me.

We were coworkers already. We were fast becoming friends. So why wasn't I content with that? What made me long for more?

CHAPTER EIGHT

FROM: "Terrance Toller" <ttoller@news9.com>

TO: "Madeline Madison" <mmadison@news9.com>

SUBJECT: ME!!!!

Madeline,

I took another look at your script and realized what the fundamental problem was. There is just not enough of ME in it. In fact, besides my voice, I hardly make an appearance at all. When viewers tune into a segment of "Terrance Tells All" they expect to see Terrance. Why would I bother even having a segment if it wasn't all about me? I am News 9's most valuable commodity. I'm sure I don't have to remind you how in 1998 I won the "Anchor You Trust the Most" award, voted by the San Diego community.

I've taken it upon myself to shoot some video of me examining different killer lipsticks. You can pepper my appearances throughout the script. Just stay away from the first few shots—the photographer completely messed up my lighting and you know how I abhor improper lighting!

Thank you for your efforts and please keep the above in mind for future stories. I know you do *not* want to disappoint my public.

Terrance

P.S. As a friend, I want to mention that you might seriously reconsider that Old Navy outfit you had on yesterday. If you're going to be interviewing people in the name of Terrance Toller, you *must* look the part. Acceptable designers would include Armani, Dolce and Gabbana, Donna Karan (which does not include that off-the-rack DKNY!) and Chanel. (And no, knockoffs are not acceptable.)

I closed my e-mail with a groan. Terrance was seriously out of control. Did he really, honestly think viewers cared if he was physically in the segment? Was he that genuinely narcissistic? I mean, hello!? He was a reporter, not Brad Pitt! Did he not get that?

But the question was, how did I explain that without having him rip me a new one? He'd already completely rewritten my "Cosmetics That Kill" script and it now barely resembled my thought-provoking, factual original. Producer-driven segment, my ass! What a laugh. Why did I even bother showing up to work if he was going to redo everything?

I could have gone to Richard and complained, but I wasn't sure what good it would do. After all, Terrance had been their number one anchor for years and held way more clout than some twenty-something, utterly replaceable producer like myself.

No, I had to pick my battles and "Cosmetics That Kill" was not worth fighting for. So I brought the mutilated script and tapes to Mike, the editor, and put the segment out of my mind.

Anyway, I was already on to bigger and better things—a story so good I could almost smell the Emmy.

The Mexico/San Diego drug cartel.

This was no everyday drug-smuggling cartel, either. Deep in the desert, the bad guys had built an underground tunnel that allowed importers to skip the high security of the Mexican/US border and instead waltz right into America with their illegal wares unchecked. Miguel had provided still photos his brother had taken of the Mexican side of the tunnel. He'd also mapped out the location of the States-side exit and promised that if we came to Mexico, he would arrange an off-hours secret tour of the Mexican entrance.

I hadn't yet pitched the idea to Richard or my executive producer Laura. I knew that they'd get way too excited and pin all sorts of hopes on it. Then, if things didn't pan out, I'd look like a bad producer and no way was I willing to take that risk. So I decided instead to work on it on the side, shoot it, and write it. Maybe even edit it in secret, while working on my other more mundane projects, then present it to them as a major sweeps story bonus. Once they saw it, they'd love it, I was sure. And if it didn't pan out, no one would be the wiser.

"So, what do you think?" I asked Jamie after he paged through Miguel's documentation and photos.

"I can't believe he sent this all to you," Jamie said, handing the papers back to me. "What a scoop."

"Yup. An exclusive investigation. All ours."

"So what do you propose we do?"

I grinned. "Head out to the desert undercover, of course."

"That could be dangerous," Jamie pointed out. "The desert is wide open. You and I would be sitting ducks with a news camera. They'd see us a mile off. If they're importing what this guy says they're importing, they probably have armed guards and everything."

"We won't bring the big news camera. We have a lipstick cam here."

"Lipstick cam?"

"Yeah. We call it that 'cause it's so tiny. Like a tube of lipstick. The whole camera fits into a purse or bag and the lens peeks out of a small opening. It's very 'stealth.'" I pulled out the contraption from under my desk. It really was cool. And so useful for getting all the important undercover video investigative stories needed.

Jamie examined the camera. "Nice," he announced. "I suppose we shouldn't take a news truck, either. Too obvious with all the antennas and stuff sticking out the top."

"Good point. We can take my car."

"If you want to be even more stealthy, we could take my motorcycle," Jamie suggested. "A car stopped on the side of the road might seem a bit obvious. Like, why are they stopped? Are they broken down? But motorcyclists stop and hang out all the time."

"You've got a point." I felt a small thrill tickle the pit of my stomach. I was going to get to ride on Jamie's motorcycle! That meant wrapping my arms around him and feeling the contours of his strong chest. Laying my head against his back and letting the desert wind whip through my hair.

Whoa, girl. You're just friends, remember. Friends don't care about that sort of thing.

Still, that motorcycle idea did make the most sense. I'd just have to control my hormones and we'd be all set.

Jamie looked at his watch. "When do you want to go?"

"Now's as good a time as any, don't you think?"

We walked down to the Newsplex and informed the girl on the assignment desk that we'd be gone for the remainder of the day "on assignment." (That was one of the pluses of TV news—no one batted an eyelash if you disappeared for the day.) Then we headed out the side door to the News 9 parking lot. Jamie's motorcycle was parked nearby: a sleek black and silver bike with the brand name "Triumph" molded onto its side.

"Nice ride," I remarked, running my hand along the body. I actually knew next to nothing about bikes—it could be a total piece of junk—but it had a cool paint job….

"Thanks. It's a British bike," Jamie said, grabbing two helmets from a back compartment. "And thus, highly superior to garish, overpriced American Harleys."

"Oh, please. You're a total Anglophile, Jamie," I teased. "Between bikes and Brit Pop. You know, there's nothing wrong with buying American once in a while."

He laughed. "Nothing except we Yanks could never make such a lean, mean, biking machine as my baby here." He stroked the handles almost lovingly, prompting me to erupt in giggles.

He handed me a black helmet and I pulled it over my head, feeling a little like Darth Vader. Jamie reached over and flipped up the visor.

"Ever been on a motorcycle before?" he asked.

I shook my head and held my hands in front of me, palms up. "Motorcycle virgin here."

"Are you nervous?"

Nervous? Me? Okay, so I had butterflies racing through my stomach like they were qualifying for the Indy 500, but I wasn't about to admit it.

"Nah," I said with a shrug.

"Good. It's simple anyway. Just wrap your arms around me and hold on tight."

"Roger that." Oh yeah, that was a definite ten-four.

Jamie flipped his visor down and straddled the bike. I climbed on behind him, annoyed at the way my body instantly tightened as it came into contact with his. It was so embarrassing the way he could turn me on without even trying. Attempting to think of unpleasant things to calm my senses, I wrapped my arms around his chest. My breasts pressed against his back and I wondered if the proximity was doing anything remotely similar to him as it was doing to me.

He looked so sexy in his black leather jacket and helmet. I never realized I had a thing for bikers before. He turned his head back to look at me.

"Are you ready?"

"Ready."

And we were off.

The wind whipped through my thin clothing as we flew down the street. I had no idea how fast we were actually going, but it felt like a million miles an hour. For a brief moment I pondered the fact that should the bike tip over, I certainly would be dead, but then put it out of my mind and simply enjoyed the ride.

As he slowed down and stopped at a traffic light, Jamie turned his head toward me and flipped up his visor. "How do you like it so far?" he asked.

I grinned. "Dreamy."

He turned back to the road and revved the engine. The light went green and we took off again. I hugged him tighter as our speed increased, enjoying being this close to him. Even through my helmet I could smell the sexy scent of leather from his jacket. This was heaven. The world could fly by us at top speed, but when all was said and done, we were completely alone together.

I definitely needed a biker boyfriend. But a cool one, obviously, not a fat, tobacco-chewing Hell's Angels type. Someone handsome, nice, and cool. Someone exactly like Jamie. I wondered if he had a twin....

Stop it, I berated myself. *You can't have Jamie. He's taken. He'll be married soon. You need to stop thinking about it.*

But I couldn't stop thinking about it, I realized. And I'd been trying for days with no luck. I still wanted him so badly it hurt. And being put in this kind of position, where I was forced to physically touch him for hours on end was driving me absolutely nuts.

To distract myself, I turned my thoughts to our mission. Truth be told, I was a bit scared going out into the desert by ourselves to find the tunnel site. What if there were guys with guns? What if they killed us and buried our bones? Would we be dug up by coyotes and eaten?

Okay, maybe I'd go back to thinking about Jamie. Hmm. Was it too late to stop the wedding?

After swinging by my house so I could grab more-appropriate desert hiking attire, we headed out to the desert. After about an hour, we exited the well-paved freeway and turned down a winding, bumpy back road—much to my butt's dismay.

Even though I was a born-and-bred San Diego chick, I hadn't spent much time out in the desert. Once in high school

I dated this loser motocross fanatic. He'd been convinced that if he dragged me out to the middle of desert nowhere and sat me in his pickup truck while he and his buddies rode their bikes around the dunes, I'd grow to love the barren wasteland. After three torturous outings, I decided dust was a bad look for me and ended it.

We passed dilapidated trailers, sun-bleached shacks, gas stations with one rusty pump, and wooden roadside stands where desert entrepreneurs displayed Native American knickknacks, hoping for some lost tourist to take pity and whip out their wallet.

But as we got deeper into the desert, the signs of humanity slipped away and were replaced by an almost creepy barrenness. A vast landscape of scrubby trees, wilted grasses, and rocky hillsides. The road's pavement began to disappear and soon we were riding on a completely dirt road. The bike's tires kicked up dust and sand, generously coating me in grime. The things I did for this job!

After an hour of this, Jamie thankfully pulled over to the side of the road and killed his bike engine.

"Can you grab the map out of my saddlebags?"

I reached back and grabbed it, handing it to him. He studied it for a moment. "According to this, the dig site is down this trail," he said, pointing to a dirt footpath off the side of the road. "I can't get my bike down there. We're going to have to walk."

I stared down the trail and gulped. I hadn't realized we'd be doing part of the journey by foot, away from the safety of our getaway bike. I looked down at my feet. Good thing I'd decided to wear sensible hiking boots. Still, I wasn't going to be able to outrun a drug dealer's bullet, should one come whizzing at me at some point.

"Okay." I agreed hesitantly as I slid off the bike, careful not to burn myself on the hot metal sides. Didn't want Jamie to think I was some wimpy girlie-girl. I could do this.

He grabbed the hidden camera from the saddlebags. We'd set it in a backpack, creating a hole in the front pocket for the lens to peek through. You'd never be able to tell there was a camera inside.

"Ready?" he asked.

"Ready," I answered, though suddenly I realized my hands were shaking and my heart beating wildly. The trip was about to get a lot more adventurous. Was I ready? Could I do this?

I took a deep breath and willed my hands to stop shaking.

Jamie studied me. "Are you okay? You look a little pale."

I masked my concern with a smile. No need for him to know what a wimp I was. After all, Diane Dickson reported live from Iraq, didn't she? I could surely brave the San Diego county desert. If anyone approached us, we'd simply tell them we were hikers, out enjoying a beautiful desert day. No one would ever guess our true mission.

"I'm fine. Let's go."

We started down the trail and into the desert. According to Jamie's map, we had about a forty-minute hike to the dig site. Luckily he'd brought a bunch of water bottles. That and a fancy high-tech GPS mapping device so we wouldn't get lost. The man was a Boy Scout with his preparedness.

The sun beat down on the dusty landscape as we followed the rocky trail. Unlike the stereotypical sand deserts such as the Sahara, San Diego deserts featured rocky cliffs and scrubby trees. A harsh landscape where only the strong survived. It was beautiful, in its own savage way. Peaceful. No modern technology to spoil it.

Jamie's cell phone rang. Of course.

"Hello?" he said, after pulling it from his pocket. "Hello?" He glanced at the phone's screen and then put it back to his ear. "Can you hear me now?" he asked the person on the other end of the line, mimicking the Verizon commercial.

After a few more "hellos," he gave up and flipped the phone closed. "Jennifer," he informed me. "But I could barely hear her. No cell towers in the desert, I guess." He shoved the phone into his back pocket.

"Do you think it was important?" I asked.

He shook his head. "Nah. Probably some kind of catering

crisis. There've been a lot of those lately."

I laughed, though inside I felt a bit like dying. It was so hard to be reminded of his upcoming nuptials. Very soon, this wonderful man would be officially and legally off the market. I had to quash this ridiculous crush I had as soon as possible.

"So, how'd you meet Jennifer?" I asked, to make conversation and satisfy my masochistic curiosity.

"She auditioned for a movie I was working on," he said. "Didn't get the part, but did get me."

"Ah, the booby prize," I teased.

"Yeah, she'd probably tell you that," he said with a laugh. "Though she was a lot different back then. She'd only recently arrived in Hollywood. Small-town girl from Missouri, desperate to become a movie star. Buck-toothed and brown-haired."

"Are we talking about the same Jennifer? Your fiancée Jennifer?"

Jamie grinned ruefully. "One and the same. Pre Hollywood extreme makeover, of course."

"Well she's beautiful now. Stunning. I mean, she looks like Paris Hilton."

"I guess." Jamie pulled a twig from a bush as he walked past and snapped it in his hand. "Though to tell you the truth, I prefer a more natural look."

I groaned. "Oh puh-leeze. Men always say that! And then they go off and ogle all the supermodels and porn stars."

"You think I ogle porn stars?"

"All men do," I insisted stubbornly. "Whether they admit it or not."

"Fair enough. I may ogle, as you call it, but I'm not going to marry one."

"Ah, here's the Madonna and whore complex!" I said triumphantly. "You want to marry someone pure—like Mom, right?"

He shuddered. "Please. You haven't met my mother."

"You know what I mean, though. You men are all the same. Sow your wild oats while young, then marry the one girl who didn't give it up."

He laughed. "Maddy, your peek into the male psyche is astounding. Did you learn all that in Psychology one-oh-one, or did you take advanced courses?"

I playfully shoved him. "Whatever, dude. Face it. You know I'm right."

"I don't," he insisted innocently. "If you were, then I wouldn't be marrying a Hollywood starlet in a few months. Jen is the anti-mom. And she'd rather commit hara-kiri than set foot in a kitchen."

"Okay, okay. I stand corrected." I giggled. "You managed to buck the trend. Marry the whore instead of the Madon—" I stopped abruptly and turned to him. "Er, not that Jen's a whore. Sorry, that came out wrong."

He chuckled. "I knew what you meant."

We fell silent after that. I felt kind of bad, teasing him about his fiancée. I didn't want him to think that I was doing it as a desperate attempt to get him to break up with Jennifer and go out with me. That was so not my intention. Had I taken the banter a step too far?

"What about you?" Jamie asked suddenly, breaking into my thoughts.

"Me?" I cocked my head in question.

"Yeah, you. Are you the Madonna or the whore?"

My face flamed. "Uh … I'm … well …" How did one answer that question? If I said Madonna, I'd be the boring, cookie-baking mom type. Which I wasn't. But I wasn't some whore, either.

"Not as easy to categorize when it's about yourself, huh?" Jamie asked. I looked up at him and could see the teasing light in his eyes.

Fine. He got me there.

"Yeah, yeah," I acquiesced. "You've proven your point."

"But you haven't answered my question." Jamie stopped and faced me. His eyes darkened and the teasing glimmer retreated from his face. "Which are you?" I suddenly felt hot in a way that had nothing to do with the desert sun beating down on us. I wanted to squirm away from his intense gaze. What was it about this guy that made me so crazy and weak in the knees? Did he have some kind of Maddy kryptonite in his pocket or something?

The phone rang again.

"Oh, for Christ's sake!" Jamie cried, dropping eye contact to grab the receiver. "Hello? Hello?" He banged on it with his hand and put the phone back to his ear. "Jen? Can you hear me?"

He pulled the phone away from his ear and pressed the 'off' button. Then he stuffed it back into his pocket.

"We'd better get hiking."

We stayed silent for a while after that as we trudged through San Diego desert, careful not to catch our clothes on the prickly cacti that lined the trail. Truth be told, I was too busy willing my heart to slow down to bother pursuing a conversation. I couldn't believe how turned on that boy could get me with a simple look. And then his fiancée had to show up via wireless transmission and ruin it all.

That was it. I had to stop putting myself in these situations. There was just too much chemistry between us when we were alone together, and it always made me hope for something more. But really, in the end, none of this was going to lead anywhere. He had Jennifer. They'd be married in a few months. That was reality and I needed to accept it. I wasn't a home-wrecker, after all.

I thought about my dad's other woman. Cindi with an "i". Did she have the same worries, guilt, and fear when she first met my dad? Did he seduce her, make her fall in love with him and then let her sit and wonder if he'd ever leave his wife? Did she try to break it off, only to find out she was pregnant? What went through her heart when the stick turned pink? Was she overjoyed at the new life she'd created with a married man? Or overwhelmingly afraid that she may suddenly find herself a single mom?

I grimaced. I didn't like thinking about Cindi with an "i" as a real person with doubts, fears, and insecurities. Better to think of her as the whore who broke up my parents' marriage.

But was she?

About twenty minutes of troubling thoughts later, Jamie stopped and looked at his map and compared the coordinates to his GPS computer. "I think it's right over that hill," he said, pointing ahead to a cliff-face drop-off.

This was it! My pulse kicked up a notch in anticipation.

"Okay," Jamie said in a low voice. "Let me turn on the camera." He casually reached into the backpack and hit the *record* button, then closed it again. We had about an hour of run time before he'd have to switch tapes.

"Ready?" he asked.

I nodded and we started walking again. Our steps suddenly seemed uncomfortably loud, and I had the weird feeling we were being watched, though there was no one in sight.

My heart beat loudly in my chest. What if we got caught? What if they found the camera? Would they destroy the tape? Or would they do more? Torture us? Kill us? Oh, why had I thought this would be a good story idea? I would never be able to get a job on *Newsline* if I were dead!

We reached the brink of the cliff and looked down. There, about hundred yards away, sat a big warehouse. I could see excavators and other digging equipment. Oil wells dotted the landscape. But no tunnel.

"Is that it?" I asked, disappointed.

Jamie pointed the camera lens to get a few shots of the building. "Did you expect mounds of cocaine piled out in the open?"

"No." I shrugged. "But maybe at least a giant tunnel. This could be anything. Looks like an oil field. Maybe Miguel was wrong."

"They want you to think it's an oil field. That way they can go about their business in secret, I'll bet." Jamie zoomed in the camera and panned the landscape below. "But would an oil field have armed guards flanking each side of the front door?"

I pulled out my binoculars and took a look. Sure enough, there were two camouflage-wearing, AK-47-carrying guards standing watch. "Wow, you're right." I set down the binoculars, hands trembling with fear. What if they looked up and saw us? Would they start shooting?

Calm down, Maddy. After all, Diane Dickson would not let fear get the best of her.

Good thing Jamie was doing the camerawork. My shaking hands would have made the video come out looking like the *Blair Witch Project.*

"Ooh! The doors!"

The guards stepped aside as the large warehouse doors swung silently open. A battered van with Mexican license plates drove out of the building. It stopped right outside and the driver killed the motor, but remained in the vehicle.

"I bet there are drugs inside," Jamie said.

I grabbed his arm and pointed over to the far left of the building. "Someone's driving up."

Jamie turned the camera to zoom in on the new car approaching down a dirt road, its tires stirring up a cloud of desert dust. When the air cleared, I realized it was a brand-new black Mercedes SUV with tinted windows.

"This is so exciting," I whispered as the door to the Mercedes opened. I'd never been on a stakeout before and the adrenaline pumping through my veins was better than any high.

"Yeah," Jamie whispered back, sharing my enthusiasm.

A skinny man with curly black hair, wearing cutoff jeans and a wife-beater stepped out of the SUV. Not the kind of guy I'd have expected exiting the expensive automobile. He rubbed a handkerchief across his sweaty forehead and walked over to the van. One of the warehouse guards yanked open the sliding side door and the man leaned inside, as if to inspect the van's contents.

I squinted my eyes. The guy didn't look how I'd imagined a drug cartel member to look. I was thinking more John Gotti, I guess, not an out-of-work plumber. But, I reminded myself, it was doubtful Mr. Gotti actually made on-site appearances. This dude was probably just a courier.

I lifted the binoculars and zoomed in, hoping for a closer

look, but I'd maxed the zoom out. "Piece of crap," I muttered.

"I wonder who that guy is," Jamie pondered aloud, still watching through the camera. "He's got to be important. Look how they're all watching him, waiting."

I looked back through the binoculars. The man had pulled out a large bag of white powder from the truck and was examining it closely.

"Ooh, ooh!" I squealed, attempting to keep my ecstatic cries at a low decibel. Thank the Lord! We had the smoking gun! Or, in this case, the smoking cocaine. This was better than I'd dared dream. *Newsline*, *Newsline* here I come! "This is too good to be true. I feel like I'm watching a movie!"

"I can't believe he's doing this out in the open," Jamie whispered back. "But then again, we're pretty far from civilization. If you didn't know where to look, you'd never find this place.

He was right. We were miles and miles from any marked roads or towns. The drug dealers probably felt they were perfectly safe. Imagine if they knew there was a TV crew above them on the ledge. That'd get the bullets flying, for sure. The thought made me crouch a little lower to the ground.

The Mercedes guy reached down to his boot and pulled out a knife. He slit open the bag and stuck a pinkie finger in the powder, bringing it to his lips.

"He's tasting it. I bet he's making sure it's real."

"This guy is like a walking-talking drug-dealing cliché." Jamie laughed.

After tasting, the guy nodded to the guard and walked back to his SUV. The guards began to empty the van and transfer bag after bag into the back of his vehicle. It appeared the dealer had some kind of secret compartment underneath the floor to stash the drugs. Some bags had the white powder. Others seemed to contain multi-colored pills. Probably Ecstasy or something.

"Look at all of that," Jamie whispered. "This isn't some fly by night operation. It's got to be from a major cartel."

After loading up the SUV, the guards slammed its back

doors shut. The man started up the engine and drove away. Once he was gone, the van driver circled around and drove back through the warehouse. The guards shut the door behind him.

"Mark the position of this building on your GPS," I instructed Jamie as I zipped close the backpack. "We can go to the nearest town and look up the property records. See who owns the land."

"Good idea." Jamie recorded our coordinates, then looked at his watch. "It's getting late, but if we hurry we may be able to catch them before they close. Save us another trip out to no-man's-land."

I personally doubted we'd get back in time, especially the way my feet were already aching from the hike out. But I was willing to give it a shot if it meant I was getting the hell out of there.

The setting sun cast a warm orange glow on the desert landscape as we headed back to the motorcycle. Neither of us spoke much, and we walked with a sense of urgency.

We made it back in record time and hopped on Jamie's bike. I thought maybe my fear would help with desensitizing the feeling of wrapping my arms around him, but evidently not. He hit the brake with his foot, revved the engine and we took off.

The desert town of Calla Verda was one of those if-you-blink-you'll-miss-it type places. There was a mayor's office, a small grocer, and four bars packed with motorcross riders come from the city to play out in the desert. It was obvious how the town made its income. We hit the mayor's office, but to our dismay it was already closed. The town evidently turned up its sidewalks at five p.m., save for the bar scene.

"Dammit," I grumbled. "Now we'll have to come out tomorrow."

"You could call."

"No. I would need to make photocopies of the records so we can videotape them. We'll have to come back."

Disappointed, we hopped back on the motorcycle and hit

the road. A few miles out we saw an orange glow on the horizon.

"What's that?" I yelled at Jamie, to be heard over the roar of the bike. I pointed to the glow.

He slowed the bike to a stop. With the land suddenly quiet, we could hear the faint, but pounding beats of techno music.

"I think it's a rave," he said.

"Ooh, we should get video for our story since we already have the undercover camera set up. I mean, raves are great to show the effects of drug use."

"Sure. No problem." Jamie gave the bike gas, and we headed for the light.

The area for the rave was a roped-off section of desert, not seemingly any different from the rest of the wasteland except for the crazy generator-powered lights and pulsating sounds. Under a small tent, a DJ spun techno and house tunes for a group of about fifty college-aged kids. They were all dressed like Lulu—with colored sneakers, and gobs of plastic kids' jewelry worn around wrists and necks. Most had several piercings—some in pretty interesting spots.

We paid our ten dollars and walked past the ropes. Someone had lit a huge bonfire and the ravers were dancing around it like shamans at an Indian tribal dance. I was delighted. This would make great video for our story.

We wandered around getting shots of the ravers. No one seemed to mind being videotaped—in fact, several kids begged us to turn the camera on them so they could watch themselves through the view screen after a rewind. We were happy to oblige. A few were curious as to what the video was for, but a vague mention of some kind of reality something or other worked to appease them. This was the YouTube generation. They were used to cameras invading every part of a person's existence.

I walked over to a vendor and waited in a ridiculous line to pay an obscene five dollars for a tiny bottle of water. As I headed back to Jamie, bottle in hand, I saw him talking to a small blond girl in pigtails, dressed in a candy-colored jumper.

Jealousy burned my gut. After all, if Jamie were going to cheat on his fiancée, it should be with me. Not some random chick.

"Who was that?" I asked. The girl had scurried away at my approach. Little desert rat.

Jamie shrugged. "No one."

I narrowed my eyes. "You look like you were having a pretty intense conversation for no one." The moment the words left my lips I regretted them. Who was I to say who Jamie could talk to or not? Even if we were together, I was not that kind of girl. What had gotten into me? Jealous of the attention someone else's guy was getting from another woman? Lame, Maddy. Truly lame.

"If you must know, she was trying to sell me drugs."

My eyes widened. "That girl? *She* was a drug dealer? She didn't even look sixteen."

He shrugged. "I guess they must be slacking down at the drug dealer licensing department."

"Ha, ha." I took a sip of my water and offered some to Jamie. He slugged a good portion down. I grabbed it back. After paying five dollars I wanted more than one sip. "Still, that's sad, don't you think? I mean, she could be one of Lulu's friends."

She probably *was* one of Lulu's friends, now that I thought about it. I guess thank God for small favors that my sister hasn't gone down that road. Yet.

"Dude, you took the wrong water bottle." A dread-locked, scrawny guy with really weird tattoos interrupted as he stalked over in our direction. He held out another, identical-looking bottle and looked expectantly at the one I was holding.

"Oh." I looked at the two bottles. Between Jamie and me, we'd drunk most of ours. "Oh well. Might as well keep it, right? I mean more for you that way."

Scrawny guy frowned. What was his problem? "Dude, I paid like thirty bucks for that."

I raised an eyebrow. "You paid thirty bucks for water? I think you got ripped off, man." I laughed and took another sip.

He rolled his eyes. "Not for the water, idiot. For the drugs dissolved in it."

I choked.

"What drugs?" Jamie demanded. "Did you dose her drink?"

"Dude, it's *my* drink. You think I wanted to waste my X on this chick? She's not even cute."

I sputtered, spitting the water out of my mouth onto the ground. Ohmigod. Ohmigod. Ohmigod. I'm drugged. I'd been drugged! I was going to pass out and wake up naked in some skanky guy's trailer.

"You bastard!" I cried. "You drugged me!"

"Yeah, so, can I have my thirty bucks since you're going to be rolling and I'm not?" Scrawny Guy whined.

"Get the fuck out of here before I call the cops on you," Jamie said, shoving him backward. Scrawny Guy must have realized he was no match for Jamie or not in the mood for cops and retreated, sad and drugless, into the sea of dancers. Jamie turned to me, grabbing me by my shoulders.

"Calm down, Maddy," he commanded. "Don't panic."

"Don't panic?" I cried. "Don't panic? I've just taken drugs! Illegal drugs. What's going to happen to me? Am I going to hallucinate? Will I see God? Oh, God, I don't think I'm ready to see God!"

Jamie groaned. "It's just Ecstasy, Maddy. I took it once or twice in college. You're not going to see anything. You're going to feel really warm and fuzzy and great in a few minutes and it'll last for about four hours. As long as we keep you well hydrated there's nothing to worry about."

"Are … are you sure?"

"Yes. You only had a few sips of water. You probably didn't even get a full dose. We'll just hang out here by the fire."

"Maybe we should find a hospital. I mean, just in case." I hated that I sounded wimpy, but, well, I was.

Jamie shook his head. "Can't. I drank the water, too. It'd be unsafe for me to drive. And we know there's no cell reception out here to call anyone."

"Great. We're going to die out here in the desert and no one will even know where to look for us."

Jamie shook me. "Listen to me, Maddy. We're going to be fine. As long as you don't panic. Just let the drug move in gradually. And soon it will be gone. And someday you'll look on this and laugh."

"I doubt it." I sulked. But already I felt my insides warming. And the concern and fear I felt a few seconds before were gradually slipping away. Damn drug. I should be frightened to death. Now all I could think about was how they called Ecstasy the "love drug."

And Jamie and I were rolling together.

The Multifaceted Jewel: Ecstasy use can lead to world healing and inner peace. The pill can catalyze a powerful experience that takes many different forms. It can induce an intense, spiritual high or lead to loving relaxation. It can connect people freely and openly with each other or promote deep inner thinking and analysis.

TIPS WHILE ON ECSTASY

- Drink lots of water to replenish bodily fluids. Otherwise you may die of heatstroke and that would be a bad thing.
- Even if you don't feel tired or overheated, stop dancing for a while—to chill out. (See above tip about heatstroke and dying.)
- Outside raves, maintain a healthy diet. Take vitamins. Get a good night's sleep. This will also ensure that your parents don't think you're a fuck-up and will allow you to go to more raves, thus giving you extra chances to explore yourself through Ecstasy.
- Watch out for impure Ecstasy—bad drug dealers will try to sell you pills laced with amphetamines, LSD, heroin, and PCP. If you want to take these drugs on your own, fine. But don't encourage dealers to skimp on the active ingredient (MDMA) in Ecstasy pills. The rest of us non-hardcore druggies will thank you.
- Alcohol reduces or changes the effects of the drug. Besides, most of you are not old enough to legally drink it, so leave the beer at home!

CHAPTER NINE

I threw the drug pamphlet in the fire. What was done was done and worrying about it wouldn't sober me up any sooner. Best to just sit tight and try to get through the evening best I could.

Jamie went to his bike and grabbed a beach towel. He spread it over the ground and we sat, as if partaking in an odd kind of drug picnic. We'd chosen a spot close to the bonfire and contented ourselves with watching the strange dance rituals of the raver kids with avid fascination.

They twirled and twirled like whirling dervishes, caught up in the power of the dance. I could see for the first time why tribes and witches used dancing in ceremonies. The power of the body's movement was almost a spell in itself.

Personally, I had no interest in dancing. And as the Ecstasy kicked in, heating my body with a pleasant fire of its own, I actually felt increasingly lazy and content to sit there in that spot, next to Jamie, all night. My mind wandered as I stared into the fire, assessing all my problems—family, work, etc.—and deeming them all inconsequential. None of it mattered. And in the end, I realized, my life was wonderful. I had so much. I'd been blessed. There were thousands of poor, starving people out there, and here I was obsessing about my pain-in-the-ass family and job that, while it could be annoying as all hell, also kept me well above the poverty level.

Truly, everything would be fine.

Gentle hands gripped my shoulder and I turned from my fire gazing. Jamie smiled and began to massage my back.

"Does that feel good?" he asked. His face was flushed and his pupils dilated. Evidently the drug had kicked in for him, too.

"Mmm, yes," I moaned in pleasure. A thousand different tingling feelings echoed through my every nerve at his touch. But it wasn't sexual this time. Just a warm and fuzzy feeling. He was just trying to keep me relaxed and not panicked until the drug wore off. Nice of him, really. I squirmed closer so I was leaning against his chest. Cozy. Comfortable. Warm. What a nice guy. A really, really nice guy.

"Good," he said, continuing to knead my back. "I'm glad you're okay. I was worried about you for a minute there."

"I appreciate that. But I'm fine, really. In fact, I can't remember a time I've felt so relaxed."

"It's been a while for me, too. I mean, I've been so stressed out. With the moving, switching jobs, planning a wedding …"

Ugh. He had to bring that up, didn't he? Major buzz-kill. But we were friends, I reminded myself. Friends should be able to talk about anything with each other. And I liked the fact he felt comfortable doing so. "How's the wedding planning going?" I, Maddy Madison, friend extraordinaire, asked.

He groaned. "I try to stay out of it as much as possible. When I first proposed, all I had in mind was a simple ceremony—maybe on the beach at sunset with a few friends. She's made it into the social event of the season." His hands traveled to my hair, dragging his fingers down my scalp, which made for more tingling feelings. I loved head massages, especially in my skin's hypersensitive state.

"Well, I'm sure it will be very nice."

"What it'll be is a chance for Jennifer to show off to all of her stuck-up Hollywood friends. In fact, I bet she wouldn't even notice if I didn't show up."

Hmm. Interesting. "You sound bitter."

"Maybe I am, a little."

Ecstasy hit different people in different ways, I realized. While I was content to simply sit back and soak everything in, Jamie's drug experience was prompting him to open up. To talk. Which was fine with me. I didn't mind hearing about trouble in Jamie and Jen paradise.

"When I first met Jen, she and I were as close as a couple could be. She wanted to pursue an acting career, and I completely supported her. But now that she's landed a few roles, got invited to a few key Hollywood parties, she wants more. It's like an addiction to fame. She doesn't want to go out for a quiet meal. She wants to 'see and be seen.' She doesn't want to drive up the coast to watch the sunset. She wants to go dancing at the Viper Room."

I yelped as his fingers caught a snarl.

"Sorry," he said, patting my head. "It just gets me so angry. Sometimes I don't even know why she's marrying me. I'm not even her type."

"No?" I turned to face him. He looked so sad. Like a lost boy. I wanted to comfort him. To hold him close and tell him everything was going to be okay. I tried to tell myself those urges were coming from my drug-enhanced state, but I knew better.

"Not at all. I've told you before that I don't buy into the whole Hollywood scene. I don't like going to parties. I don't care which celebrity was spotted at which restaurant, and I don't care about going there once they were to see if they return." He scrubbed his face with his hands. "And now that I've had to shelve my film-making career, I'm not even someone she wants to show off to her friends. At least at one time I was quote 'cool.' Someone she was proud of."

I fought back an overwhelming sadness as I contemplated his situation. Man, this Ecstasy was making me way too emotional—pity stabbing at my heart. I felt so bad for him. Here he was, the most wonderful guy I'd ever met and he was stuck with a woman who completely didn't appreciate him. Didn't worship him as he deserved.

I hadn't realized I was crying until he reached over and brushed away a lone tear from my cheek with his thumb. The gesture was gentle. Sweet. Made me want to act completely irrational and fall into his arms. Before I could act on such an impulse, he continued.

"We got into a huge fight when I took this job in San Diego," he said. "She told me I was a loser. That I was giving up my dream." He grabbed a rock off the ground and threw it into the fire. "But you know what? It's *her* dream, not mine. I'm still doing what I want to do. I'm still a photographer. Sure, local TV news isn't as glamorous as Hollywood …"

"Understatement alert!" I said with a chuckle.

"… but it's a steady paycheck. And I like San Diego, too. It's non-pretentious. Peaceful. You could raise a child here." He snorted. "Not that she probably wants children anymore. Pregnancy might force her to eat once in a while."

"I hope you don't mind me asking this," I interjected, the drug making me brave. "But why are you marrying her? You sound like you'd rather face a firing squad."

He shrugged. "Sometimes, I'm honestly not sure. But I can't call it off now. Everything's been paid for. Deposits can't be returned. Her dad's spent a fortune. How can I just walk away?"

"Jamie, once you're married it's going to be a lot worse." I folded my arms across my chest. "Can't you talk to her? Figure out what's going on? Maybe go to counseling?"

He sighed. "No. Yes. I don't know." He leaned back against a boulder. "I don't know why I even told you all that. I'm sorry."

"Don't be. We're friends, remember?"

"Friends." He smiled, reaching over to brush a strand of hair from my eyes. "It's so hard to be your friend, Maddy."

My heart caught in my throat. What had he just said? He groaned and leaned back on his rock. "Sorry," he said. "I shouldn't say things like that. It's not fair."

"It's okay," I replied, hardly able to breathe. "I mean, we have to be honest with each other, right?"

"Honest?" Jamie raked a hand through his hair. "You want honest? How about the fact that you've been driving me absolutely crazy these past few weeks."

"Crazy?" I repeated slowly. "Like in a bad way or a good way?"

"Maddy, you haven't left my mind for two seconds since the morning we slept together. You're like a sickness I can't seem to shake. And in some ways, I'm not sure I want to. You make me laugh. You give me encouragement when it comes to my writing. You're supportive and sweet and beautiful and I'm crazy about you and I feel fucking horrible about it. Especially when I'm talking to Jen. I mean, I hate the idea that I've betrayed her. Once with my body and over and over again in my mind. She deserves better than me." He slammed his fist against his knee. "God, this is such a nightmare. I don't know what to do about it."

"I-I had no idea," I whispered, my insides doing flip-flops 'til I felt like I was going to puke and it had nothing to do with drugs. I couldn't believe it. All this time I had tried to keep things friendly and not fall in love, never knowing he'd been struggling with the same thoughts and feelings as I.

He looked over at me. "I'm sorry," he apologized, his eyes beautiful and sad. "I told you it would be better to keep my mouth shut." He sighed. "It's just … well, I sit here and look at you and all I want to do is kiss you. To make love to you. To possess you in every way possible. But I can't. I can't do any of it." He closed his eyes and tipped his head to the sky. "If only I'd met you three years earlier. Or something."

I reached over and placed a hand on his knee, wanting to comfort him but having no idea what to say. My own thoughts whirled like dervishes in my head. I knew if I leaned over and pressed my lips against his, he wouldn't be able to resist. But at the same time, he'd hate himself for giving in. And I didn't want that.

He flinched at my touch and abruptly scrambled to his feet. "I've got to go take a walk," he muttered.

"Jamie, wait!"

"I'll be back. Stay here."

Helpless, I watched him step away from the fire and wander out into the wild, barren desert. I wanted to run after him, but what would I do when I got there? One thing would lead to another and we'd end up making the same mistake we made on our first night together. And we couldn't do that. It wasn't fair to Jennifer. And it wasn't fair to us either.

So I curled up on the towel, pulling my feet into a fetal position, allowing the tears to stream down my cheeks. It was one thing to fall for someone alone. But to know they felt the same, yet refused to act on it, was something else entirely.

Was I deluding myself to think he'd break up with Jen and give me a chance? Or was there a possibility—even a slight one—that he would? And was that what I really wanted in the end—for him to ditch the woman he'd promised his life to and start shacking up with me instead? Or was I being totally and utterly selfish?

*

"Maddy, wake up!"

I groggily attempted to open one eye, but the glaring sunshine seemed capable of burning out my vision, so I closed it again. Ugh. I felt like utter crap. My head pounded. My mouth tasted like cotton wool. My joints were sore and a sharp rock dug into my back. Ugh.

"Maddy. We have to get back to San Diego." Hands shook my shoulders, and I groaned.

"Five more minutes, Mom."

"Not Mom. Jamie."

That did it. I opened my eyes. Scrambled to a seated position. Jamie sat beside me, looking rumpled and sexy, though more than a bit drained. I ran a hand through my hair, trying to flatten it. I probably looked like Medusa. And there was no bathroom here to hide in.

I took stock of my surroundings. Several raver kids lay sacked out in various positions by the fire pit, the flames long extinguished. Others were still dancing, believe it or not. And a DJ manned the booth, still spinning his techno tunes. I admired their endurance. How much Ecstasy did one have to take to stay dancing from dusk until dawn?

The night before seemed almost like a dream. I remembered everything—no alcoholic blackout this time—but it all seemed unreal. Wavy. Suspect. Did Jamie really tell me he was crazy about me?

It did, however, make things rather awkward. We couldn't just say good-bye this time. We had to drive back two hours. Two hours on a bike, pressed against him.

"Morning," Jamie said. "Did you sleep well?"

"Don't remember." I stood up and stretched my arms above my head, trying to gain some sense of bodily well-being. Why was I so sore? I didn't even dance. I noticed the sun, barely peeking over the horizon. "What time is it?"

Jamie glanced at his watch. "Just after six."

I screwed up my face. "I could have slept a few extra hours."

Jamie grabbed the towel and started folding it up. "We've got a two-hour ride back to San Diego. That'll get us in by eight. I'm assuming you don't want to go to work without a shower?"

I looked down at my body. I was nasty. Dusty, dirty, and truth be told, a bit rank.

"A shower would probably be in order." I laughed, noticing Jamie didn't laugh with me. Or meet my eyes. Uh-oh.

"What's wrong?" I asked.

"Nothing," he said dismissively. "Got a headache is all."

No, that wasn't all. He had a case of the regrets. It was clearly written on his face. He wished he hadn't spent the night with me. Wished he hadn't spilled all his secrets. About him and Jen's relationship. About how he was crazy about me. He was biting his tongue to be patient, but trying to get the hell away from the scene as soon as possible. Typical guy reaction.

And I, on the other hand, was still goofy in love. Which I guess was a typical girl reaction. Go figure.

I decided against badgering him to tell me what was on his mind. In my hung over, vulnerable mental state I really couldn't deal with any more rejection. Better to let it sit. Get a ride home. Call in sick to work and stew about the whole thing from the comfort of my couch. Maybe I'd even order pizza. I hadn't eaten since yesterday morning.

"I'm ready when you are," I said.

He nodded and started walking toward the road where he'd parked his bike. I followed behind, not quite able to keep up with his speedy pace. Wow, he really *was* in a hurry to get the hell out of Dodge.

When I caught up, I found him frantically looking up and down the desert road, sheer panic written on his face.

"What's wrong?" I asked, scrunching up my eyes in confusion.

Then it hit me. I, too, looked up and down the road, panicked.

Oh shit.

"Jamie, where's your motorcycle?"

CALLA VERDA STOLEN PROPERTY REPORT

NAME: *Jamie Hayes* **DATE**: *4/15*

OFFICER: *Bradley*

AREA OF INCIDENCE: *About two miles from Calla Verda, Route 8*

PROPERTY STOLEN: *Triumph Rocket Motorcycle*

INFORMATION: *Owner of said property, Mr. Hayes, claims he and his work colleague Ms. Madison were on assignment undercover at a local rave. (Please note they have no Press Pass to back up this story and only a funny-looking home video camera, which they claim they use for "undercover work." They are also disgustingly dirty with mud in their hair. As if News 9 would hire people like that!) They ended up spending the night at said Rave even after shooting was finished. (For a reason they are unclear on.) They woke the next morning and learned that above mentioned property was nowhere to be seen. They claim they walked two miles back to Calla Verda to report the incident.*

SIGNATURE: *R. J. Bradley, Detective*

CHAPTER TEN

I wanted to throw up.

Maybe it was coming down from the Ecstasy. Maybe it was due to my lack of food for the last twenty-four hours. Maybe it was the fierce, angry sun that had toasted my skin to a crisp.

Whatever the reason, after the two-mile walk back to Calla Verda, I literally felt sick.

Jamie didn't look much better. Pale faced, save the black circles under his eyes, he looked depressed. Defeated. And why wouldn't he? He loved that bike and now it was gone. He must have felt like God had come down and swept it up as punishment for his sins.

"You have insurance, right?" I'd asked on the long walk back. Not a car in sight to beg a ride from.

He shrugged his shoulders slowly, as if each weighed two tons. "Sure. But the bike's a few years old. They're not going to give me enough to buy a new one."

"I'm sorry," I said for the umpteenth time.

"It's not your fault," Jamie replied automatically. But he thought it was. I could see it in his eyes. The way he balled his hands into fists when he answered my apology.

I gave up and we spent the rest of the walk in silence. When we got to Calla Verda, we hit the local police/fire/ambulance all-in-one building. Behind the glass reception window, the officer in charge, an obese man, stuffed like a sausage in his uniform casing, took one look at our dusty, dirty appearance and pointed down the hall.

"Methadone clinic is to your right," he said.

"We're not here for methadone," said Jamie in a tight voice. "My motorcycle was stolen."

The officer snorted. "Oh, well then. That's different. Let me call out the National Guard. Yessiree." He shook his head, chucking to himself. "You city kids. You kill me. If I had myself a dollar for every one of you who walked through that door with a missing bike …"

Well, that wasn't very encouraging. I watched as Jamie bit his lower lip and could see frustration radiating from his body.

"I know the chances of finding it are next to none," he said in a tight voice. "But I need to file a police report so I can show it to the insurance company."

"Well, thank you kindly, sir, for telling me how to do my job, then." The officer rolled his eyes and grudgingly got off his fat ass to walk over to the far wall. He grabbed a piece of paper and a pen and sat back down. "Good thing you city kids watch a lot of Miami Vice or we'd all be in trouble."

What an asshole!

"A little behind on your Must See TV, are we?" I interjected, not able to take the hick cop's rudeness any longer. "Miami Vice's probably been off the air longer than I've been alive. But I guess news travels slow out here in East Bumfuck."

"Maddy," Jamie hissed. "Be quiet."

"Watch your attitude, Missy," the cop growled back. "Or I'll have to call the sheriff. And no one likes it when we have to call the sheriff."

I fell silent, ashamed. What had I been thinking? Sure, the cop had been rude, but at the end of the day, he was still a cop. And it wasn't going to help our situation any to start mouthing off. They'd probably arrest me. Lock me up in some deep, dark desert prison and throw away the key. Not exactly how I wanted to spend my next five to ten.

"Sorry," I muttered.

"Well, you should be, little lady."

Ooh, it took all my strength to stay silent. I forced myself to smile and then turn to walk over to the plastic waiting room chair. I sank into it, head in hands. The air conditioner in the police station must have been broken because it was about eighty degrees inside. My sweaty legs stuck to the plastic in the most uncomfortable of ways. I noticed a coffee machine on the table next to me and poured myself a Styrofoam cup of thick mud. Disgusting, but hopefully it'd wake me up.

How were we going to get back to San Diego? It was a two-hour drive: too long for a taxi, not that the town probably had any to begin with. Surely no busses came through this Nowhereville.

And since Jamie knew next to no one in San Diego, it'd be up to me to call someone back home to rescue us.

How embarrassing.

I pondered my options. Dad? No. I still wasn't speaking to him. Besides, he'd probably want to bring along Cindi with an "i" and I couldn't face meeting her looking like a desert rat. There was Lulu, but she didn't have her own car and I had the keys to mine in my pocket. I'd been meaning to have a spare set made, but had never gotten around to it. Mom was probably in London, on a spending spree down Bond Street at the moment, so no use trying her.

Jodi. I'd have to call Jodi.

I didn't want to. I knew she'd be able to figure out what was going on. She'd see through my lies. Know that Jamie and I had a thing going. That I was aiding and abetting a man cheating on his fiancée. Actually, make that past tense. After this incident, I doubted Jamie would want to lay eyes on me again. Not that it was my fault.

The night had been so perfect. Jamie, opening up, sharing his soul. But tomorrow had come with a vengeance and now he looked at me with scared, mistrusting eyes. As if I were the girl who was ruining his life. It wasn't fair.

I grabbed my cell phone to call Jodi, then remembered

there was no reception out here. I looked around the police station and saw an antique-looking pay phone tacked to the wall. I rose and walked over to it.

It cost me a dollar fifty in change for three minutes. Jodi picked up after two and a half rings. "Hello?" she asked in a suspicious voice. I'm sure the caller ID area code from deep in the desert confused her.

"Jodi, it's me."

"Maddy? Where the hell are you calling from?"

"Um, a little town called Calla Verda. About two hours east of San Diego."

"What on earth are you doing there?" she asked. "Richard's looking for you. He said he tried to call you fifteen times yesterday."

"I told Alicia at the assignment desk that I was going to the desert to work on a story," I said defensively.

"And you're still out there this morning? When are you coming in? I can cover for you."

"Um, actually, that's what I was calling you about." I explained the whole sordid tale. Well, actually not the *whole* sordid tale. I kind of left out the sordid part. The drug use and the almost-kissing-a-coworker-who-had-a-fiancée bits.

"So you're stuck out there?" Jodi asked incredulously.

"Unless some wonderful best friend in the whole world comes to pick me up," I cajoled.

Silence on the other end of the line. "Jodi?"

"Uh, sorry," she said quickly. "But Maddy, how can I pick you up? I'm already at work. I can't just leave. I've got a shoot in an hour with a woman whose carpet almost killed her."

My heart plummeted. "O-oh. Oh-kay," I said, my voice cracking. My one hope. My supposed best friend was turning me down.

"Sorry, Maddy. If you need a ride after work, I'd be happy to drive down—oh, Laura's coming. I've got to go." I could hear her set down the receiver and then the dial tone buzzed in my ear.

"I'm done filing the report."

I hung up the phone and turned around to face Jamie. "I'm trying to get us a ride home," I said. "But everyone's at work."

Jamie shrugged his shoulders. "I'm not going to be much help. All my friends are still in LA."

"Jodi could pick us up, but not until after she gets out."

"Well, then I guess we're stuck here 'til then," Jamie said in a frustrated tone. "The cop said there's a hotel down the road. I'm going to get a room and take a nap."

"Oh, good idea," I said, then realized I had no money to do the same. I'd left my wallet in the bike and used up all my change to phone Jodi. In fact, I didn't even have enough money for breakfast. But I didn't want Jamie to have to pay for me. He was already in a bad enough mood. The last thing he needed was a clingy girl. "I'll, um, probably hang out here. Catch you later."

He looked at me strangely. "Here? In the police station?"

"Yeah." I tried to smile. "They have great coff—" My voice cracked and the waterworks started. Dammit. I hated that. Why couldn't I be brave for once? I cleared my throat and brushed away the pesky tear. "*Great* coffee." I raised my cup of mud. "And you know how much I love coffee."

"You're not staying here," Jamie said. "Come on, let's find the hotel."

"No. I'm fi—"

He grabbed me firmly by the arm and led me out of the police station, evidently insistent on taking control of our desperate situation. Which was fine by me, really.

It was still early, but the temperature outside had risen to a sweltering hundred and five degrees, if you believed the bank clock. Of course, it was a dry heat, the people back East would say. As if that made it any less unbearable. When it got to a hundred and five, heat was heat.

We walked down the street, passing biker bar after biker bar. I could see Jamie surreptitiously checking out the bikes parked outside. But most of these were dirt bikes to ride the dunes. None resembled his precious English Triumph.

The hotel loomed at the end of Main Street, its once cheery

blue sideboards now peeling paint. We stepped on the creaky front porch and went inside.

"I'd like to rent a room," Jamie said to the bored, gum-snapping blond girl behind the desk. She looked about fifteen.

"By the quarter hour, hour, or hour and a half?" she asked without looking up.

Jamie blushed. "How much for the day?"

The girl looked up from her magazine. Appraised me with critical eyes, perhaps wondering how I'd lucked out warranting so much time. Then went back to reading.

"Fifty bucks," she said.

Jamie handed her a wad of cash. She punched a few numbers into the register and then handed him a rusty key.

"Room eleven. Third door to the right."

We walked down the dark, floral-wallpapered hallway until we reached our room. Jamie slid the key into the lock and stepped inside. The room matched the rest of the hotel—dingy and decrepit. Dim lighting, peeling paint, and only a single double bed in the center of the room serving as furniture. There wasn't even a television.

"Oh, I'd figured there'd be two beds," Jamie said, appraising the room. "Sorry. Do you want me to get you your own room?"

So it was like that, was it? From telling me he was crazy about me, to wanting to spend fifty extra bucks just so he wouldn't have to be in the same room as me. "It's up to you," I said with a shrug. "I don't mind sharing." I stepped inside the room and looked around. It seemed clean enough, at least. As long as I didn't think about the lurid acts normally performed here by the quarter hour.

"I can sleep on the floor," Jamie said, closing the door behind me. "I could probably sleep on a rock, I'm so exhausted."

"Don't be stupid. It's your room. You paid for it. If anyone's sleeping on the floor, it'll be me." Not that I wanted to sleep on the floor. I wanted to sleep on the bed. With Jamie. Preferably with his arms wrapped around my body, spooning me close.

But that wasn't going to happen. Something had changed between us. The closeness we'd felt in our drug-induced haze had completely dissipated. You could tell he was dying to get away from me and was just being a gentleman because it was in his nature.

"Look, this is stupid," I said. "We're both adults. We can both sleep on the bed. It's just sleeping."

He nodded, agreeing without comment, kicking off his shoes and lying down. I went into the bathroom to wash up a bit and when I walked back into the room he was already fast asleep, his breathing slow and heavy.

I tried not to think of the close proximity of his warm, sexy body as I crawled into the bed beside him, resisting the urge to inch closer and seek comfort in his slumbering frame. Sure, it might give me comfort now, to press my body against his, imagining that he was mine, but in the end it would only lead to more heartbreak. Much better to hug a pillow, shut my eyes and try to sleep.

*

I woke up sometime later to the sound of a rhythmically creaking mattress coming from next door. Evidently one of the quarter-hour people had checked in. I rolled over in the bed to see if Jamie was awake. He was lying on his back, staring at the ceiling. At my movement he looked over and smiled.

"Major action next door," he remarked.

"No doubt." It was just too bad there'd be no major action on this side of the wall. But, I realized, that ship had sailed.

"Are you hungry?" he asked, rolling on his side to face me. He propped his head up with his elbow, peering at me with his beautiful emerald eyes.

"Famished."

"Think they have room service?" he asked with a laugh.

"Oh, yes. I'm sure. Probably caviar and champagne delivered to your door."

"Hmm." He scratched his chin. "I don't like caviar. And I'm way too hung over to enjoy the champagne. I guess we should go out for lunch instead."

I nodded. At least he seemed to be in a better mood. "We can get lunch and then head over to the town hall to look up those property records."

He sat up in bed, rubbing his eyes. "Good idea. Forgot about that." He stretched his arms over his head in a yawn/stretch and then turned to face me. "Maddy … before we go, we need to talk."

I raised my eyebrows. We need to talk? Wasn't that my line? Didn't I, born a female, have exclusive rights to those dreaded four words? "Okay," I agreed, bracing myself for the worst. I pulled my feet in a cross-legged position on the bed. Here went nothing.

"About last night. There was a lot said." Jamie picked at an invisible spot on his jeans, not meeting my eyes.

"Uh, yeah. I remember." Boy, did I remember.

"I … I guess what I'm trying to say is, well, I'm not sure where we go from here."

A coldness washed over me and I felt like I was going to throw up. I'd been expecting the speech all morning, tried to mentally prepare myself for it, but the reality of it actually happening still made me sick. I'd been such a fool to allow myself to think that things with Jennifer might fall through and that someday he might be free to love me. To love me as I loved him. I had no one to blame but myself. I'd put myself in a situation where I could not come out the winner. I wasn't the noble tragic victim. I was just pathetic and stupid and selfish and deserved everything I was about to get.

"And I didn't want to give you the wrong impression, make you think …"

Still, I reminded myself, it wasn't as if he were some innocent party. If anything, he'd started the flirtation. He'd told me last night he was crazy about me. And now he was trying to take it all back? What a bastard.

"I understand," I said, even though I didn't. "You want to

be with Jennifer."

"I *am* with Jennifer," he corrected, only making it worse. "I'm marrying her in less than three months. I know I said there were some things between us that weren't perfect, but really, that's true with any couple, right? I made a commitment. I can't just ditch her at the altar. I'm not that kind of guy." He shrugged. "And I do love her. I really do."

The words were daggers. "And what about what you said to me?" I spat out, not having the power to just get up and walk away, as my common sense strongly advised. "You said you were crazy about me. Just hoping to get in my pants, maybe?" My voice cracked with rage. "Nice. Real nice."

I felt sick. Cheap. Used. Not the Madonna. Total, 100 percent whore. Thank God I hadn't slept with him again. Not that it really mattered. Sex was just a physical act. The ache in my heart was much more serious.

"Maddy, calm down. I meant everything I said last night. It's just that I shouldn't have said it—do you see the difference?" He sighed. Deeply. "I can't even tell you how much you've come to mean to me over these last couple weeks. You're delightful, funny, sweet—I could go on and on. And I don't want to lose you, either. But at the same time ...I can't keep dragging you down with me. I'm trying not to be selfish here. I don't want to hurt you anymore." He ran a hand through his hair. "I'm so sorry. I wish things were different. But they're not. And I feel terrible for leading you on in the first place. Making you fall for me."

That did it. Fury slammed through my stomach. "Get off your high horse, asshole," I cried, leaping up from the bed. "You think I've *fallen* for you? You've got to be fucking crazy!" I started laughing, realized my laughter made me sound semi psychotic. At that point I didn't really care. "You know, Jennifer can have you! Not that she'd probably want you if she knew what a bastard you are! You go and cheat on her, and then expect to just walk down the aisle three months later. What a keeper!"

Jamie looked beaten. Truly beaten. Half of me wanted to go

over and hug him and tell him everything was okay; the other, more sensible half, wanted to beat him to a pulp.

"What a prize you are." I continued my rampage, settling for mental brutality over physical. "You said she was embarrassed by you? Well, I don't blame her. You're a burnt-out has-been. Pathetic. A real nothing. I wouldn't marry you for all the handbags in Prada. And neither should she. Of course, she doesn't know better, poor thing."

"You're not going to tell her, are you?" he asked, a scared expression on his face.

I drew in a breath. The thought hadn't even crossed my mind. But here he was, not concerned that he'd hurt my feelings. Just worried that he might get caught. It would serve him right. Leave him with nothing.

"Well, well. That's for me to know and you to find out," I threatened. And with that, I grabbed my shoes and made my exit, slamming the door behind me.

FROM THE DESK OF

THE CALLA VERDA ROADHOUSE

~~Dear Jennifer,~~

~~You don' t really know me, but I've slept with your future husband. I wanted to write and tell you what a bastard he is.~~

~~Jen,~~

~~Remember how we shared dinner last week? Well, that's not all we've shared...~~

~~Jennifer,~~

~~You know how some men have the Madonna/whore complex? Ever wonder who is Jamie's whore?~~

~~Jennifer,~~

~~You don' t like him anyway, so how about you go marry someone else and leave Jamie to me?~~

~~Hi Jen,~~

~~I'm in love with your husband.~~

~~Goodbye Cruel Word,~~

~~This may be my last will and testament after having my heart broken by an asshole named Jamie Hayes.~~

CHAPTER ELEVEN

"Jodi!" I cried, overjoyed, when at seven p.m. on the dot my bestest friend in the whole wide world walked through the doorway of the Calla Verda roadhouse.

The owner, a plump, motherly type with graying hair and kind blue eyes, had taken pity on me when I'd rushed in a few hours earlier, all tear-streaked and bawling. She'd cooked me lunch—didn't even charge me—and I'd told her my story. She in turn told me that all men were bastards and that her third husband had beat her to a pulp before cheating on her, which actually made me feel worse instead of better. She even gave me some stationary to write Jennifer a letter, but after several attempts, I couldn't bring myself to sell Jamie out.

"Hi, Maddy," Jodi said, sliding into the booth across from me. "I got here as soon as I could."

"I'm so happy to see you," I gushed, not being able to help myself. Then I burst into a fresh set of tears.

Jodi glanced around. The bar had filled up since I'd first arrived and several biker boys were staring at me with frank interest. Jodi stood up and grabbed me by the hand.

"Let's go. We can talk in the car."

We walked to her vehicle, a Ford Expedition, big enough to hold her four dogs. And sure enough, she'd brought the pooches with her. When I climbed in, they all clambered to the front seat of the SUV to try to greet me, as if I were their favorite person in the whole world and they'd missed me dreadfully since I'd been gone. Their enthusiastic welcome and sloppy kisses made me laugh, and suddenly I felt much better.

"Guys! Guys! Cut it out!" I giggled as the Italian greyhound took advantage of her small size to crawl under the Great Danes and hop into my lap. I cuddled her in my arms and she licked my hand.

Jodi popped in the other side. "In the back," she scolded. "Bad! Bad dogs! In the BACK!" With great effort she managed to shove them all backward, then closed the cage that separated the front seats from the rest of the SUV. The dogs whimpered behind the bars, as if having been sent to solitary confinement.

"They're so spoiled," Jodi complained as she turned the key in the ignition. "Sorry about that."

"No problem. They're cute." I stroked the Italian greyhound who had somehow managed to escape the prison sentence.

"So tell me again, why are you out here in the middle of nowhere?" Jodi asked as she pulled out onto the main road.

"I was doing undercover work for that drug cartel story Miguel told us about."

She looked over at me before turning back to the road. "And where's Jamie?"

"Hell if I care where he is. I hope he rots in this backwater town."

Jodi slammed on the brakes, causing me to lurch forward and bang my head on the dashboard. The dogs yelped their annoyance from the back.

"Ow!" I protested.

"Madeline Madison, you weren't planning on leaving him here, were you?" she scolded.

"What are you, my mother?" I growled, rubbing my head. Though of course, if she were my mother, she'd be too busy shopping in *gay Paris* to give me a lift.

Jodi steered the SUV to the side of the road. "What's going on, Maddy?" she asked. "Why are you mad at Jamie? I thought you guys were becoming friends."

I shook my head. "What can I say? He's a jerk." I really, really didn't want to tell her how stupid I'd been. How I'd had an affair with a nearly married man who, this afternoon, had informed me that he would never be leaving the wife-to-be. It was way too clichéd.

But Jodi was hearing none of it. "If you won't tell me what happened, I'm getting out of this car and searching for Jamie myself."

"You can't. The dogs and I will suffer from hot-car syndrome and die."

"I'll leave the air conditioner on."

"You'll run out of gas."

"There's a gas station a block up."

"But think how expensive gas prices are right now—"

"What happened, Maddy?" Jodi demanded. "I drove two hours to find you. And I'm driving another two hours back. That means today I've given you four hours of my life. You'd think for four hours you could come clean."

I stared at the Italian greyhound in my lap. "Fine," I muttered. "We had a thing."

"A thing?" Jodi cried angrily. "How do you define 'a thing'? Isn't the guy getting married in three months?"

"See? This is why I didn't want to tell you. I knew you'd be all judgmental and stuff."

Jodi swallowed. "Sorry. Go on."

So I told her. Everything. How we'd slept together the night I'd found out my parents were getting divorced. How he'd found me abandoned, after my date left me, and asked me to dinner with him and Jennifer. How we'd accidentally taken Ecstasy in the desert and how he'd confessed his feelings, only to take it all back the next day.

By the end of the tale, Jodi was seething with indignation. "What the hell do you think you're doing, Maddy?"

"What am *I* doing? I'm just the innocent bystander here.

He's the one with the fiancée."

"Please, Maddy. Grow up. Take some responsibility for your actions. Sure, I'm not saying Jamie's been acting like Mother Theresa here, but you haven't exactly been discouraging his behavior either."

"Oh fine. So it's all my fault."

"I'm not saying that. I'm just suggesting you gain a little perspective before you leave the guy stranded in the desert. I mean, what are you really angry about? 'Cause he told you that it would never work out between the two of you? That he needed to stay faithful to the woman he'd made a lifetime commitment to? You should have known that from the start, messing around with another girl's guy. You're not the innocent wounded party here, and I hate to say it, but you deserve everything you're getting for becoming involved with an almost-married guy to begin with."

"I know, but …" I stared out the window, shamed. "It's not some weird, dirty affair. It's sweet and innocent and good. I have real feelings for him. I can't help it."

"You need to start trying. Stop putting yourself in situations where you're vulnerable. Okay, you slept together once. Can't take that back now. But you've got to move forward. Otherwise you're spiraling down the pit of destruction."

"I know, I know. It's just … it's like I've finally met the perfect guy and I don't want to lose him. And I know he has doubts about getting married to Jen. He's admitted that."

"Trust me, everyone has doubts about getting married. That doesn't mean he's not going to go through with it. You need to prepare yourself for that reality and quickly." She reached over and touched my shoulder. "I don't want to see you hurt."

A vision of Jamie standing at the altar smiling at Jen haunted me. Jodi was right. I had to get over this ridiculous crush—and fast—or I was going to be crushed myself.

"Look, I don't know whether Jamie's a two-timing bastard or just a guy who has feelings for two women and is genuinely confused. But either way, you're not doing yourself—or him—

any good by perpetuating this flirtation. And you have no right in the world to get mad when he tells you that he's trying to honor his commitment to his fiancée. I mean, think about how you'd feel if you were Jen. Knowing some bitch in San Diego was chasing after her man?"

Ugh. She had a point. In a way, I was no better than Cindi with an i. And Jen was my helpless mother. Ugh, ugh, ugh.

"You're right," I said, swallowing hard. "You're totally right. I need to stop this now." I looked over at her. She really was good friend. "Thank you."

Jodi reached over and pulled me into a hug. "I'm sorry, sweetie," she whispered. "I don't mean to go all tough love on you. I know you're hurting and I'm sorry. I just don't want it to get any worse."

"I know. And I appreciate it. I really do." We held each other for a moment, then pulled away.

"So, you okay for giving Jamie a ride home?" Jodi asked. "I really think it is the right thing to do."

I nodded. "We can take him. I don't mind." I looked to the back of the truck and threw her a half-grin. "As long as he rides in the back with the rest of the dogs."

*

There's nothing like stepping into your own apartment after an extended absence, the sense of peace and quiet that envelops you as you open your front door and step over the threshold. No matter what's happened out in the unpredictable world, you know you can always return to your sanctuary.

Except if you have your little sister staying at your place.

I groaned in dismay as I surveyed my living room. Candy wrappers were strewn throughout. The couch cushions had been pulled onto the floor, one beige cushion now stained with some kind of grape-colored liquid. Empty bottles of Bud Light were lined up like soldiers, guarding my coffee table. But most horrifying was the presence of my bathroom makeup mirror behind the beer sentries. Laid on its side, and covered with chalky residue and rolled up dollar bills.

Dear God, no.

I approached the mirror cautiously, to get a better look. And while I was certainly no expert, I wasn't a babe in the woods, either.

Lulu and her friends had been doing drugs. In my house!

I scanned the room again, looking for more evidence of drug use. Instead I saw a trail of abandoned clothing leading to my bedroom. I took a deep breath. Could this possibly get any worse?

Half of me wanted to just retreat out the front door and come back later—after Lulu had picked everything up and kicked out whoever was there with her. Then I could return and pretend nothing had happened and not have to deal with what I was about to have to deal with.

But she was my little sister and, at the moment, I was all she had.

Stepping into my bedroom, I found Lulu in bed, an unshaven, scraggly-haired guy by her side, listlessly watching television. Except the television in question was currently spitting out static snow and neither party seemed to notice. Their blank expressions made the scene more chilling than if they'd been in the middle of some dirty deed.

"Lulu, what the hell is going on here?" I demanded.

Lulu started, coming out of her trance with a guilty, red-faced look. "Maddy!" she cried. "What are you doing here?"

"Uh, I live here?"

"Er, right. I know, I'm sorry," she amended quickly. "I just mean, well, I thought you were coming back later, that's all. I would have … cleaned."

Right. "Um, I've been gone more than twenty-four hours," I reminded her. "And I tried to call your cell about fifty times on the way home."

"You have?" She scrambled out of bed, thankfully fully dressed, and started racing past me to the other room. "Wow, I must have lost track of time."

"I've already seen the drugs, Lulu," I called after her,

realizing exactly what she was headed to do.

She stopped dead in her tracks. Turned around slowly to face me. "Drugs?" she asked, her eyes wide and innocent.

"Oh, please. Save it. Do you think I'm an idiot?"

"Oh, you think—" She laughed. A brittle laugh that sounded more hyena than human. "That's just Ritalin."

Ritalin? As in, the medication used to treat ADHD? Did she think I just fell off the turnip truck or something? "Since when does Ritalin come in a white powder?" I asked, raising my eyebrows in my best skeptical look. I felt kind of like my mother and tried to remember all the tricks I used to use when I was lying, in case Lulu tried to pull any of them on me. Not that I would have ever lied about something like this.

"It doesn't. Drummer's doctor prescribed the pills. But he's been on them so long, he's like, um, immune to swallowing them now. And his jerk doctor won't up his dosage. So he crushes them up and snorts them to get the medicine directly into his bloodstream."

She actually thought I was going to buy that? That her buddy Drummer was simply self-medicating? Would Mom have considered that a good excuse?

"It's true," the guy (Drummer?) said, also crawling out of bed. To my horror, all he was wearing was a pair of ratty flannel boxers with massive holes in some pretty distasteful spots. His legs and chest were pasty white and overly hairy, like those of a scrawny wooly mammoth. How could Lulu be attracted to such a disgusting creature? She was so pretty. She could get any guy. Did she sleep with him? And if so, how could she? In my bed, nonetheless?

"You must be Maddy. Lulu's told me lots about you." Drummer (and while we're questioning, what the hell kind of name was that!?) strode over and shook my hand. Complete confidence. As if he weren't standing nearly naked in my bedroom. As if he hadn't just admitted to bringing drugs—prescription or otherwise—into my house.

I could barely control my fury. "Get out of my house. And take your drugs with you."

"Well, hell, it's not like I'd leave them here," he drawled, grabbing a pair of dirty jeans from the floor and hoisting them over his scrawny hips. "Damn, Lu, you were right."

I could only imagine what he was talking about, what Lulu had said about me behind my back. But at that moment, I didn't care. I'd be the biggest bitch in the world if I could save my baby sister from trash like that.

After he left, Lulu flopped on the cushionless couch, a sullen expression on her face.

"So, are you mad?" she asked.

I stared at her. "Are you joking?"

"Okay, fine. You're mad. Are you going to tell Mom and Dad?"

"Lu, this isn't like being caught sneaking a beer," I cried in exasperation. I replaced a cushion—the lone unstained one—back on the couch and sat down beside her. "I don't want to be responsible for anything happening to you."

"Oh, I see. You don't care if anything *happens* to me. You just don't want to be *responsible*." Lulu snorted. "Typical. Just like the 'rents."

"That's not what I meant and you know it," I scolded. "Stop trying to twist my words." Man, I hated being the disciplinarian. "Now how long have you been doing Coke—or meth—or whatever that was?"

"It was Ritalin. A legal, prescription drug. And besides, I wasn't doing it. Drummer was."

"Bullshit," I interrupted. "I can tell by looking at you. Your eyes are black—completely dilated. Your hands are shaking like you have Parkinson's. And you're grinding your teeth. I can hear them from here."

"Okay, I tried it. One line. I didn't even like it." She reached for a pack of cigarettes on the coffee table and pulled one out, as if daring me to say something about her smoking, too.

"So, you're not going to do it again?" I asked, wanting desperately to believe her.

"Never," she promised. "Cross my heart and hope to die."

She made the crossing motions with her cigarette, grinning a little. "Stick a needle in my eye."

"Fine. I'm going to treat you as an adult and believe you," I said, too exhausted to pursue the subject further. "But if I catch you one more time, I'm going straight to Dad."

"You won't. I promise." Lulu gazed at me with a sincerely mournful-looking expression. "I'm sorry. I didn't mean to let you down."

Her sad face melted me. Against my better judgment, I held out my arms. "Come here, you."

I didn't need to ask twice; Lulu practically threw herself into my embrace. We hugged for what seemed like hours. A serene sense of almost motherly love came over me as I stroked her bleached blond hair. I could do this. I could be a responsible adult and help my little sister through this difficult time.

Maybe it really had been the first time she'd done meth, or Ritalin—whatever it really was. Most likely this event had been Lulu's way of crying for help. After all, both parents had essentially abandoned her. She was probably feeling confused. Lonely. Unsettled. A rebel with a very legitimate cause. I'd simply keep an eye on her from now on. Step up to the parental plate and make sure she didn't go down the wrong path. After all, besides me, she had no one. She was a little lost angel with a tarnished halo.

"I know you've been going through hell over Mom and Dad's divorce," I said, smoothing her back with my hand. "I'm sorry wasn't nice about you moving in."

"And I'm sorry I trashed your house," Lulu replied, sounding a little choked up. "From now on, I'll be a better houseguest."

"Roommate," I corrected.

"Really?" She pulled away, her eyes shining with happy tears. "You consider me your roommate?"

"Sure," I said, feeling generous. "And I won't even make you pay half the rent."

"Oh, Maddy. Thank you. I'll be the best roommate ever. I

promise." Lulu bounced up from the couch. "In fact, I'll start right now. I'll clean up the house."

"I'll help you," I told her. "And then we'll go out for ice cream."

"Cool!"

I watched as Lulu skipped to the kitchen to grab a garbage bag and begin Project Apartment Cleanup. She looked so innocent. Sweet. It was hard to believe she'd been up all night and day doing drugs.

It was all going to be fine, I told myself, quashing the worried gnawing sensation deep in the pit of my stomach. She'd made a mistake. We'd both made mistakes. But now the time for mistakes was over and we could move on as two responsible siblings. Together, we could take on the world and anything life threw at us.

At least, I hoped we could.

CHAPTER TEN

FROM: "Richard Clarkson" <rclarkson@news9.com>

TO: "Madeline Madison" <mmadison@news9.com>

SUBJECT: Too Much Terrance

Madeline,

I spoke with Jodi who said you're out shooting Murderous Mail (sounds like a great topic by the way!!!) but when you return, we need to discuss the "Cosmetics That Kill" piece.

I saw the finished product and I have to tell you, when I said we wanted the "Terrance Tells All" series to feature Terrance, I didn't mean to imply that Terrance had to physically be in every shot of the piece. Sure, a couple of shots sprinkled here and there would be appropriate—after all, we do want to feature our talent. But to have Terrance appear in 43 out of 47 shots seems like overkill.

Also, shooting the stand-up of Terrance applying the leaded lipstick to his own lips struck me as a bit on the disturbing side.

Please make the appropriate changes (I do not want to see Terrance more than three times total) and bring the new version for me to review.

Thanks for your hard work!

Richard
News Director, News 9

The next day at work, I sat down at my desk and clicked open my e-mail. I hadn't realized I'd been secretly hoping for a note from Jamie until I realized there wasn't one. Only spam and more work drama, joy to the world.

I wondered if Jamie had gotten in to work yet. I dreaded seeing him, facing him, working side by side with him, but what else could I do? It seemed too immature to ask Richard for a new photographer. He'd want to know why. And then what would I say? Besides, Jamie was a great photographer and I needed his expertise for my big Mexican shoot.

Tonight, fake-purse-seller Miguel had volunteered to lead us to the Mexican entrance of the drug tunnel. He knew a guard, he said, who could give us an inside look. It had the potential to be the smoking gun-type video we needed—the best video in the story. I couldn't exactly leave my photographer at home just because he didn't want to be my boyfriend. I needed to grow up. We were both adults, both professionals. We could do this.

The ride home from Calla Verda had been torturous, though. Of course, Jamie was perfectly polite, cordial. Thanked Jodi for giving him a lift and offered her gas money. But he didn't say a word to me. And when later in the trip I got up the courage to ask him a direct question, he pretended to be asleep. Even though I knew for a fact he couldn't be, since no one on earth could possibly sleep through the antics of Jodi's ultra-hyper dogs.

I turned back to my e-mail, trying to put him out of my mind. The first message was from Terrance, talking about how "utterly fabulous" the "Cosmetics That Kill" piece turned out. The second came from Richard, instructing me to make major changes to the aforementioned utterly fabulous piece—namely by taking out the utterly fabulous Terrance. And the third was from poor, tortured editor Mike, who begged me to tell Richard that it wasn't his fault that the plethora of Terrance shots had made it into the finished product. (Terrance had evidently verbally abused him for a full hour and a half, until he, as a man facing torture is wont to do, crumbled and gave the male diva everything he wanted and then some.)

I groaned. They called me a producer. Peacemaker would have been a more apt term. Or maybe crisis negotiator. I'd be so happy when "Cosmetics That Kill" finally got on the air and I never had to deal with it again.

I gnawed on the end of my pen as I contemplated how to inform Terrance that we needed to "de-Terrance" the piece before it aired. *Blame it all on Richard*, I thought. Make it seem as if I were as broken up over the whole thing as Terrance must be. *You know how news management is,* I'd say. *They simply don't have their finger on the pulse of the community.* Or some such bullshit like that. Heaven forbid he found out I completely agreed with Richard's assessment.

Satisfied with my idea, I opened up a blank e-mail, deciding it would be easier to break the news electronically. But before I could so much as type "Dear Terrance," Jamie waltzed back into my life.

I stared at my computer monitor, not turning around as he made himself at home in David's chair. I tried silently Jedi-mind-tricking him to go away, but he was either immune to the ways of the Force or I needed more lessons from Master Yoda.

"Hey, Maddy," he said in a casual tone. "What's up?" I told myself to stay calm, even as bile churned in my stomach. How dare he say "Hey, Maddy," as if nothing happened between us? As if we were just casual coworkers? Seriously, I wanted to whirl around in my chair and punch him in the face. That or kiss him senseless. One or the other. That guy who wrote the song, "Love Stinks," really was on to something.

"Oh, hi there," I said instead, attempting to mimic his casualness without much luck. Dammit, I didn't want him to know how far he'd gotten under my skin. It was too embarrassing. Too pathetic. I picked up my phone, pretending I had to make a call. Maybe he'd leave, go bug some other lovelorn producer. But of course, I was the only lovelorn producer in Jamie's life.

"Wait, Maddy. Before you get on the phone … can we talk for a second?"

Oh, no. Stop right there. I was *so* not going to fall for that one again. I deliberately placed the receiver back into its cradle and turned in my chair to face him. "What?" I demanded, my tone way too venomous for the situation. But really, the nerve of him! To sit down in my cubicle at work and insist on more talking? What, was he going to try to apologize? Say he didn't mean what he said? Well, I would have none of that.

"Yesterday, I—"

"Listen, Jamie," I interrupted. I was going to nip this in the bud. Right now. "I'd prefer if we didn't rehash this weekend's conversation all over again, no offense. I think you made yourself pretty clear, and I can accept how you feel. I'm sorry I was angry, but I've thought a lot about it and I believe it's all for the best."

There. That told him. I was firm. In control. He'd see that I wouldn't stand for his hot and cold bullshit. That I wasn't pathetic and desperately in love with him.

He frowned. "Maddy—"

"Oh, and if you're worried about me telling Jen, don't be," I continued with a bitter laugh. "You guys can live happily ever after and I'll never tell. Okay? As far as I'm concerned, it's water under the bridge. And anyway, it's not like I ever had any deep feelings for you." Okay, now the words were spilling from my lips like a cauldron bubbling over. I knew I should turn down the heat and simmer, but I couldn't stop. "You were just something to pass the time. A minor amusement." I paused. "I mean, just so you know."

He raised an eyebrow. "Well, I guess it's good to know where I stand," he said in a quiet voice. "But if you'll let me get a word in …"

I held up my hands. "Go right ahead," I said. "Say what you came to say. I just wanted to let you know where I was coming from. I am not at all upset about your decision to stay with Jen. I hope you have a long and happy marriage with many babies. And live to a long age and … stuff."

"Uh, right. Okay. Thanks. I appreciate those, um, well wishes. Now, as I was saying …" He reached into his pocket, pulled out a folded piece of paper and held it out to me. I frowned down at it, not willing to accept whatever peace offering he'd come up with.

"What is that?" I asked with disdain.

"The property record for the oil refinery," he said simply.

Oh, dear.

My face burned as I stared down at the paper. This is what he was trying to tell me the whole time? And I had gone off and said … Oh, man! I seriously contemplated crawling under my desk and dying on the spot.

Misunderstandings That Murder: Tonight at 11.

I looked up. "Jamie, I—"

He offered a small smile. "Don't worry about it," he said. "I understand."

I stared back down at the property record. It was so nice of him to have gotten it. For an utter jerk, he sure was thoughtful. Or at the very least, way dedicated to his job.

I, on the other hand, was a major bitch. And a sucky producer to top it off.

"I was going to give it to you in the car yesterday," he informed me. "But I knew you were keeping the drug tunnel story a secret. Wasn't sure if Jodi was in on it or not."

"Thank you for getting this," I said, not knowing what else to say. I wanted to apologize for my tirade, but wasn't sure how. "I mean, it was really, really great of you. It would have sucked to have to go all the way back, and, well …"

"No prob," he said with a shrug, looking a bit embarrassed.

I cleared my throat. "Look, Jamie, I'm—"

"So, uh, it says that the refinery is owned by a company called Reardon Oil," he interrupted, effectively giving me an invitation to change the subject. I stared at him for a moment, unable to read the emotion behind his beautiful eyes.

At last I gave up, keeping that last shred of dignity intact. I glanced down at the letter, forcing my thoughts to focus on more important matters than my doomed love affair.

"Reardon Oil, huh?" I repeated, giving it the old college try. If Jamie could be professional, so could I. "Never heard of them."

He shook his head. "Me, neither. But then, I'm not really up on the whole oil industry, obviously."

"True, true. Let me see what I can find out."

I turned back to my desk for some computer-assisted reporting. Last year I'd taken a course on how to use online resources to help research stories, but had never gotten a chance to put any of my newfound knowledge to use.

"So, uh," Jamie said, still awkwardly lingering. "They found my bike."

"They did?" I exclaimed, turning around again. So much for keeping the conversation professional. "That's great!"

I wanted to hate him. Wish for his misfortune. But instead, seeing the relief in his eyes, I realized I only felt delight that he'd gotten his precious motorcycle back.

"Yeah," he said. "Someone evidently took it on a joyride, then dumped it a few miles away. A patrolman spotted it and called it in. Only a few scratches. No major damage."

"That's great, Jamie. Really great." I tried to sound enthusiastic as my heart pounded at the awkwardness between us. It was as if we were strangers now. Next thing you knew he'd be bringing up the nice weather we were having lately. I couldn't bear it.

"So, um, tonight we're scheduled to go to Mexico," I informed him, trying to turn the conversation back to work-related stuff before I broke down. "My whistle-blower, Miguel, is going to take us to the other end of the drug tunnel. You up for it?"

"Sure," he said easily. "Actually, I could use the overtime."

There were probably a million reasons he could use the

overtime. Rent. Fixing the scratches on his bike. A cool computer he saw advertised on Craigslist. But there was only one reason my brain could latch on to.

Wedding expenses.

Jamie was getting married. To Jen. To have and to hold, 'til death did they part. I swallowed hard and attempted to will away the ache in my heart. I had to accept this. Start seeing him as just another coworker. A soon-to-be-married coworker. Otherwise I was seriously going to go crazy working with him. I felt my throat constrict as regret threatened to consume me.

If only I had left him alone to begin with. Not allowed myself to start something I knew in my head could only lead to disaster and heartbreak. But, no. I'd pursued a man who was unavailable. I deserved this misery.

"Um, right now, though, I have nothing for you to do," I said hastily. I could feel the tears prick at the corners of my eyes, threatening to fall. I needed him to leave. Fast. Before he saw the hurt. Before he saw how much he meant to me. "You should go check in with News. They probably have some fires for you to chase or something."

"Trying to get rid of me?"

"No!" I retorted, throwing him a glare. A glare to hide my embarrassment at being called onto the carpet. "It's just that … Richard … um, told me if I didn't have anything for you to do, I should give you to News. They can always use an extra photographer."

"Fair enough." Jamie rose from his seat and headed out of the cubicle. "Have a good day, Maddy."

I waited for a moment, until I heard his footsteps fade away, then put my face in my hands. I rubbed my eyes in frustration, probably ruining my eye makeup. Why did this have to be so hard?

"Madeline!"

What now? I looked up, surprised, as Terrance entered the cubicle. He sat down in David's chair. Oh great. I wiped my eyes with my sleeve. The last thing I wanted was for Terrance to see me crying. He was the biggest gossip on the planet.

"Did you see the piece?" he asked, his eyes shining his enthusiasm. "Isn't it fabulous?"

"I haven't seen it yet," I told him. "And I'm sure it is wonderful—Mike's a great editor. But—"

Terrance huffed. "Mike is a pain in the ass, if you ask me. I had to sit in there the whole afternoon, telling him how to do his job. If it weren't for me, that piece would look completely different."

I was pretty sure he was right about that one. But perhaps not in the way he meant.

"Anyway, Madeline, you were *so* lucky I had some time to spare to teach Mike how to do his job. I mean, did you really plan to simply leave him alone to edit without any guidance? What would you have done if I hadn't stepped in? Though, I have to say, my efforts have paid off handsomely. The piece looks—"

"Fabulous. I get it." I sighed. "But, Terrance, do you think maybe that you might have just perhaps possibly added one too many, um, shots of a certain kind?"

Terrance scrunched his eyebrows in confusion. Obviously I couldn't be subtle here.

I swallowed. "What I'm trying to say is, we need to take out some of the shots of you."

"Some of the Terrance shots? You can't take out the Terrance shots," the anchor exclaimed, shocked. "A Terrance piece must have Terrance in it! The audience expects it. The fans demand it."

I didn't know what I found more disturbing—seeing Terrance so upset about being taken out of the piece or him referring to himself in the third person.

I shrugged, taking the coward's way out. "I know you what you mean. But Richard insisted. You know how management is. I'm just a lowly producer. What can I do?"

"Well, to start, you can tell him that a Terrance piece needs Terrance. Why would I bother to do a segment if I wasn't going to be in it? The segment is called 'Terrance Tells All.' How can Terrance tell all if the audience does not see Terrance doing any of the telling? Is Terrance some sort of invisible superhero? No, I think he is not." He stamped his foot in emphasis, and I had to bite my tongue to stifle a giggle. He looked so wide-eyed and anxious. Horrified, even. An expression you might see on a man who'd been told dingos had eaten his baby.

"I'm sorry, Terrance," I managed to say, straight-faced. "I don't know what to tell you. Why don't you go talk some sense into Richard? I'm sure he'll listen to you." I wasn't at all sure of this, but at least that would take the pressure off me.

Nodding, Terrance rose from his seat and patted his anchor-perfect hair. "Yes. I will do that. Good day, Madeline." And with that he stormed off.

I sighed. If this place were filmed for a reality show, everyone would think it had been exaggerated for television.

I turned back to my computer-assisted reporting project. Who was Reardon Oil? I hit LexisNexis first, this great subscription-based web service, which archived newspaper and magazine articles. You could type in a key word and BAM! Out popped hundreds of articles. If anything had ever been written about Reardon Oil, Lexis would find it.

Only one article popped up. A story about a fundraiser for Senator Gorman, held back during his first election bid. Reardon Oil evidently gave quite the campaign contribution to our favorite Republican. Could it have been a bribe of some sort?

As if he read my mind, David picked that moment to waltz into our cubicle and sit down.

"Hey, Maddy, did you know Senator Gorman blinks twice as many times per minute than Democratic challenger Bill Barnum?" he asked with a completely straight face. "They did a study. And we're live at five with the exclusive results."

"Fascinating." I chuckled. "And this should change my vote, why?"

"Well, according to the taxpayer funded study, more blinking means you're more likely to be lying." David blinked a few times himself, in illustration.

"I see. In case anyone wasn't completely convinced of Gorman's truth-telling after his lower gas price promise last election?"

"Oh, Maddy! Our viewers can't be expected to remember something as *tedious* as campaign promises," David said. "They need something simple to focus on."

I laughed. "So true. And what is the promo department calling this story? Blinking Bad Guys?"

"Oh no, much better than that. They're calling it 'Lying Through Your Lids.'"

"Beautiful. Congrats on getting to be a part of such an election-changing story." I patted him on the back.

"Indeed, I cherish these moments and think how lucky I am to be a part of democracy in action."

"Not to change the subject," I said, "but have you ever heard of a company called Reardon Oil? Big contributor during Gorman's first bid for senator?"

David narrowed his eyes in thought. Then he shook his head. "Doesn't ring a bell. Though it'd make sense since it's an oil company. Before he was elected senator, Gorman worked for the California Environmental Protection Agency. He would have had to sign off on any oil drilling applications. Make sure they're not damaging the environment, that sort of thing."

"So whoever owns Reardon Oil could have promised him a big bribe if Gorman would sign on the dotted line for something not on the up and up?"

"Why, Maddy, It's not *bribery*! It's called *lobbying*. And what *are* you implying about our illustrious senator?" David asked in feigned horror. Then he laughed. "Sounds like the Gorman I know and love."

"Interesting," I mused.

"Let me ask Brock though. He may know more."

I grinned knowingly. "Ooh, things still hot and heavy with the senator's son?"

"Hell yeah, sister. He is the cat's meow." David beamed.

"Does his dad know you two are an item?"

"Uh, that would be a negative. Brock's still technically in

the closet. But he has one toe out. And I'm confident by the end of the month he'll manage a whole foot. Maybe even a kneecap."

I chuckled. "Okay, my patient little lover boy. Let me know what you find out."

I turned back to my computer. Now done with my LexisNexis search, I decided to try top-secret investigative reporter tool number two:

Google.

I wondered what reporters had done before the Internet. They must have actually had to use the phone. Called people and asked them stuff. But then, that was before voice mail hell. These days getting through the navigation maze of "Press one if you want …" and actually getting a live person (who then probably got paid two dollars an hour from his outsourced office in India and didn't know anything anyway) was next to impossible.

I typed Reardon Oil, but all I got back was some kind of comic book reference and a rather disturbing site about horsetail art.

I hit the "back" button to return to the search field. This time, I selected the "images" tag. Maybe I could get a photo.

However, unlike when one typed "Ewan McGregor" into Google and got 8,680 photos to gaze dreamily upon (NOT that I'd ever done that!) Reardon Oil only brought up one: a photo of an extremely heavyset man, squeezed into a tuxedo, shaking Senator Gorman's hand. Was this the owner of Reardon Oil? Unfortunately there was no caption on the photograph so I still didn't have a name. I hit "print" anyway.

Grabbing the desert undercover videotape off my desk, I headed to the viewing station to reexamine it. I didn't think Tuxedo Man was the same one out in the desert, but I had to be sure. I fast-forwarded to the spot where the Mercedes pulled in. Nice car. Drug dealers were so lucky to afford such sweet rides. The man in question opened the door and stepped out.

Disappointment washed over me. Definitely a different guy.

The man in the desert was thinner and had a full head of curly black hair, unlike the balding old guy in the penguin suit. I guessed that would have been too easy. Even if Mr. Reardon Oil did own the property, it was highly unlikely that he'd come pick up the drugs himself.

"Who are you?" I asked quietly, more determined than ever to find out.

I was about to eject the tape when I noticed something out of the corner of my eye. The Mercedes's license plate. Unfortunately in California, after some actress got stalked and killed, the DMV no longer gave out any personal info if you had a license number. But what I did notice might be equally valuable.

The car had dealer plates.

"David?" I called. "Come here a sec, will you?" David popped out of the cubicle and came up behind me. "What's up?" he asked.

I pressed a finger against the monitor. "See that? The car has dealer plates. Can you ask Brock if his dad had any campaign contributors who are involved in car dealerships as well as oil refineries?" It was a long shot, but I couldn't rule anything out.

"What *are* you working on?" David asked curiously. "It looks way too interesting to be a News Nine report."

"Well, it may be something and it may not be," I said. "So for now, can you keep it all on the down-low?"

"Sure thing, sistah. On one condition. You let me borrow your spangly tank top for Saturday night. Brock and I are going dancing."

"No problem. Just don't stretch it out with those broad shoulders of yours. And wear plenty of deodorant. I don't want sweat stains." After David swore up and down that he'd dowse with Degree before setting foot on the dance floor, I walked over to the printer and grabbed the photo with Tux Man and Gorman. I handed it him. "This is our Reardon Oil guy. If you can find out who he is, you can keep the shirt. I'll even let you have the matching skirt."

"Ooh, you know how to strike a hard bargain." David grinned. "Consider it done."

*

I always loved the look of Armani, but this dress had to be Giorgio's pièce de résistance. The black silk hugs my body in all the right places. As I sit down at the banquet table, I can hear the other guests murmuring their approval.

"You look beautiful," Jamie whispers. I glance to my right, where he sits, dressed in a sexy tux. He reaches over to squeeze my hand. "Like a winner."

I smile and return the squeeze. "So do you, my darling. As always."

"So, what do you think our chances are tonight?"

"Oh, we're a shoo-in," I say with a grin. "Our Newsline *investigative pieces have won National Emmys six years in a row. What's to stop us from taking number seven?"*

"You're amazing," Jamie says, looking adoringly into my eyes. "And to think I almost lost you due to my stupidity."

"Yes. You could have married that awful bitch Jennifer. I can't believe you were once engaged to the waitress at Deb's Diner."

"Back then she thought she'd be an actress."

"Yeah, right. Isn't that hilarious?"

"I'm so glad I fell in love with you. You are the sunshine of my existence. My perfect rose. My amazing, talented, Newsline *producer. I love you, Mrs. Hayes."*

"I love you, too, Mr. Hayes. Now, shush, while they announce the winner."

The orchestra picks up, a vibrant tune as the head of the National Academy of Television Arts and Sciences steps up to the podium.

"And the winner of this year's National Emmy for Outstanding Investigative Work goes to …"

I hold my breath. Will it be me? Will he say my name? The envelope rustles….

"Sleeping Beauty!"

Huh? Sleeping Beauty? What the …?

"Hey, Sleeping Beauty, you ready to go?"

I lifted my head from my desk, groggily recognizing the Sleeping Beauty comment to be coming from Jamie. And not gorgeous tux-clad husband at the Emmy awards ceremony Jamie, but jeans and T-shirted, engaged to another woman Jamie.

Real-life Jamie.

Thanks a lot, subconscious. We were supposed to be forgetting the fantasy, remember? Not rehashing it in our dreams.

I couldn't believe I'd fallen asleep. After David had left the cubicle earlier, I'd decided a quick eye-shutting was in order. After all, I was still exhausted from the Calla Verda adventure. But I'd only wanted to close my eyes for one second. Evidently my brain had other ideas. How long had I been out for?

"What time is it?" I asked, yawning. Hopefully no one walked by and caught me napping. Well, except Jamie, of course. I wondered if I looked cute and sleep-tousled or disgustingly disheveled. More likely the latter. At least he couldn't tell what I had been dreaming. That would be super embarrassing.

Jamie glanced at his watch. "Six. You said we were supposed to meet Miguel, right? We'd better get a move on."

"Okay." I stretched my arms over my head, trying to wake up. I'd never fallen asleep on the job before. "But I need major coffee first."

"I think that can be arranged," he said with a grin. I smiled back, unable to help myself.

I could do this. I could work with him without wanting to jump his bones. We didn't have to simply be coworkers. We could be friends. Just not lovers. Definitely not lovers.

I got up from my chair and followed him through the hallways, trying not to stare at his perfect butt. Friends did not stare at each other's butts, after all.

We hit Starbucks and grabbed ice Americanos with four shots of espresso. So strong they were barely drinkable, but I definitely wouldn't fall asleep on the job.

Now armed with caffeine, we hopped back in the SUV and drove down to Mexico. In order to not arouse suspicion, we had decided to park at the border and walk over. Then, Miguel would drive us in his car to the tunnel opening. On the way down, Jamie hooked up his iPod and blasted '80s music, eliminating the need for much conversation. It was just as well.

Getting out of the SUV, we walked through the clanging metal one-way revolving doors that led to the Central American country. Going into Mexico always reminded me of one of those Chinese finger traps: Anyone could go in—they never even checked IDs at this border. But you had to have major documentation to get out.

As we headed to the main square, delicious meaty smells wafted from nearby taco stands, tempting us to stray from our destination. But there would be no margaritas or food that evening. No fake-purse shopping. We had a more important mission. A dangerous undercover mission. I felt a little like James Bond—except, without the cool car, gadgets, and license to kill, of course.

"Hi, Miguel," I greeted as we approached his stand. He grinned back his own semi toothless greeting.

"Maddy!" he exclaimed. "Welcome back to Tijuana."

"Thanks," I said, my eyes unwillingly drawn to his wares. Wow. It looked like he'd gotten in a brand new stock of purses! Wait 'til I told Jodi. Wait—was that a Kate Spade with a sewn on label?

Maddy, stop it. You're on an important undercover mission, not a shopping trip.

I willed myself to stop looking; I could always come back another day with Jodi. Tomorrow after work. Surely no one would buy the Kate Spade purse before I could return, would they? Then again, it was pretty rare to find a counterfeit Kate Spade with a sewn on label. Most were glued. What if someone came by tomorrow while I was at work and realized what a find it was? What if they bought it before I had a chance to—

"How much for the Kate Spade?" I blurted. I could feel Jamie's disapproving gaze settle on me.

"Maddy, I thought you said we had to resist our shopping urges," he reminded me.

"Yeah, yeah, I know, but do you know how rare it is to find a good Kate Spade knockoff with a sewn on label?"

He raised an eyebrow. "In fact, I believe you specifically told me that I needed to stop you if you suddenly had an overwhelming urge to buy a purse."

I groaned. "I meant an everyday purse. Not a Kate Spade with a sewn on label. You don't understand—these purses come around once in a blue moon."

"You also said to remind you that you already had nine Kate Spade knockoffs already." He shook his head. "What do you do with nine purses?"

"You know in the time it took to have this discussion I could have bought the purse," I whined.

Miguel placed a comforting hand on my shoulder. "I put a purse aside for you, *chica*," he consoled. "But really, we must get moving to our destination. The guard who knew my brother, he is off duty at midnight. After that, it will be too dangerous to take you inside."

I reluctantly acquiesced, sure that the purse was going to be long gone by the time I got back. But what could I do?

Miguel pulled down a metal barrier over the shop window and locked it at the bottom with a padlock. Then, he motioned for us to follow him. We walked behind the store to a tiny, beat up car. We clambered inside. Jamie allowed me shotgun, and he took the rear. Miguel turned the key in the ignition, and off we went.

Two hours later, I was ready to throw up. The Mexican roads were windy and bumpy, and Miguel's car had very little shock absorption. Not to mention it had no AC and the radio blared gay Spanish tunes that only added to my nausea. To make matters worse, Miguel felt prompted to sing along. And let's just say, *American Idol* finalist he was not. The things I did to get a good story …

Finally, when I thought we would literally die from heat (and ear) exhaustion, Miguel pulled over to the side of the road and killed the engine. "Here we are," he said. "It's right over that ridge."

His statement made my pulse kick up about ten notches, drum with both anticipation and fear. This was not standing on a cliff, looking down at a distant building that we wouldn't be going near. This was actually penetrating a drug cartel facility in a foreign country where we could be shot and killed and no one would even know where to look for us. In fact, come to think of it, we hadn't even told anyone where we had gone. Pretty dumb.

When we didn't come back, there'd probably be a nationwide search. Dogs, flashlights, dredging rivers. Our faces would forever be enshrined on milk cartons. But no one would ever discover the truth—that we were complete morons who'd decided busting a drug cartel on our night off would be a positive career move.

Coyotes howled in the distance as we exited the car. Miguel pulled out a flashlight from behind the driver's-side seat, turning it on and flicking the light into the sky three times. "I am announcing that we are here to my amigo," he informed us. "Since the tunnel is only operational during the day, there is just one guard on duty at night. His job is to pay off the police if they come snooping." He laughed. "But in Mexico, they come for the money only. They do not care what goes on behind closed doors."

"So, your friend's going to give us a tour?" Jamie asked Miguel. "And he'll let us videotape it all?"

"*Si.*" Miguel nodded. "Alejandro will let you get all the video you need. To avenge his friend, my brother, God have mercy on his soul." Miguel crossed himself. "Now, let us go."

Nice. The murdered-brother story. Just the reminder I needed to get my heart rate skyrocketing again. I reminded myself that the people who did that job were not there. They were in their beds, sleeping soundly with no idea there was an American news crew invading their drug tunnel.

Jamie reached into the backseat and pulled out his camera. He'd brought the smaller, digital DVC-Pro—better quality than the hidden camera but less bulky than the full-sized beta cam. *Easier to run with if we we're chased*, he had said, and suddenly stories about killer household products that didn't really kill didn't really seem all that bad.

We walked about fifty yards down the rocky dirt road to a large dig site. The moon hung full and large in the desert sky, illuminating the landscape with a burnt yellow glow.

There was no oil refinery pretense on this side of the border. Just a bunch of rusty old digging equipment and a large ramshackle warehouse standing tall in the center. Miguel motioned for us to follow him to the building. Once at the door, he knocked three times.

The door opened and a skinny man with a straggly black mustache, dressed in a guard uniform, greeted Miguel with a big bear hug. Mexican men, unlike their homophobic American counterparts, I'd learned, were not afraid of hugging each other.

"Hola, Miguel. Coma estas?"

"Ah, muy bueno, Alejandro. Habla Englais? Para los Americanos, por favor." He gestured to Jamie and me.

Alejandro turned to greet us. "How are you doing?" he asked, switching to accented English.

"Not bad," I said. Yup, seeing as I was still conscious and not passed out from fear, I considered myself doing all right. I shook his hand. "I'm Maddy Madison, the producer. This is my photographer Jamie. Thanks for doing this."

"You are welcomed. Peter, he was like a brother. When they murdered him, I longed for my revenge," he explained. "This way I can have it, but keep my own head on my shoulders. Sure, I will lose my job if they shut down the tunnel, but there are other jobs. Jobs that will allow me to work with a clean conscience. Perhaps Miguel here will hire me to run his shop." He slapped Miguel on the back, then motioned for us to step inside. We entered a dark building with only a few lanterns scattered for light. Luckily the camera had a night-vision option or else we'd be in trouble.

"There is no electricity," Alejandro explained. "Only a generator, which makes such a noise I dare not turn it on at night."

He shone a flashlight into the darkness, revealing a large tunnel cut into the ground, angled in such a way that a truck could drive through. I drew in a deep breath. This was it.

"Follow me," Alejandro said.

Jamie lifted the camera to his shoulder and flicked on the night-vision option. Now, looking through the viewfinder had the same effect as night-vision goggles—which would give the video he shot a crystal clear, though greenish glow.

We descended into the tunnel. It was just tall enough for a van to drive through without the roof scraping the dirt ceiling. Every few feet wooden beams and wire mesh supported the infrastructure, much like a mineshaft. The tunnel descended for about a hundred feet, then flattened out.

"The tunnel is nearly a mile long," Alejandro told me, stopping and leaning against one of the dirt walls. "There have been other border tunnels built in the past. Very primitive—carved out with hand tools. Only one person could crawl through to the other side and they were so close to the border that they were easy targets for border guards to spot. Many have been busted." He gestured to the tunnel before us. "No one has ever created a tunnel this big before. Now they can import more, crossing with trucks instead of on foot. They smuggle Ecstasy, pot, and cocaine. You name it, they will smuggle it."

"The tunnels are also used to smuggle human cargo," Miguel added. "Those willing to pay a price to go to America."

It made sense. Every day there were news stories about illegal immigrants risking life and limb to cross through the desert to get to the promised land of America. But the harsh, arid climate made the trip nearly impossible and many died. A tunnel such as this where you could ride instead of walk would seem a first-class ticket to freedom.

After Jamie got enough video of the tunnel, Alejandro suggested we go back above ground. There was an office, he said, where they kept the master plans. He could do an interview explaining what he knew about the cartel's actions, as long as we didn't shoot his face and digitally disguised his voice on the finished product.

We went into the small office and Alejandro unrolled a map. Jamie videotaped while he explained. "This is where the drugs enter," he said for the camera, "and the trucks come out here, on the American side. There, they will be transferred to other vehicles and distributed for American sale."

"And who's behind this?" I asked.

"The cartel operating out of this tunnel is run by the infamous Lopez family," Alejandro explained.

I scratched my head. "I thought Ronaldo Lopez was busted a few years ago. Isn't he still in jail or something?" I remembered the News 9 report. "They said the cartel had been broken up."

"*Si*, you are right, *senorita*." Alejandro nodded. "Ronaldo Lopez is serving twenty years. But his son Felix has taken over the business. And he has even higher ambitions than his *padre*."

"In that packet of documents I sent you," Miguel interrupted, "from my brother. There are pictures of Felix on the scene the day the tunnel first opened. They told him he should never come to the actual site—to be implicated like that—but he is bold and likes to take risks. On that day my brother took secret photos of Felix with his camera phone."

"Yes, I saw those pictures," I said, wondering if Miguel's brother had remembered to turn off the clicking sound on his phone before he took them. Maybe not, considering how he'd ended up.

"He took the photos thinking he could bribe the Lopez family and get a share of the business. Instead of accepting his proposal, they simply killed him." Miguel shook his head. "He was young and foolish, my brother."

"I'm sorry," I said, bowing my head in respect. I'd have to go back through those documents now that I knew what they were photos of. I'd had no idea the guy in them was head of the infamous Lopez Cartel. How perfect for the story. The smoking gun, so to speak.

"Does the Lopez family own the property?" Jamie asked.

"Oh, no. They do not own anything," said Alejandro. "If

they did, the *policía* would be on them immediately. They lease the land from a third party and pay them off in a combination of drugs and cash in exchange for the use of the land."

"Do you know who they lease it from?" I asked, getting excited. That transaction we saw in the desert—that must have been the guy they were leasing it off of. It made finding out who owned Reardon Oil even more important.

He shook his head. "I do not know for certain. I would assume someone from the American side. Someone with a clean record that the Feds would not suspect. A business leader, perhaps. A—how do you say it?—pillar of the community."

Curiouser and curiouser, as Alice in Wonderland would say. It all starting making perfect sense. Reardon Oil paid off Senator Gorman to approve their digging for oil on that property. With government approval, no one would suspect anything illicit going on. And since it was so far out in the desert, most likely it didn't get inspected on a regular basis. Then, Reardon Oil leased the land to the Lopez family to transport their drugs. They made a huge profit for doing absolutely nothing.

Only one question remained. Who owned Reardon Oil?

Before I could ask any more questions, voices, speaking in Spanish, suddenly echoed through the warehouse. Someone had arrived.

All four of us froze. Alejandro glanced at Miguel, a scared expression on his face.

"Eduardo," he said in a whisper. "The other guard. I do not know why he is here. He is not on duty for another hour."

Jamie and I exchanged horrified looks. This was exactly the nightmare situation we'd feared. To be caught by drug lords! Tortured. Killed. Buried in the desert. Our lives could be over in a matter of minutes! I felt like I was going to puke. Why had I thought this was a good story?

"Quickly. Through the window!" Miguel pointed to a small, dingy window on one wall. Could we even fit through that? The voices were coming closer. We'd sure as hell have to try.

Alejandro ran to the door and locked it.

"This will not buy us much time," he said. "Please leave. I mourn the loss of your brother, Miguel. But I do not wish to join him in hell."

We didn't wait for a second invitation. Propping a chair against the wall, I stood on it and pushed up the window. It opened with a resounding squeak that I was sure would give us away. Any second the door could open. We could be caught.

Focus, Maddy!

"*Alejandro?*" a male voice called. "*¿Dónde está usted?*" I nearly fell off the chair as the doorknob rattled. Thank God Alejandro had locked the door. That would have been it.

"*Un momento, Eduardo. Ha, ha. Usted me ha cogido que tomaba una siesta*," Alejandro said, motioning for us to hurry.

"What did he say?" I hissed to Miguel, praying it wasn't Spanish for selling us down the river.

"He says they caught him taking a nap."

Phew. With great effort and much adrenaline, I pulled myself through the window. For a moment, my child-bearing hips stuck against the sides of the small frame, but I managed to wiggle my way out and jump to the ground. Short, skinny Miguel came next, slipping through easily.

My breath caught in my throat. *Jamie.* He was a much broader build than either of us. Would he be able to fit?

His head poked through the window and I could see that he was struggling. He was just too big for the narrow frame. Terror choked me. He would get caught. They'd kill him. KILL him! I couldn't let it happen. Not to Jamie. Well, not to anyone, if it came to that. But especially not to Jamie.

I raced back to the window and grabbed his hand. "Let me help you," I cried. "I'll pull you through."

"I don't think I'm going to fit," he said hoarsely, out of breath from his struggle and fear. "You should go on without me."

"No!" I cried, tears streaming down my cheeks. "I'm not leaving you here." Inside we could hear banging on the door.

"*Alejandro?*" the voice demanded, not so amused this time.

"*Abra la puerta inmediatamente!*"

"Maddy, it'll do no good to have both of us caught," he scolded me. "Go. Now!"

"No!" I upped my grip to his arms and yanked as hard as I could. "I'm not going to leave you!" I tugged again, using my full weight for leverage.

It was amazing what someone under a severe adrenaline rush can do strength-wise. The last pull prompted the window frame to crack and give way. Jamie came crashing through, I fell backward and he landed on top of me, his weight crushing my rib cage.

I looked up. His face was inches from mine, his expression, a mixture of shock and relief. Then he leaned in closer—giving me a quick kiss on my surprised mouth.

"Thank you," he whispered, and then just as quickly rolled off of me.

We scrambled to our feet; there was no time to think, to feel. We dove into the darkness.

"Hurry," Miguel hissed from a distance, his voice guiding us as we ran through the desert to the car. A few moments later, a light flashed from the window into the darkness and we ducked to avoid catching its glare. My knee slammed into a sharp rock and I bit my tongue to keep from crying out as hot blood flowed from my kneecap.

"Stay down," Miguel commanded.

Crawling on hands and knees, it took next to forever to reach the car. I prayed over and over that they hadn't left anyone as a guard waiting with an AK-47 to blow away whoever came to claim it. This sure seemed a lot more glamorous when it happened to James Bond. Of course, he had an Aston Martin as a getaway car. I wasn't too sure Miguel's subcompact hatchback would have much of a chance if it came down to a car chase.

Jamie and I hopped into the back of the car and Miguel pulled the gearshift into neutral. Then he got out and pushed the vehicle down the hill until we picked up speed. He jumped into the car as we rolled silently down the desert road. Once we were a distance away and the hill flattened out, he turned the key in the ignition and shut the door.

"We should be safe now," he said.

I let out the breath I'd been holding for God knew how long. I turned to Jamie, panting for air, still not able to speak. He grabbed me and forcefully pulled me into a crushing hug that said more than words ever could. I clung to him, burying my face in his shoulder, sobbing with relief. Miguel stepped on the gas and we sped off into the night.

"Quite the adventure, no?" he asked, turning to look at us.

Jamie released me from his embrace and nodded. "Quite," he said, his voice still unsteady.

I leaned back in my seat and shut my eyes. I didn't want to talk. To think. Emotions ran too fast, too hard. I felt a hand squeeze my own and I opened my eyes and looked beside me. Jamie gave me a sad smile that spoke a thousand words.

"Thank you," he whispered.

"For what?"

He paused for a moment. Then answered: "For just being you."

Normal Heights

Community High School

10777 Alta Vista Road

San Diego, CA 92116

Dear Ms. Madison,

By law, every child at Normal Heights Community High School must attend an average of 180 days per fiscal school year. We do allow for occasional absences due to illness, family emergencies, even an occasional vacation.

However, Lulu's extended leave has become unacceptable. She has fallen behind in her studies and is in danger of flunking out.

While I am sorry to hear of your recent bout with bird flu from your visit to China and understand Lulu's fervent desire to be with her sister in her time of need, as Lulu's new legal guardian you must agree that her studies should come first.

I hate giving ultimatums, but if your sister does not start attending school immediately, she will be expelled.

Sincerely,

Walter Sott

Principal

PS. I'm also sorry to hear about your parents' tragic death by car accident. It's odd, I must have missed their obituaries in the paper.

CHAPTER THIRTEEN

The clock had struck three a.m. long before I inserted my key into the lock of my front door. I couldn't be more exhausted if I'd run a marathon. In a way I had, I guess—a mental marathon, anyway. My heart literally ached from the rapid beating it had been forced to drum during our desert adventure. And my scraped knee throbbed its annoyance at the horrid mistreatment it had suffered under my watch.

It was funny. James Bond never came home sore and exhausted. He'd go on high adventures—espionage, chase scenes, gun fights—much more strenuous than mine and still have plenty of energy to pleasure a Bond girl the same night.

He must have had better gym habits than I did.

I tiptoed into the living room, assuming Lulu would be sound asleep on the couch. At least I hadn't come home to another wild party; tonight I wouldn't have had the wherewithal to deal with San Diego's pierced and tattooed.

But Lulu wasn't lying on the couch. Nor, as further examination confirmed, had she passed out in my bed. I began to worry. Was she out partying again? The girl was going to flunk out of school. I'd already gone through the roof when she sheepishly presented me the note from her principal the night before. I had no idea she'd been skipping. The devious little bitch had been waking up at six a.m. and leaving the apartment on time to catch the bus; how was I supposed to know she'd detoured somewhere along the way? And to lie to the administrators? Tell them our parents had died and I'd contracted some weird disease?

Seriously, if I ever managed to get married, I was so not having children.

I noticed the answering machine's blinking light and pressed the "play" button. Maybe Lulu had called. Maybe she'd decided to sleep over a friend's or went back to our parents' house.

"Um, hi, Maddy? Can you, like, come down to the police station when you get home? I've been, um, arrested."

Or maybe she was in worse trouble than I'd even imagined.

Damn it all to hell! All I wanted to do was curl up in my warm, inviting bed and sleep for a year. Was that so much to ask for at three a.m. on a work night? And now I had to go down to the police station to bail out my little sister for God knew what reason? Seriously, whatever I'd done in another life to deserve such karma must have been pretty darn bad. Like Attila-the-Hun bad.

I thought about calling my father. Letting him know the consequences of his neglect. Lecturing him on how he should be sorting out his old family before starting in on his new one. Force him to parent—to deal with Lulu's juvenile delinquency. But luckily for dear old dad, at this moment I didn't have the mental energy to deal with his disappointment in me for not looking after Lulu the way I should have. As if it had been my job all along.

No, I'd go and bring my sister home myself. But he'd be sure to hear about the incident first thing in the morning. I should have gone to him to begin with, before things got so out of control.

I headed to my bedroom to grab money out of my underwear drawer. I had stashed it there before going to Mexico—didn't want to bring a ton of cash to a foreign country. Of course, if I'd known the funds would be called upon to bail my crazy sister out of jail, I might have handed them out willy-nilly to the far more deserving Mexican beggar children. Or at least bought that purse.

I reached into the drawer and fished around under my collection of lacy thongs (hardly used) and granny pants (somewhat threadbare) for the cash.

I didn't feel it.

Puzzled, I started pulling out the underwear and tossing it on top of the dresser. It had to be there.

Nothing.

Three hundred dollars had just disappeared.

Lulu. The thought hit me like a ten-ton truck. It had to be Lulu. Oh. My. God. She was soooo dead.

Seriously, I should let her freaking rot in jail. I wondered how long they'd leave someone there if no one came to bail them out. If we were lucky they'd incarcerate her until her thirtieth birthday.

What a fool I'd been. She was a drug addict. That stuff on the mirror? That hadn't been no stinkin' Ritalin. That'd been meth. Or cocaine. Oh, why hadn't I trusted my first impulse? Called my father? He could have gotten her into rehab. Now she'd stolen from me and gotten arrested. How was she supposed to get into college with a criminal record?

No longer tired, adrenaline kept me pumped as I ran to my car and burned rubber to the police station. When had my sixteen-year-old sister become a drug addict? And why hadn't I noticed the signs? This was all my fault. Mine or my parents'. How dare they be so selfish—go on living their own lives as if they'd never had children tying them down?

If I ever got married, I would get my tubes tied before the ceremony. Just in case the birth control pill, diaphragm, and double condom somehow failed.

A half hour and a hundred and fifty dollars later (thank goodness for ATMs), a pale, withdrawn, stony-faced Lulu walked through the police station door. I rose from my seat, half delirious with exhaustion and ran over to hug her. She shrugged me off.

"I'm tired. I want to go home."

I wanted to yell at her. Shake some sense into her. Beat her to a pulp for being so stupid even. But the officer on duty suggested I wait until morning. Until she'd slept it off. At the moment she was coming down from the drugs and would most likely be combative, unremorseful.

She'd evidently been picked up buying meth from an undercover cop at a nightclub. It was pretty common, the cop said. Meth was huge among San Diego teens. Cheap and available and highly addictive.

As he explained this, I wanted to cry. To tell him that the officer must have made some mistake and arrested the wrong girl. That my baby sister would never do hardcore drugs. Meth was for white trash desert rats, not middle-class all-American girls from normal nurturing families.

But then reality smacked me upside the head and I stayed silent, bearing the cop's judgmental look as he spoke to me. *How could you let her get so out of control?* he seemed to ask. *You're her sister. Why couldn't you stop her?*

The sun had peeked over the horizon when we finally arrived back at my apartment. I tucked a listless Lulu, who refused to speak, into my bed and took my place on the sofa. As exhausted as I was at that point, I couldn't sleep. I think I was secretly worried she'd try to sneak past me and out of the house. Just in case, I got up and strategically stacked a few soda cans in front of the door. At least then if she tried to open it, I'd wake up.

By that time it was late enough to reasonably call in sick at work. I phoned and left a message on Laura's voice mail, coughing a little for effect. It sucked to call in because I wanted nothing more than to work on my Mexican drug piece. The one time in my life I actually wanted to go to work. But Lulu's problems couldn't be put off any longer. I had to go to my dad.

I finally fell into a restless sleep. When I awakened, it was past noon. The soda cans still stood like sentries guarding the front door. I rose from the couch and peeked into the bedroom. Lulu lay there, sleeping like the dead.

I called my dad.

"Maddy!"

He sounded overjoyed to hear my voice. Well, he damn well should be. If it weren't for Lulu, he'd still be getting the silent treatment. Unfortunately I couldn't sign her into rehab without parental consent. And since last I heard by e-mail, Mom was climbing to Everest base camp, that left the family terminator—aka Dad—to sort out the mess.

"We've got to talk."

"I'm so glad you called," he gushed, ignoring my tone of voice. "You know, when you said you never wanted to talk to me again, that was the hardest day of my life."

I almost felt guilty. Almost.

"Can you come over? It's about Lulu."

He paused. "Well, actually, today's kind of bad…."

I gritted my teeth. Why did I bother? Then I reminded myself he didn't know the seriousness of the situation.

"This is important, Dad."

"I'm sure it is. It's just—well, I promised Cindi I'd go shopping for cribs with her today."

That was his excuse? His daughter was on the fast track to self-destruction and death and he had to go freaking shopping for an unborn baby who wouldn't even need a crib for another six months?

"Fine. Whatever. Forget I called." I'd figure out some other way to get her in treatment. Forge his signature, whatever it took.

"No, wait! Don't hang up."

I stayed on the line. "What?"

"I'll come by," he said quickly. "I'll just tell Cindi I'll meet her afterward."

"Fine." I hung up the phone and slumped back over to the couch to await his arrival.

To his credit, he showed up ten minutes later, dressed in khakis and a polo shirt. Divorce evidently agreed with him—he looked refreshed, tanned. It made me even more annoyed.

Against my will, he immediately grabbed me in a huge bear hug. The type he used to give me after coming home from a business trip when I was little. He'd ring the doorbell three times in a row, so I'd know it was him. I'd come rushing to the front hall and throw myself into his arms. He'd spin me around the house until my mother forced him to stop, lest I throw up on her carpet.

Who would have thought Super Dad would end up Super Asshole?

"I've missed you, Maddy," he murmured into my ear. "So much."

I could feel my defenses melting, but forced myself to stay strong. This man may have donated a sperm to me, but he'd also betrayed our family. He'd left his youngest daughter to fend for herself way before she was ready.

I pulled away from the embrace. "We need to talk about Lulu."

He glanced around the room. "Is she here? When is she coming home, do you think? I miss having her around."

I stared at him. "Why did you even let her come here in the first place? She's not old enough to live on her own."

He sighed as he made his way over to the couch and sat down. "I tried. She won't talk to me."

"You didn't try hard enough," I rebuked him. "Now she's almost flunked out of school. She stays out all night partying."

His eyes widened. "What? Why are you letting her do that? You're her big sister. You should be—"

"Be what? Standing over her every second of the day?" I snorted. "Be realistic, Dad. There's only so much I can do. And besides, technically none of this is my job. You and Mom are the parents, not me. And neither of you seem to give a shit that your youngest daughter is going off like a suicide bomber in Baghdad."

I didn't realize how angry I was until I started bitching him out. It felt good, actually. Relieved some of the pressure that had built up inside me.

Dad stared at his hands. At least he had the decency to look remorseful. "Your mother and I are going through what the psychiatrists call a selfish stage," he explained. "We spent the last twenty-four years as parents. It's time for us to spend some time making ourselves happy as well."

What?! Oh, puh-leeze. He thought I was going to just bend over and take that load of bull?

"Well, I hate to burst your bubble of selfish joy, Dad, but we have a problem." I took a deep breath. "Lulu got arrested last night."

"What?" Instantly Dad popped back into parent mode. "What for?" he demanded.

"Drugs."

He stared at me. "Dr-drugs?" he asked, his voice trembling. "You mean, like pot, right?"

"No, Dad, I mean like fucking crystal meth. I mean like one of the most addictive drugs on the planet. And this wasn't her first time, either. The girl is a major druggie."

"Oh, God." He leaned back against the couch and shut his eyes. "I had no idea. My little baby girl. My Lulu. A drug addict?" He opened his eyes. "Are you sure they didn't make a mistake?"

"I'm sure."

He moaned, staring at the ceiling. "This is my fault. I should have been there for her."

It was hard to watch. Growing up, my dad had always been in perfect control of every situation, never displaying any emotion. He was a rock, my dad. But to see him now, looking so guilty, so defeated, I felt myself soften.

"It's no one's fault," I told him. "She hid it well. But now that we know, we need to help her." What a surreal feeling, to be reassuring one's parent. Before now, it'd always been the other way around.

He nodded. I could almost see his brain working, formulating an in-control Dad plan. "We'll get her into rehab. Twenty-eight days. I'll call some places right now." He rose from the couch. "Where's your phone book?"

I sighed in relief and went to retrieve my Yellow Pages. It

was so nice to have Dad back in control. To have the responsibility and stress lifted from my shoulders. I should have gone to him in the first place.

I handed him the phone book and he put a hand on my shoulder, pulling me into a warm hug. This time I didn't resist and buried my face in his chest. "I'm so sorry you felt you had to deal with this by yourself, Maddy," he said. "I wish you had come to me in the first place." He squeezed me tighter. "I love you. And nothing can change that. Not Cindi. Not a new baby. You and Lulu are still my girls and I love you both to death."

I leaned closer into the hug, feeling warm and safe for the first time in what seemed like forever.

Daddy was back. Now everything would be okay. I hoped.

CHAPTER FOURTEEN

FROM: "David Johns" <fairyprincess@queermail.com>

TO: "Madeline Madison" <mmadison@news9.com>

SUBJECT: Reardon Oil

Hi Baby Doll,

Guess what? Brock and I are getting married! Isn't that sooo wonderful? Last night, he decided to leap out of that proverbial closet in a single bound—like Superman, only in Armani instead of that tacky spandex outfit! His dad, Senator Gorman, is absolutely pissed, of course, which makes the whole process even more delicious. Yes, I know, I've only known him a couple of weeks, but Maddy darling, when it's love, it's love!!!!

Oh, I asked Brock about that Reardon Oil company and while he said he never heard of such a business, he immediately recognized the guy in your photo. Evidently the fatso's name is Ronald "Rocky" Rodriguez and he's president of the Association for California Car Dealers. He and Brock's dad evidently go way back. UCSD frat buddies or some shit like that. Rocky owns Pacific Coast Cars in San Diego. You remember those cheesy ads you always see on News 9, don't you? "If I can't beat their price I'll drown myself in the Pacific!" That's him. I totally didn't recognize him without that goofy llama he always has with him on the TV ads.

Anyway, on to more important topics. I found the most fabulous Vera Wang and put down a deposit. I'm going to be a June bride—isn't that so wonderfully clichéd? Oh, and if you can make it up to San Fran, I'd love for you to be a bridesmaid.

Love and Kisses,
David

I was still pretty exhausted. Yesterday my father and I spent the whole day trying to find a teen rehab facility that would take Lulu. It seemed every single place was booked solid. (Which, I thought, didn't bode well for the future of San Diego's youth.) In the late afternoon, we finally found a small private hospital with an extra bed. It took some major convincing, dragging her against her will, but we finally got her checked in.

At least work was going well. Getting an e-mail from David revealing the identity of the guy in the Reardon Oil photo was a major coup. (Though I wasn't convinced he and Brock should get married so soon ...) Now it made perfect sense why the car with dealer plates had been there to pick up the drugs. Evidently Mr. Rocky Rodriguez had a little side business going on. Now I just needed to prove it.

"You're back!"

I looked up to see Jamie enter my cubicle, an overjoyed expression on his way too handsome face. All work matters fled my mind and my heart panged its appreciation of seeing him again. One day off and I'd missed him terribly.

Things had changed between us since our near death escape. It was like we had this deep connection now. Something beyond sex. Beyond words. Beyond a boyfriend/girlfriend thing. Unsaid and unrefined, but definitely there.

"Hi, Jamie," I said with a small smile. Did he feel it, too? The tension in the cubicle? He sat down in David's seat.

"How are you doing?" he asked, studying me with those heartbreaking eyes of his. "When you weren't here yesterday, I worried that …"

"I'm fine," I reassured him. "I just had to deal with a family thing."

"Do you want to talk about it?" he asked, his expression illuminating his concern. I suddenly realized that I did want to talk about it. I wanted to share my grief and worry with him. Let go of the heavy burden I'd been carrying around.

I looked around. News 9 Cubicle Land, however, was not the best place to off-load.

He caught my glance. "Let's go to Starbucks," he said.

I nodded, relieved. It was as if he could read my mind.

A few minutes later we sat down in the comfortable purple velvet chairs to sip our coffees and I told him the whole sordid Lulu tale. He listened with rapt attention and, when I'd finished, he placed a hand on my knee and squeezed. I knew it was meant to be a comforting gesture, but it sparked something else inside. Something I was trying very hard to ignore.

"I'm so sorry you've had to go through all that," he said, removing his hand. "You've had quite a week, huh?"

I nodded, feeling my throat constrict. I willed myself not to cry.

"And what I did to you probably didn't help much," he said with a sigh, staring down at his coffee. "I feel terrible."

I shook my head. I didn't share my story with him to gain his pity. "Listen, Jamie. There's no need to apologize," I insisted. "You said what needed to be said. You gave me my much needed reality check. You have a fiancée. Period. End of story. It's better that you laid it on the line before …" I trailed off. I'd begun to stupidly say before I fell too deeply in love with him. But I couldn't say that. I'd sound like a total loser.

"What I said in Calla Verda—in that motel room—I said out of fear," Jamie said slowly. "You see, I thought I had my life all figured out. Then you came along and turned me completely upside down. What I had with you—what we shared—started becoming more important to me than my relationship with my fiancée. I started looking forward to talking to you more than her. And that scared the hell out of me, to tell you the honest truth." He raked a hand through his hair. "I've always considered myself a decent guy. If I make a commitment, I follow through. And yet, suddenly I was having all these doubts. Like, what if Jen and I really had grown apart and I had been in denial all this time? Would marrying her make everything okay? Would we reconnect and fall in love all over again? Or would it be a huge, huge mistake that was going to make me miserable for years to come?"

I stared at him, my head spinning, not knowing what to say. Was he doing another reversal on me?

"None of this has anything to do with you, exactly," he continued. "Only that I started really caring about you and thinking about you all the time and wanting to be with you. But at the same time, I realized how completely unfair I was being to you—forcing you into the role of the other woman because I couldn't resist having you in my life. I'm not a jerk, Maddy. I'm really not. And so I realized I had to do something."

He paused for breath and I wondered if I should say something. But he didn't look finished, so I remained silent, contemplating what he'd just revealed. It made sense, really, and explained a lot of his mixed messages. But the question was, what would it all mean for us in the end?

He continued. "So I did the cowardly thing—I pushed you away. Tried to make you hate me. I guess I figured in the end that would make it easier for both of us. You'd think I was a jerk who didn't deserve your love and I'd never be able to go back to you, even if I was tempted. I'd marry Jen like I'd committed to and things would slowly get better between us as memories of you faded away."

He cleared his throat. "But at the same time, I couldn't bear the idea of you hating me. And I don't want to hurt or disappoint you, either. Especially since I have real feelings for you. Strong ones. And I don't know what the hell I'm supposed to do about that."

I held my breath, nervous butterflies flapping through my stomach as I tried to figure out what the hell he was trying to say.

"I went up to LA and met with Jen yesterday evening," he blurted out at last, staring into his coffee cup, not ready to look me in the eyes quite yet. "And I told her I couldn't marry her."

I stared at him, unable to believe my ears. He'd called off the wedding? He was no longer engaged? He was a free man?

"I told her that I felt we'd been drifting apart for a long time. I no longer felt a hundred percent into the relationship and I didn't think it was right to go through with it when I was having so many doubts. It wasn't fair to me and it wasn't fair to her either."

I nodded slowly. "How'd she take it?"

"Really well, actually," Jamie admitted. "She told me she wasn't shocked I felt this way and that she'd felt the growing distance between us as well. In fact, I think in a lot of ways she was relieved, to tell you the truth. This way she gets to stay in LA and not give up her career and her friends. Which I totally understand and support, you know? She told me she loved me, but realizes that we are two very different people, destined to live two very different lives." He stared down at his hands. "I can't say it wasn't a little weird to have her be so accepting about it, but in the end, I know it's best."

"Did … did you tell her about me?" I asked.

"Yes. It was probably the hardest thing I've ever had to do, but I figured it was better to be honest," he said. "She was bound to find out sooner or later anyway, and I'd rather she hear it from me. She told me she knew I had a crush on you from that first night at dinner. Something about the way I looked at you." He shrugged. "As usual, you women are a lot more perceptive than us dumb men."

"I don't know what to say," I said truthfully. "It's a lot to take in."

"I know. And I'm sorry. Don't think this puts any pressure on you," Jamie added. "In the end, this is something I had to do for myself and had nothing to do with my feelings for you. Well, in a way it did, but it goes much deeper than that. So you shouldn't feel guilty or anything. You were just a catalyst for something I should have done a long time ago."

Okay, I was confused. Was he interested in dating me now that he was free? Or did he need time on his own for a while to figure things out? "I understand," I replied at last, even though of course I didn't.

He chuckled. "Do you? I'm glad to hear that. I'm not sure I understand it all myself." He rose from his Starbucks chair. "Do you mind if we swing by my apartment on the way back?" he asked abruptly, his voice sounding almost nervous. "Jen had been dog-sitting for me in LA. Once we had the wedding conversation she sent the pooch back with me. I want to make sure he's adjusting to his new surroundings."

I hesitated. Go to his house and check on his dog? Was this some kind of lame pretense to hook up? And would I mind if it was? After all, he was suddenly a free man. And he'd definitely admitted he had strong feelings for me. Maybe it was time to see where this potential relationship could go—for the first time without feeling guilty about it all.

Then again, what if he suddenly pulled another reversal on me? Loved me and left me? I had no desire, after all, to play rebound girl. It could only lead to more hurt and I'd already had more than enough of that to last a lifetime.

I glanced up at him and he smiled shyly at me, his gaze hesitant but hopeful, and it made my heart melt as I saw the love in his eyes. Whether he would admit it or not, he had broken up with the girl he was supposed to marry and a lot of it had to do with me. He'd taken the first step toward a new life path and he clearly wanted me along for the ride.

Really, how could I say no?

"Oh, a dog?" I forced myself to coo. "I'd love to see him."

*

We arrived at Jamie's apartment a few minutes later. It was a cute courtyard building with a pool in the center, à la Melrose Place. He unlocked the door and we stepped inside. He hadn't been lying about the dog. A bundle of brown fur attacked me with excited yelps the second we walked through the door.

"This is Bowser," he said, kneeling down to play wrestle with the pooch. "Bowser, this is Maddy."

"Hi, Bowser," I greeted, crouching down to pet the dog. He responded by licking my face with his sloppy pink tongue. He was some kind of terrier mix and extremely cute.

Jamie rose. "So do you, uh, want a tour?"

I took a deep breath, reminding myself this was no mere dog visit. The sexual tension in the room was so thick you could cut it with a knife. I sucked in a breath. "Sure," I said, squaring my shoulders. Too late to back out now. Wait—did I put on good underwear this morning? I so had not planned this. I tried to nonchalantly lower the hem of my skirt to catch a glimpse.

"This is the—are you okay?" Jamie asked, catching my skirt-lowering maneuver. My face flamed in embarrassment.

"Oh, yes. Fine, thank you." I stammered. I quickly pulled my skirt back up. "Just, uh …" Checking to make sure my panties were appropriate for sex? Probably not something I needed to admit at that moment. "… had an itch."

Blue cotton. Not terribly sexy, but not ripped at least. Not huge like Bridget Jones's had been, either. Still, if only I'd had some clue today would be Sex Day, I would have grabbed one of those barely worn thongs I'd been saving for just such an occasion.

"Well, as I was saying, this is the kitchen …" I followed him into a rather large farmhouse-style kitchen with a center chef island, lots of counter space and a small table with a cheery red checked tablecloth in one corner. "I love to cook," he said, running a hand over the island. "Sometime I'll make you something, if you'd like."

"That'd be nice. I'd like that," I said, feeling awkward and shy all of a sudden. Wanton sex goddess I was not. And besides, what if I'd completely misread the situation? What if all that had been on his mind was dog walking and today had not been Sex Day after all?

"Did you want to give Bowser a treat?" Jamie asked.

"Uh, sure," I said, trying to come out of my haze. To be completely truthful, I'd have preferred to give Jamie a treat, but I was getting less and less sure he'd be interested in such a thing. Or maybe he was too nervous to follow through, now that we were here. I leaned against the counter, kind of wishing we'd never left work.

"They're up here." He pointed at the cabinet above my head. "Duck for a minute, will you?" I ducked out of the way only to have my head smack into his solid chest, which did nothing for soothing my raging libido. He closed the cabinet and I raised my head.

He was standing very, very close. And there could be no mistaking the look in his eye.

A moment later, he was on me, the box of treats crashing to the floor. (Bowser was going to have a field day.) His body crushed against me as he attacked my lips with his own. I struggled to breathe as want consumed me and fire burned in my belly. No longer shy, I clawed at his shirt, yanking it above his head so I could run my fingers along his chest.

He scooped me up onto the counter, spreading my legs. I wrapped them around his waist, feeling his desire, pressing against me. He wanted me, too. Badly, by the feel of it. He tugged up my skirt and peeled off my panties, not even giving them a second glance, which was probably for the best. As his mouth lowered to nibble at my neck, his hands fumbled with my button-down blouse, parting it and exposing my Vicky Secret's lacy bra underneath.

God, his touch felt so good. Delicious torture. "Hurry," I begged between kisses. "You're going to make me explode."

He grinned against my mouth. "Good things come to those who wait," he murmured, reaching under my skirt and stroking me with a rhythmic pulse as his other hand cupped and teased my right breast. I shivered as the sensations coursed through me, too many to catalog individually.

"Jamie, please," I moaned, dying for him. I reached in front of me to unbuckle his belt, then unbuttoning and unzipping him until his pants fell to his ankles.

I realized he wasn't wearing any underwear at all. My gaze dropped down, taking him in. I couldn't believe he and I had already had sex once and I'd blacked it out. I mean, how the hell did a girl forget a man like him?

He grabbed my ass and pulled me to the edge of the counter. Then, after slipping on a condom I didn't see him grabbing, he pushed himself inside of me, filling me completely. I cried out in pleasure and bit his bare shoulder. I'd wanted this for so long. Maybe my whole life. And I was determined to enjoy every minute of it. At this moment, rocking against him as one, nothing else in life mattered. Nothing except his burning mouth, relentless fingers and hard, fast thrusts against me. Soon I was seeing the stars that heroines in romance novels always blabbed on and on about. And, let me tell you, they were more beautiful than I'd ever imagined.

Jamie came a moment later, crying out then collapsing against me, burying his face in my hair. His breathing came hard, fast, erratic, tickling my ear. I could have come again just from that.

"Gurp," I managed, not ready to form real English words yet.

I could feel his smile against my neck. "Gurp," he agreed. Then he scooped me up in his arms and carried me gently into the bedroom. He lay me down on the bed and climbed in next to me, pulling a soft blue comforter over us and cuddling me close.

"Maddy," he said, stroking my cheek and looking at me with big puppy dog eyes. "Oh, Maddy."

I knew exactly what he meant. I felt the same way. Words were completely unnecessary. Useless to describe what had just taken place between us.

I leaned forward and planted a kiss on his nose. I wanted to lighten the mood. Otherwise I'd probably break into helpless tears of joy.

I'd never thought this would happen. I didn't even dare pray or wish for it. But now here he was, mine all mine, no strings attached. I could scarcely believe it.

"Great tour." I grinned. "I feel like I know the place … intimately."

He brushed a piece of hair from my face and studied me with thoughtful eyes. "Are you okay?" he asked. "Was what happened … okay with you? I mean, I know it was kind of sudden. It's just—well, I've been holding back for so long … and I just couldn't wait a second more."

"Trust me, I know the feeling. And it was very, very okay. More than okay, actually. Pretty awesome, to be exact."

He kissed me on the mouth. "Good," he said with a shy smile. "'Cause it was pretty awesome for me, too. But I don't want to rush things, either. So I'd like to start over. Do it the right way this time." He sat up in bed. "Ms. Madison, would you consider going out on a date with me?"

I nodded and grinned. "I'd like that very much, Mr. Hayes."

From the Desk of Madeline Madison

Maddy Hayes

Mrs. Maddy Hayes

Mrs. Madeline Madison -Hayes

Mrs. Madeline Leigh Hayes

M. L. Hayes

Mrs. Jamie Hayes

Mrs. Hayes

Mr. and Mrs. Jamie Hayes

The Future Mrs. Madeline Leigh Madison -Hayes

CHAPTER FIFTEEN

Unfortunately what often happens when one leaves work for wanton sex first thing in the morning, one must return to work before one's coworkers and, more importantly, one's boss realizes one has left the building. So while Jamie and I would have much rather cuddled in bed all day, at noon we were instead sitting in my cubicle, discussing the drug cartel story and trying to keep our hands off each other.

"So," I said, explaining my findings. "According to the records you found in Calla Verda, the property's owned by Reardon Oil, right? Well, on the Internet I found a photo of some Reardon Oil guy shaking Senator Gorman's hand. Evidently the company was a campaign contributor the first time Gorman ran for office. I gave David the photo to show Brock, Gorman's son. He and David are having a hot affair, by the way."

"Oh, my. What does Gorman say about that?"

"Evidently he's through the roof." I snorted. "Anyway, Brock says the guy's an old crony of his dad's—named Rocky Rodriguez. He owns that Pacific Coast Cars dealership down in Mission Valley and is also the president of the Association for California Car Dealers."

"The guy with the llama commercials?"

"Yup. One and the same."

"So he owns Reardon Oil?"

"I don't know. No one's ever heard of Reardon Oil. And I have no idea how it's connected to Rocky Rodriguez and Pacific Coast Cars. But they're connected somehow. That's for sure."

"Maybe Reardon Oil is part of a larger company that owns both?"

"Maybe." I thought about that for a moment. It would make total sense. I turned to my computer and pulled up Internet Explorer, then went to the Secretary of State's business-lookup Web site and entered "Reardon Oil" in the blank field.

Corporation
Reardon Oil

Date Filed: 1/1/2000
Status: Active

Jurisdiction: California

Mailing Address
PO Box 9003, San Diego, CA 92110

Agent for Service of Process
COASTAL KINGS

"Coastal Kings, huh?" I mused. I could feel Jamie's breath on my neck as he peered over my shoulder, and had to fight the urge to turn around and ravage him.

Totally not appropriate workplace behavior, Maddy!

I clicked over to the Dunn & Bradstreet company reports Web site and typed in *Coastal Kings*. I entered my credit card number to pay for the report and then pressed "enter."

"Bing-fucking-o!" I cried as the report came up.

It appeared from the report that Coastal Kings was a

holding entity that possessed several companies under its umbrella. All of these were Southern California and Mexican car dealerships. Except one.

Reardon Oil.

"Why would this car dealership chain own an oil refinery place out in the desert?" I asked rhetorically.

"The better to smuggle drugs with, my dear," Jamie teased, while massaging my shoulders, which made it even tougher to focus.

"Cute. But not good enough for an investigative story. We're journalists. We've got to answer all the 'w' questions. The who, the what, the where, the why and the how." I ticked off the questions on my fingers.

"Um, 'how' doesn't begin with a 'w.'"

"Yeah, but it ends in one. Close enough." I pulled up a blank Microsoft Word document. "Let's start with the 'who.'" I typed in the word *who* at the top of the screen, then centered it and changed it to a fancy font for effect.

"Okay, well 'who' in this case would be Felix Lopez of the Lopez Cartel whom we know is behind the smuggling operation," Jamie said. "We have photos of him on-site and the interview with the guard naming his involvement."

"Right." I typed *Felix Lopez* beneath the 'who' column." And we know that the Lopez family can't own the tunnel property because it will be a major red flag to the Feds."

"They need a middleman," Jamie finished. "Our second 'who.' And so they pick an upstanding car dealer from San Diego. Not only a car dealer but president of the Car Dealer Association in Southern California."

"Who just happens to be buds with the government official who gives out the oil permits," I said, typing *Rocky Rodriguez* and *Senator Gorman* under Felix Lopez.

"Yeah. And used car salesman jokes aside, you can't get much more upstanding." Jamie laughed.

"So, Rocky Rodriguez takes money from Felix and gives it to Gorman while he was still working at the EPA. Gorman signs off on the fake oil digging operation. Then they start work on the tunnel, under the guise of drilling for oil."

Jamie nods. "Because the whole operation has all the proper permits and the company is privately owned, no one's going to bat an eyelash that the oil digging operation never actually sells a drop of oil."

"'What' and 'where' are easy." I said, managing to talk and type at the same time (prompting more than a few typos). "'What' is an underground tunnel to smuggle drugs. And 'where' is our video of the tunnel itself, its entrance and exit, and the drugs being passed off."

"Which leads us to another 'who,'" Jamie pointed out. "The guy in the Mercedes."

"Well, the Mercedes's dealer plates suggest he's associated with Rocky and his car dealerships."

"But we can't jump to conclusions on that."

"True." I scrolled up and typed *Mercedes Man* under the 'who' column. Then I added a question mark. "We should probably hit Pacific Coast Cars at some point and see if we can find the Mercedes there."

"Good idea."

"So, what do we have left?"

"'Why' and 'how.'"

"'Why' is easy," I said. "Money. Greed. Opportunity. Family business. But 'how' is a little more complicated. As in, how did Lopez and Rodriguez hook up?"

"And that's the big remaining question. We answer that one and we have our story."

I flashed him my biggest smile. "Exactly," I said triumphantly. "You know, Jamie, you're so much more than a great photographer. I mean, you're practically my co-producer. My partner."

He stroked my arm with his fingertips, sending tingly feelings down to my toes. "I like helping you on your stories. It's fun unwrapping the mystery. Challenging. On the documentaries I used to do, I was simply the guy with the camera. You make me feel part of the team."

"And what a good team we make," I declared. "I'm never

going to let you go."

"Don't worry." Jamie grinned. "I won't let you."

*

"You what?" Jodi demanded. "You slept with Jamie? Are you insane or just really, really stupid?"

It was Sunday and we had headed out to the nearby island of Coronado to let her pooches romp on its popular Dog Beach. After parking, Jodi opened up the SUV's back door and all four came bounding out, the three Great Danes nearly trampling her husband's scrawny Italian greyhound with their exuberant exit.

"You were wrong about him, Jodi." I argued, shutting my door. I had debated on whether to tell her—I knew she'd flip her shit. But things had been so wonderful between Jamie and me that I would have had to come clean at one point or another. I mean, what if we ended up getting married? She'd need time to get fitted for that fuchsia bridesmaid dress I was going to make her wear.

"Maddy, this guy cheated on his fiancée and then left her high and dry. Is that the kind of man you want to have a relationship with?" Jodi asked as we ran after the dogs down the trail leading to the beach.

"It wasn't like he left her at the altar. They weren't getting married for three months," I argued. "And in my opinion, it's far better to come to your senses before the wedding than live an unhappily-ever-after in married hell."

"And you don't feel one bit a home wrecker?"

"Hey, it's not my fault I'm soooo irresistible," I joked, twirling around in the sand. I tripped and fell on my butt.

Jodi snorted. "Yes, I can see how he couldn't help but fall for your graceful charm."

"But seriously, Jo'." I scrambled to my feet. "You're looking at this all wrong. Jamie was already unhappy in his relationship before he even met me. I was merely the catalyst that caused him to see the truth."

"Or so he claims."

"Not all men are assholes, you know."

"You're right. Not all. Just most."

I rolled my eyes. "Fine. But Jamie's not one of them."

"If you say so … Oh, shit, hold on." Jodi broke into a run across the beach. I looked over to see what had gotten her worked up. Oh yeah. Great Dane number one had his head buried in a nearby picnic basket. Typical.

"No! Harley! Stop it! Bad dog! Bad!"

No sooner had she dragged Harley away from the picnic basket than Great Dane number two took advantage of the situation and hit the off-limits smorgasbord himself. I stifled a laugh. It was worse than having kids!

"Dee! No!" Jodi cried, releasing Harley into my care to grab the other dog.

"I'm sorry," she apologized to the annoyed-looking couple, who most likely hadn't planned on having their lunch devoured by dogs as big as horses. I, however, couldn't help bursting into laughter as Great Dane number three walked over and lifted his leg to mark the basket in question as his own.

"Ralph! Oh no, Ralphie, no!"

Jodi dragged Dee over to me and I held both him and Harley while she went back to retrieve Ralph. Meanwhile, the Italian greyhound, probably embarrassed by her adopted brothers, hightailed it back to the SUV and sat, waiting patiently to go home. (She wasn't big on exercise….)

"Good job, guys," I whispered to Dee and Harley. "Way to take the pressure off me."

Harley burped in response, leaving me to wonder whether his motives had been as altruistic as first appeared.

After leashing all four dogs (they'd lost their freedom privileges, Jodi scolded, as if they could possibly understand what that meant—or cared for that matter. After all, they'd just gotten a delicious meal!) we each took two leashes and walked down by the water. I kicked off my flip-flops and splashed in the shallows, dreamily reminiscing about the last week. I'd been doing a lot of that lately. But who could blame me? No matter what Jodi wanted to believe, life was good. Great, in fact.

All week Jamie and I had been inseparable, spending basically all nonworking hours in bed. But it wasn't all about sex, though there was plenty of that and it certainly was wonderful. We also spent hours talking, sharing, laughing. Never had I felt so comfortable with someone of the opposite sex. If there were such things as soul mates, I'd found mine. And in the nick of time, too. How awful it would have been if I'd lost him to an actress/model/waitress marriage-from-hell.

"How's your sister?" Jodi asked, bringing me back to the present.

"Good, I assume. They don't allow her to have much contact with the outside world the first couple of weeks, so we haven't heard from her," I explained. "Next weekend is family weekend, though. So Dad and I are going to that."

"What about your—? No! Harley! Don't eat that!" With effort, she dragged the dog away from his delicious decomposing-seagull snack. Poor Harley looked greatly affronted at being denied his meal. "Naughty dog! I should send you to the pound." She shook her head. "Sorry. What about your mother?"

"Safari in Tanzania, we think. I sent her an e-mail, but I don't know when she'll get it. Not too much Internet access in the Serengeti," I explained. "But Dad's been great. Really great."

"That's good."

"Yeah. Everything seems to be working itself out. Even News Nine's going good if you can believe that. I've managed to work on all the inane consumer stories they've assigned and still had time to produce the drug tunnel one."

"Ooh, yeah, how's that going?"

"Amazing. Seriously, I think this could be the one to win me my Emmy."

"That's awesome."

"It's got all the elements. International drug scandal aided by government greed. And the video is superb."

"Excellent. When are you going to tell Richard and Laura about this secret segment?" Jodi asked.

"I want to get it all done first. I'm supposed to interview Rocky Rodriguez—drug dealer aka car salesman extraordinaire, on Monday. Then I'll edit it and show the powers that be the final product."

Jodi's eyes widened. "This Rocky guy actually agreed to be interviewed?"

"Oh, yes. Of course, he thinks it's 'cause he won San Diego's Best Car Dealership…."

"Maddy!"

"Well," I protested defensively. "I know it wasn't completely, completely honest…."

Jodi's hands went to her hips. "Not completely honest? Why, it's an outright lie."

"Yeah, but he'd never agree to talk otherwise."

"But that's getting an interview on false pretenses."

"Who cares? He's a drug dealer. It's not like he regularly plays by the rules." I kicked a seashell.

"Man, he's going to be pissed when you start asking those kinds of questions."

"Oh, I'm not stupid," I corrected her. "I'm not going to ask him about the drug tunnel. He'd probably whip out a gun or something. I'm only going to get video of him for the story. And then we're going to see if we can find that Mercedes we saw out in the desert—the one with the dealer plates. See if it's on the lot. To dot all our i's and cross all our t's."

Jodi frowned. "They're not going to simply let you snoop around the car dealership. Especially if they have stuff to hide. There's probably major surveillance. And what if they suspect you have an ulterior motive?" Jodi's face echoed her concern. "These are drug dealers, Maddy. And you know they already killed Fake Purse Man's brother."

"I know, but—"

Jodi shook her head. "I know you'll never listen to me, anyway. You're too stubborn. But do me a favor and be careful, okay? You can't apply for a *Newsline* job if you're dead."

"Okay, Mom."

"Well, someone's got to take on the role."

"I know." I gave her a warm hug. I did appreciate her concern, even though I didn't warrant it necessary. "And I'm glad it's you."

We embraced for a moment—until Jodi suddenly pulled away and started running down the beach.

"Oh, no, Ralphie!" I heard her cry. "Please don't eat Dee's puke!"

I watched her run down the beach, chasing her beloved but mischievous pets. Even though her mothering could be a pain in the ass sometimes, she was a great friend and I knew she only did it for my own good.

But this time I couldn't follow any of her advice. Not about the interview with Pacific Coast Cars and not about Jamie. I had to follow my own path. Make my own mistakes. See where life led me.

Man, I sounded like a Jerry Springer Final Thought.

CHAPTER SIXTEEN

FROM: "Laura Smith" <lsmith@news9.com>

TO: "Madeline Madison" <mmadison@news9.com>

SUBJECT: re: Story Idea

Hi Maddy,

I see that you had pitched me a story idea on how kids are being sexually abused at summer camp. It's great that you have the police reports and statistics and a kid willing to talk. But since we're also doing our already sponsored "Kids Love Camp" campaign this summer, it seems to me that it might be a conflict of interest. I mean, we can't exactly be promoting camps on one newscast and then showing the icky things counselors do to kids there in the next, now can we? (And since one's already paid for, guess which one sales wants us to go with?)

If you're looking for something to work on, may I suggest you contact the author of that new "How to Marry a Millionaire" book? I was thinking we could give our viewers "Nine Tips to Marry Rich." (Unfortunately in his book he only offers seven tips—but since we're News 9 it'd be more promotable to do nine. We can make up the last two, I'm sure—how hard can it be?)

Hope all is well with you. It's great to be back.

Laura Smith

Executive Producer, News 9

Monday morning, Jamie and I headed over to interview Mr. Ronald "Rocky" Rodriguez. I had determined to do the interview outside in the lot instead of his office. After all, he'd be less likely to shoot us with a concealed weapon in broad daylight. Not that he'd want to shoot us. As I'd told Jodi, we were going in under the false pretense that his dealership had won an award. But still, you could never be too careful.

Pacific Coast Cars was located in the Mission Valley section of San Diego, off of Route 8. There were a number of other cookie-cutter dealerships along the same road. For easy comparison shopping, I guess. Pacific Coast Cars was the farthest down the road and had the requisite colorful balloons and streamers to celebrate its "low, low prices!"

We parked near the front and headed into the glass-walled showroom. The cold blast of air conditioning hit us as we walked inside and wove through the shiny new cars to the information desk.

"You must be Madeline from News Nine," a male voice drawled from behind me as we reached the desk.

I whirled around, a bit too nervously. No doubt about it, it was the man in the Internet photo. Of course today, the heavyset, fifty-something car dealer wore a completely different outfit—this one complete with spurs, jodhpurs and the stereotypical ten-gallon hat. He looked so silly that I had to stifle a giggle. Then I reminded myself that while this man may look like a total fool, he was involved in aiding and abetting a huge, illegal drug cartel, which made him somewhat less funny and a hell of a lot more scary.

"Yes. Hi. You must be Rocky. You can call me Maddy." I

held out my hand. "And this is my photographer, Jamie Hayes." My boyfriend and the love of my life, I almost added. But I guessed Rocky wouldn't really care about that little piece of trivia. It was funny how some things seemed monumental to you and meant diddly-squat to the rest of the world.

He shook my hand in one of those manly finger-crushing grips and I made every effort not wince. Then he motioned to the door.

"You said you wanted to do the interview outside. Well, let's get out there then. I've only got about ten minutes before I start shooting my TV commercial."

"Okay, sounds good." Ah, a TV commercial. At least that explained the outfit. It was strange to think this John Wayne wannabe ran with an international drug cartel crowd. He looked so fat and stupid. Guess you couldn't judge a drug dealer by his cover....

We walked outside, past a menagerie of animals that were, as Rocky explained, props for the commercial. I never really got why car dealers thought llamas and elephants and fifty thousand helium-filled balloons would help them sell cars, but who was I to judge? I couldn't have sold life rafts to Titanic passengers.

We reached a good spot to do the interview (far, far away from the zoo animals) and Jamie set up his tripod. I realized my hands were shaking like crazy and shoved them behind my back. No reason to get nervous now. Okay, so there was a very big reason to get nervous, but I refused. Besides, what could happen? He had no idea why we were really here. How could he?

Jamie signaled he was ready and I started with a warm-up question.

"So, tell me a little bit about this dealership, Mr. Rodriguez."

He grinned a toothy grin. "Well, little lady, my grandpa started this dealership back in 1954 ..." He launched into a long speech about the history of Pacific Coast Cars and how he had single-handedly made it into the successful dealership it was today. He was so long-winded I felt like asking him for a hit of his drugs just to stay awake.

"Okay, thanks," I interrupted when he paused for breath. "I think we've got what we needed."

He looked surprised. "Really? But I didn't tell you about all the great deals we offer our customers. Like how if you come in right now, we'll give you a free toaster."

Wow. How generous. "I'll be sure to squeeze that into the piece," I assured him.

"And when is this going to be on the TV?" he asked. Oh shoot, I forgot he might be wondering about an airdate. "I'm not sure," I bluffed. "A couple weeks, maybe. I'll be sure and let you know."

"Great. 'Cause I want to get my whole family to watch it. Just don't wait too long. My grandpa—the dealership's founder—is ninety-five years old and has a bad heart. Could go any day now. But when he heard I was going to win an award, he said to me, 'Boy, you give me a reason to hang on to living. To see my life's work honored by a major TV station like News Nine.'"

I stole a guilty look at Jamie, who raised his eyebrows back. While I had no qualms about exposing a guy involved in dealing drugs, I didn't like thinking I'd be making an elderly gentleman keel over in shock, his whole life's pride and joy crumbling during his last few breaths. Still, what else could I do?

"We'll make sure to get it on the air soon," I forced myself to assure Rocky. "For Grandpa."

"Well, that's great." He shot me another toothy grin. "If we're finished then, I've got to get over to the llama. These commercials don't shoot themselves, you know."

"No problem. Thanks for doing the interview. Do you mind if we go around and shoot some video of the dealership?"

"Go right ahead. Just make us look good, you hear?"

Score! I resisted the urge to high-five Jamie as Rocky walked away and left us unescorted. Time for our real assignment to begin.

"Okay, let's pretend we're looking for stuff to shoot," I said in a low voice. "And we'll start hunting for that Mercedes."

"Sounds like a plan." Jamie hoisted the camera off the tripod and onto his shoulder. "There's got to be an employee lot where the cars that aren't for sale are parked."

"Cool. Let's go walk around the back."

Casually, as if we really were there to shoot San Diego's best car dealership, we sauntered around the parking lot. Jamie made it look as if he were shooting various cars and signs on the way. A couple customers gave us curious glances, but were surrounded by eager salesmen, arms full of toasters before they could think to ask us what we were up to.

We reached the back of the lot, closed in by a wire gate. The padlock had been left hanging unclipped and we could easily open the door. I looked around, nervously wondering if anyone was watching.

"What do you think?" I whispered.

"Go for it."

Before my normally cautious nature could dissuade me, I detached the padlock and pushed open the wire gate. We slipped inside, pulling the gate closed behind us.

As we had guessed, it appeared we'd entered an employee parking lot. Several fancy cars—Jags, Beamers, and Mercedes—sat parked side by side. But it was one car in particular that caused my breath to catch in my throat.

The Mercedes SUV from the desert.

I knew it even before I checked the license plate. It sat by itself at the far end of the lot, the desert dust still clinging to its tires.

I grabbed Jamie's arm and pointed with a shaky finger. His eyes widened and he nodded silently, lifting the camera to shoot video of the vehicle. After getting a few shots, he motioned for us to go closer.

"Do you think it's unlocked?" I whispered. "Maybe we could shoot the secret compartment where we saw them storing the drugs."

Jamie shot me a worried look. "Aren't we going a little bit too far? What if they have security cameras and see us?"

"We'll make up some excuse," I said, reaching for the back door hatch. The handle turned easily. Not locked. "Yes!" I cried in delight. I motioned for Jamie to start shooting as I lifted the top hatch and lowered the bottom gate. Then I crawled into the back, feeling along the floor for an opening. The James Bond feeling was back in full force and this time I would definitely still have enough energy to shag a Bond Boy when I got home.

"Did you find anything?" asked the Bond Boy in question, still shooting from outside.

"Not yet—wait …" My fingers curled around an indent in the floor and pulled. The secret compartment sprung up. "Open sesame," I muttered. It'd almost been too easy. "Are you getting this on tape?" I asked.

"Getting what on tape?" asked a male voice—definitely not belonging to Jamie.

Oh, shit. We were caught. Fear shot through me like a lightning bolt as I released the trapdoor, which closed with a damning thud.

In the meantime, Jamie had turned around to address the man who'd approached. "Hi," he said, and I could distinctly hear the tremble in his voice. "I'm Jamie Hayes, photographer at News Nine. We're shooting 'San Diego's Best Car Dealership.'"

I stared at the man who'd approached us, the fear now crawling from my fingertips down to my toes. No doubt about it. The black curly hair was unmistakable. It was the guy from the desert who had shown up for the drugs! And now he'd caught us shooting video of the SUV he'd stored them in.

"Yeah, well, these cars aren't for sale. I don't know how you got back here, but this is the employee lot," he said with a growl.

I scrambled out of the back of the SUV, ready to turn on every ounce of charm my body had in it. "Oh, really? I'm sorry. It was just that there are some really, really cool cars back here. I mean sure out there you've got your Toyotas and Fords, but these Jags and BMWs are truly stunning. Take this Mercedes SUV," I said, gesturing to the car. "I was just saying to Jamie what a roomy interior it has."

"I'm going to get Rocky," the man said.

I felt my face flush with horror. "Oh, no," I said with a nervous laugh. "No need to trouble Mr. Rodriguez. He's busy shooting that commercial and all and ... well, we've got what we needed anyway."

The guy narrowed his eyes. "And you needed the inside of Rocky's personal Mercedes, why?"

I gulped. He wasn't going to let us go. He was on to us—saw through our weak cover story. Any minute now he was going to pull out a gun and shoot me in the head. "Well, it's just such a cool car," I stumbled. "And …"

"I'm getting Rocky."

"No need. We're done. We're off." I grabbed Jamie's arm and tried to lead him away as fast as possible. "Thanks again!"

"Hey!" the guy called after us.

"Yes?" I turned around, trembling with fear.

"Who else won?"

"Huh?"

The man narrowed his eyes. "San Diego's best car dealership. Who were the other finalists?"

I swallowed hard. Think Maddy, think!

"Um ... there was …" Blank mind. Completely blank mind. Probably a hundred car dealerships in San Diego county and I couldn't even think of one of them. "Actually, I can't tell you," I said with what I hoped looked like a sorry shrug. "It's a secret 'til the segment airs."

The man gave us a grimace. I just knew that he wasn't buying my excuse. That he knew we knew about the drug tunnel. My heart pounded as I waited for him to call me on it.

But all he said was, "Yeah. I figured. You have yourself a nice day."

*

It took about three hours of Jamie's reassurance before I finally felt able to breathe normally again. Every time I heard a noise, I jumped a mile, thinking it was the drug dealers come to get me. I was that scared.

"He had no clue what we were doing," Jamie insisted for the thousandth time. "How the heck could he know?"

He was right, of course. There was no way they could know. I'd made up this whole drama in my head. But knowing that didn't help my state of mind. I couldn't wait to get this story on the air and get the bad guys behind bars.

I somehow managed to get through the rest of the workday, even scheduling an interview with the Drug Enforcement Agency the next day. They were going to be a key interview for my piece.

At six, Jamie came to my cubicle and told me he was kidnapping me and taking me to Moondoggies for K9-Kosmos. Just the idea of sipping frozen drinks and breathing in fresh open air made me relax a bit.

Even better, when we got there and ordered our drinks, Jamie whipped out his surprise—pages of his brand-new novel in progress. Ecstatic, I practically ripped them from his hands.

"You can wait 'til later to read them," he protested.

"No way! I'm reading them right this very second. After all, I loved your first book."

He sat patiently as I slurped my drink and devoured the chapter. When I finished, I looked up with a smile.

"Oh, Jamie …"

"So what do you think?" he asked, looking a little nervous. It was so adorable how sensitive he was about his writing.

"It's so good!" I exclaimed.

"I want your honest opinion," he insisted.

"Okay, then." I grinned. "It's so very, very good. It's uber good. Fantastic."

He groaned. "You don't have to say that."

Honestly, for a guy who normally had so much confidence, he certainly became a real basket case when it came to his own writing.

"What makes you think I'm just saying that?"

"I don't know." He shrugged. "Maybe so I'll continue to do this to you?" He pulled his chair closer and nipped at my earlobe, sending a chill of delight down to my toes. "Or this?" His mouth traveled down to my neck.

"Mmm. You must be right. The book sucks, but I can't bear to tell you for fear you'll stop molesting me." He groaned and pulled away.

"I'm kidding!" I cried, tugging him back to face me. "I'm so kidding! It's great. Wonderful. Pulitzer prize–winning."

"I'm pretty sure they don't give Pulitzers to sci-fi writers." But he grinned nonetheless.

"Well, maybe yours will be the first," I said stubbornly. "This is great, Jamie. You have a real talent."

The thing was I wasn't exaggerating one bit. It was good. Really good. And I was sure I wasn't the only one who'd recognize it.

"Thanks," he said, blushing a bit. He took the pages and shoved them back in his messenger bag. "I hope you know I never would have written this if it weren't for you."

Now it was my turn to blush. "Yes, you would have."

"No. I'm serious. Until we had that talk in Starbucks, I'd all but given up writing. When you made me promise to take it up again, I had to force myself to sit my butt in that computer chair and stay put. I didn't feel like it at all when I started. But a few minutes later, my hands were flying over the keyboard. And the story started gushing out of me. It was like a dam had burst or something." He shook his head, remembering. "It was such a great feeling. I remembered why I used to get such pleasure out of writing."

"Why did you give it up in the first place?"

He shrugged and took a sip of his beer. "You're going to think this is completely stupid, but Jen used to make fun of it."

"What?" I asked, incredulous.

"Yeah. You know how she's all into the Hollywood snobbery and stuff? Well, she thought I shouldn't be wasting my time on 'pulp-fiction trash' as she called it. Thought I should be writing scripts instead."

"But you didn't want to?"

"Well, I gave it the old college try and all that. But found it wasn't for me. Completely different style of writing—I just couldn't get a good handle on it. In fact, I got so burnt out on it that I decided to just quit altogether. Which was fine with Jen. She'd rather have me on her arm at her insufferable Hollywood parties than locked in my study typing away."

"Well, I like the idea of you locked away writing." I grinned. "I think it's kind of sexy, actually."

He smiled, leaning forward to plant a kiss on my lips. "Well, you're welcome to come over and play my little muse anytime you like. We'll lock ourselves away together."

"Sounds perfect. What are we waiting for?"

*

Normally News 9 producers didn't really dress up for the job. Only reporters and anchors, armed with a station-funded clothing allowance, donned smart business suits every day before work. Producers, having the luxury of being behind the scenes (and lack of money to hit Armani), usually settled for sloppy chic.

But on the morning I was scheduled to go interview the Drug Enforcement Agency—the DEA as everyone knows them—I decided that jeans and a cute top might not cut it and instead wore my best interview suit. I wanted to look as professional as possible so they'd take me seriously.

It had taken some major hoop jumping to even secure the interview in the first place. The DEA's public affairs officer had been very suspicious when I told her I wanted to interview them about drug tunnels. She demanded details, which I wasn't about to give up. After all, there were still missing pieces to this puzzle and I wanted to have a solid case before I aired the piece and alerted the Feds. My plan was to give them the completed story and the documents the day the story was scheduled to air. That way they would have all the evidence they needed to arrest the bad guys and I'd have my exclusive story to impress *Newsline* with.

The San Diego branch of the DEA's offices was located in San Ysidro, right on the border of Mexico and the United States. Guess they wanted to be close to all the drug-smuggling action. Jamie and I parked the News 9 SUV and headed inside the building.

The public affairs officer, a smug-looking woman with a pinched nose, black-rimmed glasses, and a severe-looking navy suit greeted us at the door and demanded our IDs. Evidently they ran a tight ship at the DEA. After proving we really did work for News 9 and didn't just pick up a professional video camera and tripod at our local Wal-Mart, she allowed us inside and into a small conference room. As Jamie set up the lights, a thirty-something man with sandy blond hair entered the room. His tailored suit screamed "narc" and I hoped he didn't specialize in undercover work as any druggie in a fifty-yard radius could probably point him out.

"Hi, I'm Maddy Madison, News Nine," I said, holding out my hand.

"Hello, Ms. Madison. I am Mr. Mann."

I had to do everything in my power not to laugh when I heard his name. How ironic. "The Man" was literally named Mann.

Jamie motioned that he was ready for me to begin the interview, so we took our seats and I started asking my questions. "First off, tell me a little about drug tunnels," I said. "Are they common?"

"The Mann" (ha!) nodded. "We've found several tunnels over the years. And most likely there are more that exist. Border patrol keeps a constant eye out and we keep our ear to the ground as well. The thing about tunnels is you can't move them. So, sooner or later some druggie, hoping to get a lighter sentence, drops the dime on the tunnel's location and a bust becomes imminent."

"And has the infamous Lopez cartel ever been involved in a

tunnel?"

He paused for a moment, thinking. "No. I think Ronaldo preferred to send lackeys over the border the old fashioned way. That's how he got busted a few years back."

"What about his son, Felix? Do you think he might have taken over his dad's business?"

"No," Mr. Mann said, "There's no evidence at all of that. Felix is an upstanding citizen and businessman. He graduated magna cum laude from UCSD back in the day and hasn't looked back to his family for years."

UCSD? Excitement pumped through my veins. It was probably a coincidence, but wasn't that where David said Senator Gorman and Rocky Rodriguez had known each other from? Maybe they had been pals with Felix, too! Of course, lots of people had gone to UCSD. But still, they all seemed around the same age….

"Is this Felix Lopez?" I asked, switching topics by pulling out Miguel's brother's photos from my manila folder. I knew it was, but I had to get videotaped confirmation from the expert for my story.

"Yes. That is Felix Lopez," Mr. Mann agreed, after studying the photo. "Where was this taken? And when?" He looked agitated and suspicious all of a sudden, and I wondered why.

"It doesn't matter," I said, grabbing the photo and sticking it back into the envelope. "I just wanted to make sure it was him."

"Ms. Madison, what is this all about? Do you have something you'd like to share with me?" the official demanded.

"Not yet. Maybe soon, though," I replied, doing my best to keep my cool. Couldn't let The Mann get me down, after all. "And when I do, I swear you'll be the first to know." Which reminded me, I had to tell Richard about this story soon so we could schedule an airdate. He was going to be so psyched when he learned about it. Surely it'd be the best story all year.

"I hope so," Mr. Mann said. "Because keeping this kind of information from your government in hopes of getting a lead story on the evening news isn't very patriotic. Or"—he added, narrowing his eyes at me—"very legal."

The intercom on his desk buzzed. Saved by the bell. "Senator Gorman is here to see you," a female voice announced. "He says he's ready for your golf game."

I felt a chill spin up my spine. Not so saved after all. They were buddies? Thank goodness I hadn't spilled my suspicions to this guy. How deep did this corruption go?

Mr. Mann broke out into the first smile I'd seen since I entered the place. "Excellent," he said. "I'll be right out." He shot me a pointed look. "We're all done here."

*

"You sure this is the place?" I asked as Jamie pulled the News 9 SUV down a dusty, unpaved driveway in the desert town of Ramona. At the end of the road squatted a dilapidated trailer, its vinyl siding a dingy white. The yard around it had the stereotypical junkyard motif going on, and there was even a faded pink flamingo standing watch over a weedy garden of cacti.

"Fourteen Meditation Road," he said, glancing down at the directions. "It's got to be."

"When Switchboard dot com said Meditation, I was kind of thinking Koi ponds and Japanese pagodas. What is this guy meditating on—the ancient American art of white trash?"

Jamie laughed appreciatively and put the SUV in park. "You are too much, Maddy."

Seriously though, even he had to admit, this was the weirdest twist to the drug tunnel story yet.

Yesterday, on a hunch after the DEA interview, I'd gone to the UCSD student library and hit the yearbook section. I already knew what year Gorman went to business school there—his bio was on a billion Web sites. So I'd grabbed what would be his senior yearbook and dragged the dusty thing over to a table.

I flipped through it, trying not to pause and check out the funny outdated hairstyles and bell-bottoms, looking for some connection. Some tiny clue that would link Gorman, Rodriguez, and Lopez together.

Well, I found a clue all right. And it wasn't little, either. In fact, it was downright Mr. Snuffleupagus sized.

Not only did I find a picture of all three men together, but they were wearing crowns. Celebrating the launch of their student company. And not just any student company. A student company named Coastal Kings. The same umbrella company now owned by Rodriguez and encompassing his car dealerships and Reardon Oil.

Even more intriguing was the fact that there was a fourth "king" in the photo. A king named Bob Reardon.

I couldn't be more excited than if someone handed me a platinum card and pointed me to a Prada sample sale. Not only did I now have proof all these guys knew each other, I had a completely new "who" to add to my list. A man whose last name just happened to match the faux oil company I wanted to find out about.

I had to talk to this Reardon guy. Pronto. I had this feeling he'd know the answers to every one of my questions.

So, now we were here. Not exactly the kind of place I'd expected an MBA to hang his hat. To make matters worse, I couldn't find a phone number, so he had no idea we were coming. What if he was some crazed psycho?

I raised my hand to knock, but before I could, the door swung inward. A man with a shock of white hair that made him seem older than he probably was stared at us from behind the screen.

"Can I help you?" he asked.

"Um, yeah, hi. I'm Maddy Madison of News Nine and this is my photographer Jamie."

The door slammed closed.

Oh-kay then. Not exactly the greeting I'd been hoping for. I banged on the door, not willing to give up.

"Mr. Reardon? I'm sorry to intrude and all, but really we just had a few questions."

Silence.

"A, uh, few questions about Reardon Oil and Rocky Rodriguez, that is." As soon as the words came out of my mouth, I regretted them. What the heck was I doing? What if he opened that door with a rifle and shot me to kingdom come?

The door opened and Reardon (sans gun, thank the Lord) peeked through again.

"What the hell do you want to know about Reardon Oil?" he asked.

"Please, sir." I took a deep breath. "I just want to ask you a few questions."

"You best ask Rocky. He owns Reardon Oil now. I don't have anything to do with that shit. I got kids, you know." He paused, peering at me with watery blue eyes. Then he raked a hand through his already ruffled hair and sighed. "You know about it, don't you? That's why you've come asking."

I nodded, wondering if that was the right move. I could barely breathe.

"Right. I knew one day someone would find out. That's why I wasn't about to get involved with it all. I always said someday the shit would hit the fan and when it did, my nose would be clean."

"Can you tell us the story?" I asked.

He thought for a moment, then shrugged. "Sure 'nough I guess. Long as you make sure it's clear I had nothing to do with anything illegal. I don't want the cops knocking on my door. But if this is all going to be made public in any case, might as well have the truth on record."

My heart pounded with excitement as he ushered us inside. This was it! He was going to tell us everything. I stole a glance at Jamie, who still looked a little wary.

At least the interior had undergone a decent house-cleaning. It was small and the furniture worn, but it was clean and smelled like lemon-scented pledge. It could have been much worse. Like the time I did the story on Backyard Breeders and we went undercover to a woman's house who kept fifty dogs (literally!) in a trailer. Bleh!

"I know it ain't much, but it's all paid for with honest, hardworking money. Not drug money," said Reardon.

We sat down across from each other, him on a ratty armchair and me on the flowered couch and chatted about the weather while Jamie set up a few lights. A few minutes later Jamie touched me on the shoulder to let me know he was rolling tape.

"So, Mr. Reardon …" I began.

"Bob. Call me Bob."

"Okay, Bob." I smiled. I was calm. I was poised. I wasn't going to get up and run screaming from the room at the first sign of trouble. "I wanted to talk to you a little about Coastal Kings. I understand you and three others started the company back in college?"

"Yes. Me, Rocky, Felix, and Senator Gorman," he said. "Of course, Gorman wasn't a senator then, though I think the slime bag had political ambitions even then." He gave a toothy grin. "The man was always a smooth talker."

Interesting. Evidently Bob wasn't too keen on his former classmate. Then again, neither was I and I'd never even met the guy.

"So when you graduated from business school, what happened then?"

"Well, we all went our separate ways, I guess. Gorman got a staff assistant position with the EPA, Rocky took over his dad's car business, Felix went back to Mexico to squander his family's wealth, and I started my own company, Reardon Oil."

I felt the excitement tingling all the way to my toes. I could barely stand to sit there and act cool, calm, and collected.

"The same Reardon Oil located by Calla Verda? Now owned by Rocky?" I asked, wanting to be extremely clear. "Under the Coastal Kings umbrella?"

"There's only one Reardon Oil," Bob replied. "Though back then it had nothing to do with Coastal Kings. You see, my grandfather willed me the land and he died right before my graduation. He always told me he had high hopes that oil would be found there." He glanced over at a tarnished frame containing a black-and-white photo of an elderly gentleman. "But he never had the money to do the digging."

"But you did."

"Not really, but I took out a loan. A big business loan. And I purchased all the equipment to dig oil, to fulfill the dream of my grandfather. The dumbass." He shook his head. "There's not a drop of oil on that damn property. Never has been, never will be."

I made a note in my notebook. "So then what happened?"

"Well, it took me a few years, of course, to realize my life investment wasn't worth diddly-squat. 'Bout ten, I reckon. And by that time I had a million creditors after my ass." He picked at a worn spot on his easy chair. "Not a pleasant situation to be in, let me tell you."

"I can imagine," I said sympathetically.

"So then I hear on the TV that Felix's dad was busted for drug smuggling. We'd all heard rumors Felix was related to the Lopez cartel when we were in school, but of course no one ever had any proof. But still, the guy was my friend. So I contacted him to offer my condolences. And while talking to him, I happened to mention about my failed oil property. He seemed very interested, though at first I had no idea why.

"A few weeks later, Felix showed up on my front stoop, dressed to the nines and asked me if I wanted to go out to dinner, his treat. I was broke as a joke and he was my friend, so I said yes. That's when he introduced his plan."

I raised my eyebrows. "Which was?"

Reardon shook his head for a moment. "Can't believe I'm telling you this," he muttered. "But I've lived so long with the guilt, it feels kind of good to come clean. Besides, you know most of it anyway or you wouldn't have come calling in the first place."

He scratched at his bug-bitten forearm. "Felix had taken control of the cartel now that his dad was behind bars. But he didn't want to smuggle drugs the old-fashioned way. Too small-potatoes for him, sending one mule over at a time. He told me he wanted to build a gigantic underground tunnel to cross the border—one that could fit truckloads of drugs. Told me we could get rich and there was very little risk. All I had to do was keep Reardon Oil in business—in name only. He'd do the rest."

"And under the pretense of digging for oil, they could really dig an underground passage," I mused.

"Exactly. But let me tell you, I wanted no part of that," Reardon said, his eyes flashing. "I may have been broke and my life savings down the tubes, but I still had ethics. Morals. I wasn't going to aid and abet a guy who wanted to smuggle in foreign substances that were killing Americans. I'm a church-going guy."

"So you told Felix no."

"Right. And I guess after that he went to Rocky. 'Cause the next week Rocky showed up, just like Felix, dressed to the nines and wanting to take me out to dinner. I knew what he was going to ask me before he even opened his mouth."

"Which was?"

"He offered to buy off Reardon Oil for twice what it was worth. Told me he wanted to try his hand at digging for oil. Like I was stupid or something."

"So what did you do?"

"I sold." He shrugged. "What was I supposed to do? I'd married by then and my baby girl needed diapers. And baby food ain't cheap. So I pretended to believe Rocky when he said he wanted to dig for oil. And I turned over the property to him."

"And then they built the tunnel."

"Guess so. I stayed out of the whole thing so I couldn't tell you for sure. They got our buddy Gorman to do an EPA sign-off of the property. My oil business hadn't produced any oil in ten years and some nature lovers were trying to put me out of business. Once I sold, Gorman made sure that all got buried and Reardon Oil continued to exist for ten more years—far as I know they never sold a drop of oil."

"And now?"

"Now they're living large. And I'm stuck in a damn trailer.

My wife left me. Took the kids." He sighed. "Sometimes I tell you, Maddy, there are days I wished I hadn't had any morals and pride. But you know what? I'm honest." He cleared his throat. "And now that you're investigating all this, something tells me I'm going to be real happy I'm not involved."

"Yes, sir, you are." I motioned for Jamie to turn off the camera. "Listen, Bob," I said. "Are you sure you want to be telling me this stuff? I mean, not that I don't appreciate you doing it, but isn't it dangerous?"

Bob shrugged his thin shoulders. "Don't matter much if it is," he replied. "Truth is, I'm dying. Got the cancer. Doctors say I only have about a month to live. And I'm itching to get into Heaven, though I ain't done much to deserve it. Maybe this will end up helping me out some with Saint Peter at them pearly gates."

My heart went out to him. What a rough life he'd lived. "I'm sorry," I said.

"It's all right, I've come to terms with it all. And I'm glad the other two are finally going to get their just desserts. You let the DEA know that I'll be happy to talk to them once they open the investigation."

I thought of Mr. Mann and wondered, once again, what side he was on. "I will," I replied.

We thanked him again and walked back to the SUV in silence. I didn't know for sure about Jamie, but I for one was blown away by the revelation we'd heard inside. It was like every puzzle piece fit into place. Every "i" was dotted, every "t" crossed.

Now all I had left was to write my story and get it on the air.

SAMPLE EMMY-AWARD WINNING SPEECH

(Just in case!)

Oh, wow. I'm so surprised. I didn't even prepare a speech because I honestly didn't think I'd win. After all, there were so many great entries in my category. *(Name competition here—you will seem like a good sport.)*

First of all, I'd like to thank the Academy. And God. And Jamie Hayes, amazing photographer and love of my life. Check out the big rock he just put on my finger, ladies and gentlemen. (Hold out big engagement ring (hopefully!) and pause for applause.)

I'd also like to thank our main anchor Terrance Toller, star of "Terrance Tells All," who actually did absolutely *nothing* but read the piece and make sure his hair looked good for the stand-ups. *(Pause for laughter.)* But Terrance, we love you anyway—even if you are a pompous ass most of the time.

Oh and I would *not* like to thank my family. After all, my dad's infidelity and my sister Lulu's drug abuse nearly caused me to lose my sanity before the piece even had a chance to air! And mom—wherever in the world you're currently shopping—you'd better bring me back something cool. And not one of those T-shirts that says, "My mom went to such-and-such a place and all I got was this lousy T-shirt" either.

And lastly, I'd like to thank you. My adoring fans. Especially Diane in the front. Diane Dickson, that is. Who flew all the way out from New York to offer me a position at *Newsline*. And yes, I've accepted the position!

(PAUSE FOR TREMENDOUS STANDING OVATION!)

CHAPTER SEVENTEEN

I held my breath as Terrance scanned the script. Waited for him to whip out his red pen. To mutilate the words that I'd spent so long crafting. To tell me that I sucked as a writer and his pet Chihuahua could have written better.

So I waited. And waited.

He flipped to the last page without making a single mark, then replaced the other pages on top. He looked up, wearing a strange expression I couldn't read.

"You can tweak it," I said, lamely, when he didn't speak.

"Are you kidding? This doesn't need tweaking."

Oh, great. He hated it that much? "Or rewrite it from scratch," I amended. "If you want."

Please don't want to, I begged silently. *Please let me have this one story the way I want it.*

"Rewrite?" Terrance looked down at the paper and then up at me. "Are you kidding? I wouldn't change a word."

I almost fell over backward. "You ... you wouldn't?" Was this some kind of sick joke? I figured he'd at least ask if we could shoot him doing a ride-along with border patrol or something equally lame.

"No. This is the best piece of journalism I've seen in the last ten years. You've covered all the angles. It's fair. It gives all the facts. You're uncovering a major scandal that has been going on for years and no one—not even the DEA—has any clue about it."

"Well, um, thanks," I said modestly. Inside, my reaction was a bit livelier.

Oh, yeah! Maddy Madison, getting a compliment from Mr. Toller .Who rules the universe, bay-bee?

It took every bit of willpower not to start doing the Snoopy dance right then and there.

"You know, Madeline," Terrance said, after not so surreptitiously checking his reflection in the mirror, "I was wrong about you. I assumed you were one of those cookie-cutter News Nine producers who had no brains and simply went along with whatever plastic surgery story of the week was assigned to her. But this …" He looked down at the script and back up at me. "This takes guts. It takes brains. It takes courage. I'll be proud to put my name on this story."

"Um, thank you," I repeated, still at a loss for words. I knew I was blushing. Probably deep purple at this point. But at the same time I was pleased as punch. He liked my story! The fussy old anchorman liked my story!

"So, what's your next move, Madeline?" Terrance asked. "After News Nine, I mean. If you're writing stuff like this, you're not going to be stuck in this hell-hole much longer."

Wow. The compliments kept coming. I wondered if he was serious. Or if I told him about my *Newsline* dream he'd start making fun of me? Oh, what the heck. Let him. Having goals and dreams was nothing to be ashamed of.

"My ultimate dream goal is to become a *Newsline* producer," I said, squaring my shoulders and daring him to put me down.

But he didn't. He simply nodded thoughtfully. "Yes," he said. "That would be a good move for you, I think."

"Really?" I asked before I could censor my enthusiasm.

"Produce a few more stories like this and you're a shoo-in," Terrance said. "And I'd be happy to give you my recommendation."

I stared at him, still unable to get over his enthusiastic

reaction to the script. I thought for sure, no matter how good it was, he'd tear it apart simply because it hadn't been written by him. I would have never guessed in a million years that he would be offering me a reference to my dream job.

"Thanks. I'll take you up on that," I said, finding my tongue.

"Now, about this story. Anything else you need me to do? A stand-up? Maybe some teases?" He paged through his Daytimer. "I'm available tomorrow afternoon after my Botox appointment."

Here it was. He wanted to be in the story. He wanted thirty-seven of the fifty shots to be pictures of him.

"Terrance, can I ask you something?" I queried. I might as well lay all my cards on the table, even if that meant the compliments would cease.

He looked up. "Sure. What is it?"

"Why do you think it's so important for you to be physically present in the story? I mean, what's wrong with it just being your voice? Do you really think it adds to the piece to see you in it?"

He stared at me for a moment, as if in disbelief that I had asked him such a question. I bit my lower lip, waiting for the yell-fest to begin. Why couldn't I have kept silent? Terrance opened his mouth, then closed it, then opened it again. He was beginning to resemble a goldfish.

"Have you looked around News Nine, Maddy?" he asked. "Counted how many people work here over the age of thirty-five?"

"Um, there's.. ." I tried to think. My mind went blank. Surely there were one or two middle-aged people. "Well, there's Don," I said, referencing the old engineer that'd been working at News Nine since the days of black-and-white film.

"I mean on air. Reporters. Anchors," Terrance clarified. "Don't think too hard. There's no one. I'm sixty-five years old and the next oldest reporter is thirty-three." He cleared his throat. "Every time contract time comes around the station bosses ask themselves, why do we want to keep an aging, overpaid anchor around, when we could buy a hip, leather jacket–wearing, twenty-something replacement who will work for a quarter of his salary?"

I nodded slowly. I'd never thought about that. But it made perfect sense. There were hundreds of reporters banging down the door to work in "America's Finest City."

"The only thing I have going for me is name recognition. The viewers know who I am. They watch News Nine to see me and management knows it. If I ever lost that, I'd be kicked out the door with not so much as a 'thanks for the memories.'"

"Right," I mused. I hadn't thought of it that way before, but what he was saying made perfect sense. In this business, approval ratings were everything. The viewers knew and trusted Terrance Toller to bring them the day's news. And he'd built up that trust over years of hard work. Who could blame him for wanting to hang on to what he'd earned for as long as possible and not give it up to some random twenty-something who looked good in Jimmy Choos?

Terrance paused, fiddling with his pen. "So, yes, it may seem silly for me to put so much effort into getting my mug on TV, but the bottom line is, the viewers like it. And they're what's kept me on the air all these years." He looked up at me, his eyes fierce and proud. "So I think I'll carry on, if it's all the same to you."

I nodded at him with a newfound respect, and then, on impulse, stuck out my hand. "Sounds good to me," I said as we shook. "It's been a pleasure to work with you, Mr. Toller." And strangely enough, I meant it.

"Likewise, Ms. Madison," he replied. "Now let's go bust some drug dealers!"

*

Mike popped the tape out of his edit deck and handed it to me with a smile on his face. "Your story, madam," he quipped.

I grinned, taking the tape and bringing it to my lips to kiss it. "It came out great, didn't it?" I said.

The editor nodded. "It's way too good to be a News Nine piece."

I laughed. "Well, your editing helped a lot." Mike had done an amazing job merging the undercover video with the interviews we'd done. It wasn't overly edited, or too flashy like many News 9 pieces. It looked more like … well, to be completely honest, it looked like a *Newsline* piece. And I couldn't be happier with it.

"I aim to please," Mike said, blushing a bit. "When does it air?"

"Well, I've got to go show it to Richard first," I explained. "I've sort of been saving it as a surprise."

Mike nodded. "He's going to be thrilled."

"I hope so."

I exited the editing booth and walked through the newsroom to Richard's office, still clutching my precious tape. I couldn't wait another second to show him. To hear his praise. His admiration for a job well done.

If only all my producers were as talented as you, he'd say.

"Hi, Richard," I greeted, entering his office.

He looked up from his computer with a smile. "How are you, Maddy? Enjoying your new position?"

"Yes, sir." I nodded, holding up the tape. "I thought you might like to see my latest story."

"Sure." Richard gestured to the tape deck. "Pop it in. Let's see."

I inserted the tape, pressed "play," and sat down in a chair, holding my breath. The piece played out and I couldn't help being impressed all over again by how it looked. Each frame was perfect; I wouldn't have changed a thing. Finally, Terrance tagged out and the video faded to black.

I hopped up to push the "stop" button. Then I sat back down in my chair and waited breathlessly for the accolades. The applause. The pat on the back. The *good job, Maddy, you're the most brilliant young producer to come through the ranks of News 9 in years.*

You've probably figured out by now that I got none of the

above.

"What the hell was that?" Richard asked instead, twirling back in his chair to face me, his expression stony.

"Huh?" It was the only reply I could come up with on short notice, since all my planned comments had been of the "Awh shucks, thanks boss, all in a day's work" variety.

"I thought you were working on 'Murderous Mail.'"

"I am. For, um, next week." Why did he look so pissed?

"I don't remember assigning you this story."

"Well, that's because, you, um, didn't. I got a hot tip and took the initiative to run with it."

"I see." Richard motioned for me to sit. "Maddy, can I ask you something?"

"Sure." Though I knew for a fact I wouldn't like the question.

"Who signs your checks?"

Oh. That was easy. "Brenda in accounting," I said promptly. Why the heck was he asking me that?

"I mean," Richard clarified in a tight voice. "Who makes sure that when you cash your check, there's money in the account to cover it?"

"Oh! You mean Mr. Bur—err, Mr. Michaelson, that is." Oops, I'd almost slipped and called News 9's owner by his behind the scenes nickname: Mr. Burns. Dubbed after the old miser in *The Simpsons*. Trust me, he looked and acted the part. And our salaries were as pitiful at Homer's.

"And where do you think Mr. Michaelson gets the money to pay you?"

"Could you stop the twenty questions routine and let me know what's wrong?" What did any of this have to do with my story?

"Advertisers!" Richard proclaimed, as if he'd stumped me.

I stared at him, realizing where this was heading. "Rocky Rodriguez," I mumbled. Damn it all to hell. I couldn't believe he was going there. Not with such an important, big story.

"What was that?" Richard asked.

"Rocky Rodriguez," I said louder, staring him in the eye

with my most defiant expression. "You don't want to run the story because one of the bad guys selling drugs is Rocky Rodriguez. Owner of Pacific Coast Cars. A News Nine advertiser."

"Bingo! Give the girl a gold star."

"Yeah, but …" I didn't know how to argue this. I understood his point: News 9, as a rule, did not make negative statements about its advertisers on the evening news. But this was different, wasn't it? This wasn't saying a bakery lied about the fat content in their blueberry muffins. Or that a popular chain restaurant's pint glass only poured out to fourteen ounces of brew. This was a San Diego business leader smuggling drugs and human cargo into the United States of America. Certainly that called for a different set of standards.

"No buts. Pacific Coast Cars is our number one advertiser. We would have no newscast without them. And if we have no newscast, you and I have no jobs. Got it?" Richard pounded on the desk for emphasis. "Not to mention the absurd amount of cash Senator Gorman has spent on commercials for his reelection campaign. Not only would we lose those, but we'd likely be sued by his office for slander."

I stared at him in disbelief, my heart sinking to my knees. He wouldn't run the story. My potential Emmy-winning, *Newsline* demo tape story. The story I'd risked my life to get. The best story I'd ever produced. And because of corporate fucking greed it would never see the light of day.

"Look, Maddy." Richard's tone softened. "You're a great producer. The piece is excellent, I'm not denying that. But we don't live in an idealistic world, here. That ivory tower of journalism? You should know that's just a myth."

I did know that. But it still hurt to hear him admit it out loud. I thought back to the day I graduated from college, journalism degree in hand. I had such high expectations. I was going to right society's wrongs. Expose the bad guys. Make the world safe for democracy. But it would never happen, I now realized.

"This is such an important topic," I argued without much

life left. "It'd save millions of lives." Like he really cared. He only cared about his own life. His own job. "Maybe I'll turn it over to the Feds if you won't run it." Though deep inside, I knew that wasn't enough. After all, without widespread exposure to bring on public outcry, Gorman's golf buddies could just bury it all under years of bureaucracy.

"Did you know Laura was leaving?" Richard asked suddenly.

I squinted at him, trying to follow the subject change. Our executive producer was quitting? "No! I had no idea. Why?"

"She's off to join some PR firm. Decided to go for the big bucks instead of slaving away in a newsroom her whole life. Can't say I blame her, really."

Wow. I always knew Laura didn't really have her heart in the whole TV-news thing, but I never thought she'd actually quit. Evidently she'd found a new career that would still get her invited to all the industry parties and at the same time pay the bills.

"Did you find her replacement yet?" Maybe it'd be someone cool. Someone with good taste in story ideas. Someone who would once in a great while allow something remotely journalistic to slip through.

"Actually, we did." Richard looked pointedly at me.

"Who—?" I caught the look. "Not … You don't mean … Me?"

"Why so surprised? You're a talented producer with a great sense of story. I think you'd be great for the job."

I stared at him, confused as all hell. First, he rebukes me for producing a story that implicates News 9's biggest advertiser as a drug-dealing criminal. Then he wants to promote me? It didn't make sense.

Unless … Unless he was trying to buy me off. Was he that scared I'd go run the story somehow? Or go around telling all my coworkers that he'd axed it because he was afraid of losing a sponsor? I felt a little sick to my stomach.

"I'm honored that you thought of me, sir. But—"

"Great. Then it's settled. You start tomorrow. Laura will

show you the ropes before she leaves."

This was happening too fast. I couldn't process it all. Was it a genuine opportunity or a bribe to keep my mouth shut?

"Oh, and here's what we'll be raising your salary to." Richard scribbled a number down on a sticky note and slid it across his desk.

I stared down at it, thinking at first my dyslexia must be playing up and I was seeing the numbers in the wrong order. But no, after a few blinks to focus, they remained, clear as day. They wanted to pay me *that*? I mean it wasn't a PR salary by any means, but it was nearly double what I'd been making as a regular producer. I'd never have to worry about making the rent. And I could buy good bottles of wine instead of that dreadful blush in a box I'd been stocking in my fridge.

Not to mention it was a huge career move. I'd get a lot of added responsibility and I'd have a staff. And even better, I'd get to assign stories to the producers that had journalistic integrity. I could even do away with the *Household Products That Kill* series. Sure, I'd lose this investigation, but I could assign ten others, equally as important that didn't happen to involve advertisers. For the first time, I, Maddy Madison, could make a difference.

Maybe I should take it.

Of course, that would mean giving up my *Newsline* dream. Going into management was another career track altogether. But, hey—maybe it wasn't such a bad thing. After all, who wanted to move to NYC or LA to slave away at some entry-level position at the national news magazine show? I had family here. Friends. My wonderful boyfriend Jamie. This was my life.

I'd probably hate it at *Newsline* anyway, I justified. I'd have to leave everyone behind and rent some stuffy, rodent-infested studio in Queens. Or New Jersey, and everyone would always ask what exit I lived off of.

"I'll take it," I declared. "Thanks. It's really an honor."

"You deserve it." Richard held out his hand, a big smile on his face. I shook it, pushing the nagging guilt of selling out deep inside. "Welcome aboard."

Back in Cubicle Land, I found Jamie sitting at my desk. I leaned down and gave him a warm hug. "You'll never guess! I'm going to be executive producer."

"Really? Great," he replied in an automatic voice. Almost as if he hadn't heard me.

I narrowed my eyes, studying him closely. He looked bad. Pale-faced, hands trembling bad. Something was definitely up. "You okay, Jamie?"

"We need to talk."

Oh, God, I hated those words. What now? This was turning into a roller coaster of a day.

"Oh … okay." I could feel my pulse kick up a few notches as my good mood vanished into the shadows.

"Not here, though. What time are you leaving?"

I glanced at my watch. "Um, in like a half hour."

"Fine. I'll meet you at your apartment." He rose and turned to leave.

I grabbed his arm. "You're scaring me. What's going on?"

He attempted a smile and failed miserably. Whatever it was, it had to be bad. Really, really bad. "I'll be by around six thirty."

"S-sure." I reluctantly let go of his arm. What was going on? My stomach knotted in apprehension. After he walked away I realized I hadn't even gotten a chance to tell him they'd axed our drug tunnel piece.

"So, how'd Richard like the story?" Jodi asked, bounding into my cubicle a moment later. "Did he fall over backward at how awesome it was? I bet he did, right?"

"Um, not exactly." I briefed her on how it went down. "And then he offered me a promotion, if you can believe it. Evidently Laura's leaving to go sell out as a publicist and they need a new executive producer."

Jodi shook her head in amazement. "I hope you told him where he could shove that promotion," she said with an angry voice. "I mean, really. What a slimeball."

"Well …"

"But … you didn't." Jodi stared at me with a horrified expression on her face. "You didn't actually agree to …?"

I hung my head, unable to look her in the eye.

"Oh, Maddy! How could you? It's so obviously a bribe."

"Yeah, but—"

"First he tells you to suppress the truth about News Nine's biggest advertiser and then offers you a huge promotion completely out of the blue?"

I picked at a hangnail. "Maybe it's a coincidence."

"Don't be an idiot."

"Well, it could be," I said, feeling more than a bit defensive. Mainly because I knew she was completely right.

"So, what, you're going to just throw away the best story you've ever produced and become one of them? Become management? Become the person who axes all the stories with journalistic integrity?" Jodi frowned. "I expected more from you. I thought you were better than that."

I looked up, furious at her condemnation. "You don't understand," I retorted. "It's a great job. And it's a ton of money."

"What about *Newsline*? You're not going to be producing stories as an executive producer. How are you going to finish your *Newsline* résumé videotape?"

"Look, Jodi, let's be realistic. We both know *Newsline* was a total pipe dream. It doesn't matter how much crap I produced for News Nine. I'd never get there. My lot in life is here. In San Diego. I'm a local news kind of girl. And it's high time I started living in the present and stopped striving for some glamorous dream job I'll never get." I held up the slip of paper where Richard had scribbled my new pay. "Look. It's a good salary. I can start saving for a house. Get married. Become a mom. Live the good life."

Jodi rose from her seat. "You disappoint me, Maddy. I never thought you'd be the one who settled."

Anger rocked through me. "I'm not settling."

"You are and you know it. But whatever. You've obviously made up your mind. Congratulations on your new job. I hope it makes you very, very happy." And without another word, Jodi stormed off.

I glared at her retreating figure. How dare she be so harsh? She should be happy for me. She was probably jealous. Maybe she wished Richard promoted her instead of me. Maybe she didn't like the idea that I'd be her boss from now on.

Or maybe she's telling you something you need to hear, a nagging voice at the back of my head pestered.

Was I selling out? Sacrificing my journalistic integrity for a cushy position I didn't even really want? But at the same time, what choice did I have? Me refusing the new job wasn't going to suddenly convince Richard to air the drug tunnel story. And I couldn't exactly sneak it on. Sure, I could mislabel the videotape with another story's name to trick them into airing it. But it'd probably play for exactly three seconds before Richard realized what it was and called the control room to pull the plug. So, really, taking the executive producer job didn't make a lick of difference in the short term and in the long term I could possibly make a difference around here. It was win-win.

So, why did I still feel so conflicted?

CHAPTER EIGHTEEN

FROM: "Laura Smith" <lsmith@news9.com>

TO: "Madeline Madison" <mmadison@news9.com>

SUBJECT: Now that you're me …

Hi Maddy,

Congratulations on getting promoted to executive producer. I'm sure you'll do great. And now that you're me, I wanted to let you in all on this job's perks! As executive producer, you have power over a company's public relations and marketing staff. And if you use this power for good, you can walk away with a ton of free stuff.

For example, if you want to go to an amusement park, concert, or sporting event, all you have to do is call the public relations rep and ask them for tickets. They'll give them to you—free! Sure, you may have to promise to do a segment on them at some point—something that gives them some free advertising. I once got a whole ski weekend comp'ed just by promising to feature them in an upcoming News 9 report. (Oh, crap, that reminds me—can you assign someone to do a Southern California's Best Ski Resort story? Make sure White Mountain wins first place.)

You can also get a ton of great stuff in the mail. If you like a new product, simply do a story on it and they'll send you one free. (Even expensive stuff!) Sometimes they'll only send it as a loan, but I've found that if you keep it, they eventually give up calling to get it back. Also, you're already signed up to get every new DVD, music CD, and book that comes out. Once in a while, you might want to share the wealth (especially if the CD is rap or something you don't want). Leave your leftovers on the freebie table and your staff will think it's Christmas! Or there's always eBay if you're short a few bucks. Some of those press—only promo items really rack up the bids.

Okay, that's all for now. I'll write again later to fill you in on how to meet movie stars, get your speeding tickets fixed, and solve personal problems with places like banks, etc., all by saying you work at News 9. Also, please consider doing a story about my new client's line of home facial products. I promise we'll hook you up with tons of free samples so you'll be able to hide all those stress wrinkles you'll get from taking the new job. LOL.

Laura

I arrived at my apartment and kicked off my sandals. No sooner had I poured myself a glass of Callaway Chardonnay then the doorbell rang.

Jamie.

I invited him in and handed him a glass of the wine. He looked as if he could use it. Actually, he looked as if he could use a straight up shot of Jack. He walked over and sat down on the couch. He looked so serious. Dazed. Kind of devastated, even, with his distracted eyes not meeting mine, and his rumpled shirt only half tucked into his trousers. What the heck was wrong with him?

I sat down beside him, placing a hand on his knee. He flinched a little at the touch, but didn't move his leg. "What's wrong, Jamie?" I asked, seriously concerned at this point. "You can talk to me."

He took a long sip of wine before beginning. Practically drained the glass. This was not looking good.

"Before I begin, I want you to know that I care about you deeply," he said, setting down his glass and placing a hand over mine. "And these last few weeks have been some of the best in my life."

I gave him a small smile—the best I could manage in my freaked-out state. I took a deep breath and tried to ready myself for whatever his next words would bring.

He scrubbed his face with his free hand. "God, this is so hard," he mumbled. "I don't know how to tell you this."

"Maybe the Band-Aid method would be best," I said. "Like pulling it off all at once instead of prolonging the torture."

"Okay, then." He swallowed hard. "Here goes. Jen's pregnant."

Oh. My. God.

After getting over the initial slam of horror, my stomach caught up and I wanted to be physically ill. This could not be happening. It could not be happening.

Every possible scenario I had played in my head as to what his bad news could have been was not nearly as horrible as what reality had chosen to throw in my direction. I felt like I was on some bad episode of Jerry Springer.

My brain threw questions, fast and furious, but my mouth didn't know where to begin.

"Wh-when did you find out?" I finally managed. As if that question even mattered. Who cared *when* he'd found out? The point was, he had.

"She wrote me an e-mail a couple days ago, asking me to come to LA. Said she had some news." Jamie stared at the floor, kicking at the rug with the toe of his sneaker. "I made the trip yesterday. She told me when I got there."

"Is she … sure?"

He nodded. "After she did the home test, she went to the doctors to confirm it."

"And it's definitely … yours?"

He swallowed hard. "The day I broke up with her. I was really nervous and stressed about the whole thing. So I suggested we have a few drinks. Figured it would calm my nerves. Then we ended up having a few more. I soon realized I was too drunk to have such an important conversation, and decided to wait until morning. Problem was, she wanted to have sex. And I didn't know how to say no without getting into the discussion."

"Oh that's nice. Really, really nice," I retorted. Visions of Jamie—my Jamie—naked and writhing in Jennifer's arms invaded my mind. I wanted to puke.

He squeezed his hand into a fist. "Trust me, Maddy, it wasn't like I enjoyed it. All I could think of the whole time was you and how you'd be hurt if you knew what I was doing."

"How noble of you to think of me while fucking another woman."

"Look, I'm not proud of what I did. But it wasn't like you and I were a couple then, you know?"

I knew he had a point, but that didn't make any of this any easier. He'd had sex with her. And now she was pregnant with his child. The whole relationship house of cards I'd built was toppling before my eyes and I didn't know what to say or do. Tears welled up in my eyes and I choked back my sobs. I felt so dirty for some reason. So violated.

"Didn't you guys use … protection? Were you that stupid?" My voice cracked as I hurled my accusations. I had to lash out. I couldn't keep the anger inside.

"She's been on the pill forever," he said wearily. "Maybe she forgot to take it that day? I don't know. She doesn't either."

Nor did it matter, I realized. The fact remained: Jamie was going to be a dad. And not to my imaginary future babies. There was a real baby now—one he'd created with another woman. A baby that in nine months was going to arrive screaming out of a birth canal, demanding a father. Everything in Jamie's life from that moment on was going to change.

"Maddy, I'm sorry. I know this is a lot to take in. I had no idea, believe me." His voice sounded sad, pleading. I wanted to beat him senseless. And I wanted him to pull me into his arms and tell me everything would be okay.

But that would be a lie.

"Is she going to keep it?" I asked.

"Yes," he said in a low voice. "She's really excited about the baby, actually."

Of course she was.

"Maddy, I know this is weird and awkward, but at the same time, you need to know, this doesn't change things between you and I."

I stared at him. Was he serious? "But it does, Jamie. It changes everything."

"It doesn't have to."

"Look, are you going to want to be involved in the kid's life?"

"Well, yeah. I mean—"

"Go to ultrasounds, birthday parties, graduations? Have visitation on weekends? Are you going to move back to LA to be closer to it?" I couldn't manage to think of this monster in Jen's belly as a him or her just yet.

He sighed. "I don't know yet. I just found out. I haven't made any decisions."

But he would have to, I realized. And he'd be making them soon. His priorities. His life. Everything would change. And I wasn't ready. This relationship was too new. I couldn't move to LA for him—I'd just gotten promoted at News 9. And I wasn't going to suffer through a long-distance relationship only to find out he'd decided in the end it would be best for the child if he went back with its mother.

There was no other decision to make. This relationship had to be nipped in the bud. I didn't want it to be. I loved Jamie so much. Even as I sat here, furious with him, I wanted to cradle him in my arms and tell him everything was okay. Yet reality had reared its ugly head and I couldn't turn my back on it. I wasn't going to be one of those girls who got walked all over by their boyfriends. Jamie had made his bed. I was no longer interested in lying in it.

"It's over, Jamie," I said, my heart breaking as I spoke. My spacious living room suddenly felt too small. Cramped. Stifling. "It has to be."

He looked at me with his beautiful eyes, pleading for me to change my mind. "No, Maddy," he cried. "Don't do this. Please. I love you."

I love you. The words that once would have sent me spiraling into a delighted haze now only served to make me sick.

"Guess you should have thought of that before you had sex with the ex," I retorted.

Jamie scowled. "That's not fair and you know it. You're being a baby."

"And you're having one." I shot back. "Look, Jamie, let's just cut our losses and move on. This relationship has been a train wreck since it started. It was always doomed to fail." I couldn't believe how in control my voice sounded, when my insides were breaking apart, piece by piece.

"But—"

"Don't you see?" I interrupted. "You were meant to be with Jen. I stole you away. Now the universe is telling you to go back. It's not too late—you can have a nice little family together. You can have your wedding, be happy. You wanted children. Now you've got your wish."

"I wanted your children. Not hers."

"Again, something you should have thought of before you orgasmed," I said bitterly. "Now could I please ask you to leave? I need to do some thinking." *And crying,* I added silently. *A lot of crying.*

"No. I won't leave until you've let me have my say," he said, grabbing my arm as I tried to rise from my seat. I shook his hand away.

"Jamie, please. Just go," I begged with my last shred of

dignity. I didn't know how long I'd be able to hold out before I melted into a sloppy, tear-stained puddle on the floor.

"No."

Suddenly, the phone rang. Grateful for the distraction I grabbed the receiver.

"Hello?"

"Maddy?" It was my dad, though I barely recognized his voice, he sounded upset.

"What's wrong?" I asked. Oh man, what now? I was already at my breaking point. I could so not deal with more bad news.

"It's Lulu. She escaped from the rehab."

I white-knuckled the receiver, my heart slamming against my rib cage. All thoughts of my love life evaporated instantly as worry for my sister flooded my brain, my heart. "Do they know where she is?"

"Yes."

"Thank God." I exhaled in relief. I had had visions of search parties, combing the streets of San Diego, calling her name. "Where?"

I could hear my father's hard swallow on the other end of the phone line. "She's in the emergency room."

"What?" I sank back down to the couch, my legs no longer able to withstand my weight. I felt Jamie staring at me, his eyes concerned and questioning, but I couldn't look in his direction.

"The nurse who called said someone dropped her on the hospital's front sidewalk and took off. They think she overdosed." My father's voice broke on the other end.

"Over—?" I couldn't even say the word. "Is she … going to be okay?" Did I really want to hear his answer?

Silence, and then, "They're not sure yet."

Lulu. Oh, my baby sister! What have you done to yourself?

"Okay," I said, using my last reserves of talking strength. "Are you at the hospital? I'll be right down."

"What's wrong?" Jamie asked as I hung up the phone. "What happened? Are you okay?"

"No." It was all I could manage without breaking. I had

one shred of control left, and I wasn't about to lose it in front of him. I knew he'd be concerned and comforting and I'd find strength in his arms, but they were no longer my arms to find strength in. The sooner I accepted that and moved on, the better.

I stood up, my legs wobbly. I needed to get to the hospital, though how I'd actually manage to drive in my current state of shock, I wasn't sure. "I-I have to go somewhere," I told him. "Please. I need you to leave."

"No."

I stared at him. "What do you mean, no?"

"What part of the word didn't you understand?" He rose from the couch. "Something's obviously happened. And I'm not going to just take off and leave you."

He held out his arms, tempting me to collapse in his embrace. And I wanted to. Oh, how I wanted to. But I couldn't. I had to stay strong.

"Jamie, none of this is your concern. It's a family thing I have to take care of. I'm asking you to leave. Now."

"And I'm saying no." He reached out and grabbed my hand, pulling me to him. I had no more will to resist. I buried my head in his chest and started sobbing.

"Tell me what happened," he murmured while stroking my hair.

"Lulu's in the emergency room," I sobbed. "She OD'ed and they think she could die."

"Oh, Maddy, I'm so sorry." Jamie pulled me tighter, nearly crushing me against him. He felt so good. So warm. Safe. I wanted this to be my reality. To have a rock like him to cling to. But I couldn't allow myself to get used to this. He belonged to Jen. To their unborn child. Things would never be the same between us and the sooner I accepted that, the better.

I abruptly forced myself away from his embrace. "I have to get to the hospital. My family's there."

"I'll take you."

I shook my head. "No."

"Maddy, look at you. You're in no shape to drive."

As much as I hated to admit it, I knew he was right. "Okay. Fine. You can drive me to the front door. But you're not coming in. I need to be with my family right now."

His shoulders sagged. "I understand."

But did he? Did he really get the fact that I needed him to stay away for good?

It didn't matter. All that could be discussed on a later date. Right now, I had to get to the hospital. To Lulu. A vision of her, strapped to life support, unable to breathe on her own, gripped me and wouldn't let go.

Oh, Lulu, why? Was it worth it?

We jumped in my car and sped to the hospital. Jamie pulled up to the emergency entrance, promising to return my car to the driveway and take his motorcycle home from there.

"I'll call you," he said, grabbing my hand before I could exit the vehicle.

"Please don't." It killed me to say, but I had to. I removed his hand from mine. "It's hard enough without you being so sweet."

"Maddy, please. I don't want to lose you." His eyes were pleading. And they broke my heart.

"Don't you get it, Jamie? You already have."

I got out of the car and slammed the door too hard, bursting into tears. I ran into the hospital without looking back. It was the hardest thing I ever had to do.

I scanned the waiting room, looking for my dad, and found him in the far corner. Next to him sat a mousy brunette in black-rimmed glasses who, for a moment, I couldn't place. Then her slightly bulging stomach clued me in.

This was Cindi with an "i"? For some reason all this time I'd assumed the woman who broke up my parents' marriage to be a gorgeous blond bimbo. But Cindi looked average. So girl-next-door. For a moment that made me feel better. But then I remembered the monster growing inside her belly. It made me think of Jen. And how Cindi had done the same thing to Dad as Jen just did to Jamie.

I wished my mother were here.

My dad rose from his seat, his face ashen and worn. We embraced and then he gestured to Cindi.

"This is Cindi, Maddy," he said, looking extremely nervous. "Cindi, this is my daughter, Maddy."

"Hi," she said shyly, holding out her hand. "I'm so glad to finally meet you, though I'm sorry it has to be under these circumstances."

"Nice to meet you, too," I said, shaking her hand briefly, distracted. There was no time to assess her, judge her, pick apart any faults. I turned back to my dad. "How is she?"

"They haven't told us much. They think she had a stroke." He brushed a tear from his cheek. I'd never seen my dad cry before. It made me very uncomfortable. "The doctors don't know yet whether it's caused permanent brain damage." His voice broke and Cindi took his hand, squeezing it in her own.

I sank into a plastic waiting room chair, the world spinning out of control. My sister. Having a stroke. Sixteen-year-olds weren't supposed to have strokes. Strokes were for old people. People who had already lived long, happy lives. Not people whose lives were just beginning.

What had happened to her? Where had things started going wrong? If I hadn't let the first time slide—the time she said it was Ritalin—would she have gotten help before she'd gotten so bad? Was this somehow all my fault?

"But she was in rehab," I said. "How did she get out?" My dad stared at the ground, not able to answer. "They think she bribed one of the orderlies," Cindi told me. She paused, then added, "With sex."

Oh, God. I didn't want to hear any more. It didn't even seem real to me. My sister sold herself to some random guy so he'd let her out and she could do more drugs? That didn't sound possible. Then again, maybe it was. A vision of her, in my bed with that disgusting Drummer guy popped into my brain. I had to face facts. My sister was a drug addict. And drug addicts did any damn thing they had to in order to support their habit.

*

The hours passed slowly. The worst thing about hospitals was the waiting. No matter which hospital you found yourself in, there's never much to distract you from your worry and grief.

Hospitals were much worse than airports, which at least had shopping and restaurants and booze. The hospital gift shop with its sappy get-well cards and brightly colored beanie babies couldn't entertain even the most desperate shopaholic for more than ten minutes. And the bland Salisbury steak and lime green Jell-O specials at the cafeteria made for a minus two star rating from food critic Maddy Madison.

So you sat there. Waiting. Feeling bored and then feeling guilty that you were feeling bored. You should be thinking about the patient inside and you were, but you also wanted to think about other things even though you feel that's completely disloyal to the person you were there for.

In other words, I desperately tried to keep all thoughts of Jamie out of my mind. But even had I been busy, I doubt the replays of our conversation would have ceased running through my brain. And since I was completely unoccupied, sitting in my chair, the visions became relentless. His sad eyes. His warm touch. His awful, heart-breaking news.

Oh, Maddy, what are you going to do?

My dad got some exercise at least, pacing back and forth across the waiting room floor until I wanted to reach out and trip him to physicalize my annoyance. I'd been in such a rush I hadn't even brought a book, and the romance I'd picked up at the hotel gift store only made me angry.

In romance novels, the heroes, no matter how bad they start out, always redeemed themselves in the end, becoming loving husbands and fathers—to the heroine's children, not the ex-fiancée's. Then again, perhaps Jen was the heroine of my story and I was the villainess. It made sense, actually, since I'd stolen Jamie away from her. She was pure as the driven snow. Madonna incarnate who just wanted to marry the man who'd asked her. I was the whore who'd seduced him. And that meant she was the one entitled to the fairytale ending.

I threw the book against the wall and it landed with a thud on the floor. An elderly woman huffed at my blatant cruelty to literature and retrieved the novel. I watched her page through it and wondered if she still believed in that naive kind of love.

With nothing else to read, I sat in my squeaky plastic chair, waiting to see if my sister had destroyed her brain. I sat and thought. About life. About the universe. About everything. But mostly about life and how fucked up mine had become.

It was funny how things could turn on a dime. Yesterday the world had been my oyster as the saying went (though I never was quite sure what that was supposed to mean). My sister had been recovering in rehab. I'd just finished editing an Emmy-worthy news piece. And I was living a happily-ever-after with the man of my dreams.

And then in a few hours it all went to hell.

I glanced over at my father and Cindi. He'd stopped his pacing and sat with his head on her shoulder. She held his hand on her rounded lap and was stroking his palm. They looked very much in love, which kind of weirded me out.

I wanted to think of Cindi as some horrible home-wrecker who'd swept in and destroyed my family, but these days I was starting to realize that sometimes life just wasn't that black and white. I only had to think about the Jamie situation to see that. Had Mom and Dad, like Jamie and Jen, grown apart over the years? Had they stayed together out of habit, each inadvertently making the other miserable and complacent? And when my dad did stumble on a second chance for happiness, did he have the right to go after it like he did? Or should he have honored the thirty-year-old commitment he'd made to my mom, no matter what the current state of their relationship? They'd tried counseling and even an open marriage and nothing had worked. Was it better in the long run to call it quits? Even if in the short run, several people—my sister, for example—got caught in the crossfire?

It was a tough call. I didn't have the answer. Heck, I couldn't even figure out my own sorry love-life. All I knew was that even though I was furious with him, I missed Jamie with a vengeance, and a big part of me wished I hadn't pushed him away. Still, it was better in the long run, right? This way I didn't have to deal with a baby and possible future rejection down the road.

I rose from my chair, too confused to sit still a moment longer.

"I'm going to get some air," I told them, motioning to the door. Cindi smiled and nodded.

I stepped out into the crisp night, wishing I had taken a coat. People who didn't live in Southern California never understood how cold nights could get here.

I stared at the sidewalk in front of the emergency room. This is where they had left Lulu. Her so-called friends had abandoned her on the pavement. Just in case they would be held responsible for her death.

Not that she was going to die, I reminded myself.

"Maddy!"

I looked up from the sidewalk and my eyes widened as I saw my long-lost mother stepping out of a cab. She waved and then turned to pay the driver.

She had returned.

In reality, she hadn't been gone all that long. Only about a month. But so much had happened within that month it felt like a lifetime.

"Hi, Mom," I said as she approached me. The words sounded lame, coming from my mouth, concealing the anger that bubbled beneath the surface of my calm exterior.

"Honey!" She threw her arms around me and smothered me in a huge maternal hug. Behind her, the cab sped away. I didn't know whether I should hug her back or pull away. I was happy to see her. But I was also quite pissed off.

"You've returned," I said, stating the obvious.

"Yes. Your father phoned me and told me about Lulu. I took the first plane home."

"How self-sacrificing of you."

She frowned at my sarcasm. "If you have something to say,

young lady, why don't you go ahead and say it?"

I shook my head. I didn't want to start in on her. Not under these circumstances. Not with Lulu a few rooms away.

"You blame me," she said simply. "You blame me for what happened to Lulu."

Okay, fine. She wanted to know what I thought? Fury rose inside me and I couldn't hold back. "Yes, I fucking blame you. You took off on your daughters when we needed you the most. Was around the world in eighty days fun? Was it worth maybe losing your youngest child to drugs?"

I knew I was shouting and I knew some of the EMTs by the parked ambulances had started paying attention—intrigued by the nighttime drama—but I didn't care. I was so mad I was shaking.

"No. It wasn't worth it. I hadn't thought out the consequences," my mother replied, not raising her voice. "I only thought about me and my grief."

Her grief. I snorted. "And what about the rest of us? We were grieving, too."

"It's not the same," she said, looking at me with a fierce expression I'd never seen her use. "You didn't lose your marriage. Your partner for thirty years. You didn't have a man leave you to start a completely new family. You have a career. A life. Friends. You still have your dad even. I spent my whole life taking care of a man who one day decided the sacrifice I'd made wasn't good enough. Do you have any idea how that feels?"

I shook my head no. Though actually, now that I thought about it, the whole thing had a weird parallel to my short relationship with Jamie. Maybe Jen and Cindi could set up play dates for their evil spawn.

"You're goddamn right. You don't know." Now my mother's voice had risen, to a screechy desperation. "So let me tell you. It feels like you're dying. Like your world has burst apart. So I'm sorry you think I was selfish by going a little crazy. But you're twenty-four years old, Maddy. It's time you stopped believing this fairy tale that your parents are perfect.

That we don't make mistakes or have feelings. That we just live to serve you children. This may seem astonishing to you, but before I was Mom I was a person named Diane."

I stared at her. I'd never thought about it that way before. To me, she had always been Mom. Cookie-baking, stay-at-home, drive-me-to-gymnastics-practice Mom. But her words made sense. Women in her generation gave up all sense of individuality when they got married and had their husband's children. In my short years on this planet I'd already accomplished more and experienced more than she had in her fifty-three. How must she have felt when all that came crashing down? Of course she'd gone a little nutso. She was trying to make up for thirty years all at once.

"Believe me, Maddy," Mom continued. "I had no idea Lulu was so close to self-destruction. If I had I never would have left. At the time I guess I figured she'd be fine with your father—better, probably, because she wouldn't have to deal with my mental collapse. I had no idea he'd shirk that responsibility and put it all on you. I guess I should have though."

"It's okay, Mom," I said, starting to understand what had happened. How she felt.

"It's not though," she insisted. "If Lulu suffers permanent brain damage ... if she …" My mother gulped. "If she dies …"

I opened my arms and allowed my mother to collapse into my embrace. Sobs shook her thin shoulders as she released all of her upset.

Once again I was stuck in the responsible-one-who-took-care-of-everyone-else role. But I was happy to offer comfort to my mother—especially after all she had gone through.

Still, I wondered, when would someone be there for me? To comfort and give me strength when my world fell apart? Until yesterday, I'd thought that person might be Jamie. But I'd pushed him away. I was destined to face life alone.

My mother pulled away from the embrace. "I'm sorry, sweetie," she said. "I didn't mean to burden you with all that."

"Mom, it's okay. Really."

"Let's go inside."

I paused. "Dad's in there, you know. With …"

"Oh." My mother was silent for a moment. "Wow. This is awkward." She gave a shaky laugh. "Now you see why I thought it'd be better to take a trip."

She looked so sad. I felt awful for her. She probably wanted nothing more than to seek comfort from the man she'd committed herself to for so long. But he was inside, being comforted by someone else.

"I could use a cup of coffee," I lied to relieve the situation. "Want to hit the caf?"

My mother gave me a half smile. "Thanks, Maddy. You're a good kid, you know that?"

"Yeah, yeah."

We walked into the cafeteria and ordered two coffees, then sat across from each other at the table. I filled her in on Lulu's activities, how we'd discovered her drug use, bailed her out of jail and sent her to rehab.

Mom shook her head. "I can't believe my daughter got involved in something like this. Little Lulu. Though she always was a bit of a hellion."

I giggled. "Yeah. Remember the time she set the living room on fire playing Barbie Apocalypse?"

"Or the time she ran away from home and they found her trying to set up a tent at the San Diego Zoo near the panda exhibit?"

We laughed together, reliving the past and reducing the pain. It was so nice to have my mother back. I hadn't realized how much I missed her until now, and I told her so.

"I missed you, too," she said fondly. "You and Lulu." She pulled her hand away and rubbed her forehead. "I just hope my little Lulu is okay," she said with a long sigh.

"I know, Mom."

She pounded her fist on the table. "It's terrible how things have gotten," she continued. "The government's so strict with the drinking laws in this country. Heaven forbid a twenty-year-old sips a beer. But a preteen can purchase illegal substances on any street corner. War on drugs indeed." She huffed in indignation. "If it's a war, we've already lost, big time."

I nodded wordlessly, thinking back to my own axed drug tunnel story. How Rocky Rodriguez wasn't satisfied by the fortune to be made in the car-selling business and had funneled money into a much more successful illegal venture. How Senator Gorman had enabled his buddy to easily import drugs in exchange for a hefty campaign contribution. And how News 9, the supposed journalistic watchdog of such actions, had turned a blind eye—all to ensure they didn't lose an important advertiser.

It was a sick world we lived in. Everything was based on money. Greed. No one cared about people like my sister. All they cared about was making a buck. Getting ahead.

Including me!

Realization hit me like a ten-ton truck. I was just as bad as the rest of them. I'd willingly tossed my exposé in exchange for a cushy job and a big pay raise. I was as guilty as Senator Gorman. As Rocky Rodriguez. As Felix Lopez himself! I knew how, when and where drugs were being imported into the United States. Drugs dealt out to young kids like my sister. In fact, it was very possible the same drugs that landed Lulu in the hospital had come from that very tunnel.

I had to get the story on the air.

Somehow, some way, that story needed to be told. For my sister's sake. And for the sake of all the San Diegan children seduced by drugs. Getting the information out was more important than any job. Any raise. Let them fire me. I'd know I did the right thing. I'd saved lives.

A plan formulated in my head. I knew what had to be done. And I knew just how to do it.

CHAPTER NINETEEN

"How are you feeling?"

"Like hell." Lulu said, as she lifted her right hand and placed it over mine. She looked pale and weak lying in her hospital bed. But she was alive. That was the important thing.

Early that morning, a nurse had found my family, uncomfortably napping in waiting room chairs. She informed us that Lulu had been released from the ICU. She was awake and talking. And, thank the Lord, she didn't seem to have suffered too many permanent injuries. Her left side had slight nerve damage but doctors were confident that with intensive rehab she'd regain full bodily function within a few months.

I leapt out of my chair and hugged the doctor. Lulu was going to be okay! I wanted to laugh and cry and scream all at the same time. At that moment, nothing in life mattered except this. My precious baby sister would live. Not only live—but be fine. Fine! She would be able to go to the prom, apply for college, graduate high school, meet a guy. Live happily ever after. Tears of relief streamed down my flushed cheeks as I released the doctor and shared hugs of joy with my mother, my father, and even Cindi with an "i".

"She's a very lucky little girl," the gray-haired physician told us sternly after the hug fest had completed. "But if she doesn't stay off the drugs, I can't say she'll do so well next time."

The statement sobered our elation. Lulu was out of the frying pan, but still in the proverbial fire. Could she resist the drugs? I honestly didn't know. But if there was any way I could help her, I would.

My mother and father had gone in to see her first, while Cindi and I waited in the lobby. Though my parents still looked a bit uncomfortable talking to each other, they'd bonded through this common adversity. Who knew, maybe someday they'd even form a weird sort of ex-spouse friendship. But even if they didn't, both of them had learned an important lesson about responsibility. Neither would drop the parental ball when it came to Lulu again, that was for sure.

Visiting hours in her ward were short, so after about ten minutes my parents came out and said Lulu wanted to see me before her time was up.

Walking in and seeing her swaddled in hospital bedding, her skin porcelain white and her eyes hollow and vacant made me want to burst into tears. But I knew I had to be strong. For her sake and my own.

"I was so worried about you," I said, stroking her forehead. "If I had lost you …" I found I couldn't form the words I wanted to say. But she knew, of course.

"I'm sorry," she whispered. "I'm such a loser, huh?" Her mouth quirked up in a weak, self-deprecating grin.

"You're not a loser," I replied, fiercely. "Drug addiction is a disease. Just like diabetes. You had a relapse. But you can beat this thing, I know you can." Actually, I didn't know any such thing, but I wasn't about to let her in on that.

"I'm glad *you* think so," she replied with a snort. "I, myself, am not so sure." She gestured to her body with her good arm. "Look at me, lying here, sick as a dog, and I'm totally jonesing for more drugs. Even though I'm positive if I were to do them, they'd kill me. Pathetic, huh?"

Waves of nausea swept through me as I tried to imagine what she was going through. It seemed completely unfathomable to me that someone could become so addicted to something they'd rather die than go without. But it happened every day. And I was no longer blind enough to think someone like my sister could be an exception to the statistics. Being a white, middle-class, all-American girl didn't give you any sort of immunity to this kind of thing. At this moment, Lulu was as bad off as any street crack whore.

But she had one advantage. Her family. Me. And I was bound and determined to help her through her recovery in any way I could. No more being pissed off about responsibility. No more thinking it was "not my job" to parent her. Whatever she needed, I would be there for her. That's what you did for people you loved.

"I don't even know how this all got so out of control," Lulu continued. "I mean, at first it was just a joint or two at parties. Then some Ritalin to keep me awake and focused at school after being out all night. Then Drummer introduced me to meth and it was so awesome at first. You feel like you're flying—like you're queen of the world and none of your problems matter anymore. Which was just what I needed at the time. You know, with all the family shit going on. But then the come-downs got so horrible, I needed more and more drugs just to feel normal. And then … well …" She shrugged. "You know the rest. I'm an addict, plain and simple."

"But you'll get better," I assured her, feeling like I was offering her empty promises. "One day at a time, right?" Isn't that what they said in rehab? It sounded stupid coming from my mouth.

Lulu nodded. "I'd been doing good, you know. At Shady Oaks? I'd even stopped feeling sick from detoxing. Then that stupid guard offered to let me out and …" She trailed off. "Some of the things I've done, Maddy. It's so embarrassing. When I saw Mom, I could barely look her in the eye."

"You don't have to apologize for the past," I said firmly. "Just get well. That's all we ask." I petted her head.

"I'm going to try," Lulu said, nodding and then wincing from the pain of doing so.

A manly-looking nurse with a mustache that desperately needed bleaching picked that moment to enter the hospital room. She checked Lulu's IV and fluffed her pillows before turning to me. "Visiting hours are over," she coldly informed me.

I nodded, grasping my sister's hand a last time and stroking it with my fingers. I leaned forward to kiss her cheek. "I won't give up on you," I whispered. "I love you, Lulu."

"I love you, too, Maddy," She whispered back, tears streaming down her face. "And I won't let you down."

*

I still couldn't believe I was actually doing this.

Clutching the videotape in one trembling hand, I strode down the hallway, heading for what in the TV news world, we called Receive. The place where my story could broadcast to the world. Well, at least the world of San Diego. Receive was the gateway to the air-waves and its guardians had no idea what they were about to let loose.

In just minutes, my five-year career at News 9 would be over forever. Heck, they'd probably blacklist me from ever setting foot in a TV station again. My dream of working at *Newsline* would never come true. But it didn't matter. I didn't want to work in a business that was as corrupt as I'd recently determined it to be.

The truth was more important. My sister and the others like her were more important.

My heart slammed against my rib cage as I pushed open the door to Receive. The coordinator gave me a stressed smile before going back to organizing the videotapes for the night's broadcast. I smiled back, knowing from her look that no one had time to check to see what was on the tape I delivered.

I took a deep breath. This was it.

"This is for you, Lulu," I whispered to myself, then handed the coordinator the tape.

"Here's tonight's feature story," I informed her. "Cosmetics

That Kill."

I held my breath as she took the tape and examined the label. *Please don't check, please don't check.*

"Great." She smiled, filing the tape in its appropriate slot for the five o'clock news. "Thanks, Maddy."

It was done.

*

After leaving Receive, I raced down the hall to Richard's office, as fast as my flip-flops could carry me. Forgetting to knock, I burst into the office. He was sitting watching the newscast and looked up when I entered.

"Madeline?" he asked, looking bit worried at my brash entrance. "Is something wrong?"

"Oh, no," I assured him, trying to catch my breath. "I just stopped by to chat."

"Can it wait? I'm watching the newscast right now."

Which is exactly what I need to stop you from doing, I thought as I deliberately walked in front of the TV. T minus two minutes. How was I going to pull this off?

He leaned to the side, trying to see the television. "Madeline, could you move over to the—"

"So, Richard. I was thinking. Since we barely know each other, and now as fellow managers we'll be working together on a daily basis, I thought it'd be best if we could chat for a bit."

Richard stared at me like I was a crazy person. "Now?" he asked.

"Sure, why not? So, first off, I need to inform you that my name's actually Maddy, not Madeline. No one's called me Madeline since birth. So if you don't mind, now that we're colleagues and all, can you please call me Maddy from here on out?"

I could hear the broadcast behind me. "And now tonight on 'Terrance Tells All' … Could those cosmetics you keep in your cabinet actually kill you? Terrance has our News Nine exclusive …"

This was it!

I grabbed the remote off Richard's desk and pressed mute.

"Hey," he protested. "I was watching—"

"Oh well, you've already seen this segment. Cosmetics That Kill?" I willed my voice to remain casual, even though my heart was beating like mad. "I showed you the story earlier, remember?"

"Yes," Richard admitted, looking seriously pissed. "But I like to see how it looks on air."

"So, anyway, as I was saying, let's get to know each other," I said, ignoring his request and not dropping the remote. "What are your likes and dislikes? Hobbies? What do you do on weekends? I myself am a big fan of eighties music and movies. Did you ever see *Pretty in Pink*?"

"Maddy, I don't know what's gotten into you," Richard said in a tight voice. "But if you don't give me back the remote control right this second and get out of my office, I'm calling security."

Oh-kay. Time to make my exit. The piece still had a couple minutes to play, but I had an idea.

"Sure, no problem. Sorry." I handed him the remote, while wrapping my toe around the phone cord on the floor. "I guess I'll come back when it's a better time."

"What the—?" Richard said with a gasp.

"Records show that the land is owned by this man, Rocky Rodriguez of Pacific Coast Cars," Terrance was saying over the airways.

Richard stared at me, his face quite literally turning purple. "What the hell have you done, Madeline?" he demanded. He grabbed the receiver to his phone and punched in three numbers. Probably dialing Receive to have them pull the tape. Couldn't have that.

"Okay, I'll just—" I yanked my foot, still wrapped around the phone cord, as hard as I could, forcing it out of its socket.

"Hello?" Richard cried, not realizing I'd disconnected him. He looked like Grimace from McDonald's at this point, and I hoped he didn't have any heart problems. "Hello!?"

I quickly exited the office and ran upstairs to Cubicle Land. Just had to grab my purse and I was out of there, mission accomplished. I knew that there was no way Richard could reach another phone before the end of the piece. The drug tunnel story had aired on News 9 and there was nothing anyone could do about it.

My illustrious career in TV news, on the other hand, had warbled its swan song. It was sad in some ways. But I knew I'd done the right thing. This wasn't about me. This was about Lulu and the thousands of others like her. I'd gone into TV news to make a difference. Now I felt I actually had.

It was only a week after Lulu's overdose, but it seemed like a lifetime ago. After three days of hospital recovery, she'd been admitted into another rehab—this one maximum security—for further treatment. Doctors said she was extremely lucky. We all were. They warned us about her tough road ahead. But I had faith in her recovery. This time, unlike when first admitted, she wanted to quit. I knew desire wasn't always enough, but it was a good start.

I had taken the week off from work to deal with Lulu's affairs and be with my family, so I hadn't seen Jamie since the night of the overdose. The night he'd told me Jen was pregnant. He'd phoned me though, every day, leaving messages, begging me to return his calls. But I couldn't bring myself to pick up the phone. Every time I thought of him, I could only envision Jen, growing huge with his child inside her belly. It was too much to deal with. As much as I loved him, I couldn't get past her pregnancy. I wanted desperately to move on with my life.

My cell phone rang. Jodi.

"I'm watching the news," she screamed through the receiver. "And I can't believe what I just saw. How did you get them to go along with it?"

"I didn't," I admitted, walking down the stairwell to the front desk. I needed to make a quick exit. "There was a tape label malfunction."

"But Maddy, Richard will fire you…."

"Oh, I'm sure the paperwork's already been started," I agreed, pushing open the door and heading outside. "If Richard isn't in the hospital facing cardiac arrest."

"They'll blacklist you from TV. No one will hire you."

"Then I'll find a job in another field." I reached my car and rummaged for my key while balancing the cell phone against my ear.

"But—"

"Listen, Jodi," I said soothingly. She was taking this harder than I was. "It's fine. I don't mind. It was something I had to do. And I feel I made the right choice. The story got told, that's the important thing. What matters is people are now aware of the drug tunnel's existence. It'll be shut down. The borders will become stronger and it'll be harder for drugs to be smuggled into the US. That's the bottom line. That's all that matters."

"Wow," Jodi said softly. "That's so brave and noble of you. And here I had accused you of selling out by accepting the executive producer position. I'm sorry, Maddy. I was wrong."

"You weren't." I shook my head. "At the time I would have ditched the story for the chance to get ahead. But then after what happened with my sister … Well, I started to see things in a new light."

"I think that's great, what you did. You are truly a credit to the profession of journalism."

"Yeah, yeah," I said, blushing. I got into my car and turned the key in the ignition.

"So what will you do now?" she asked, concerned.

"You know, Jodi?" I said with a small grin. "For the first time in my life, I have absolutely no idea." And also for the first time, I was okay with that.

CHAPTER TWENTY

FROM: "Richard Clarkson" <rclarkson@news9.com>
TO: "Madeline Madison" <mmadison@news9. com>
Re: (NO SUBJECT)
Madeline,

PLEASE COME TO MY OFFICE … IMMEDIATELY!

Richard
News Director, News 9

So I was fired. No big surprise there. The next morning, as I packed my things into one of those big cardboard boxes companies always had on hand for such occasions, I felt oddly sad. Even though News 9 had time and again thumbed their nose at journalism and didn't give a rat's ass about all my years of service, it still felt like my home in a way. My family. I'd miss all the people—the photographers, producers, reporters, and editors, who worked so hard and put out such an amazing product for so little reward. They were the ones who gave me hope for the future. Perhaps when the old regime retired, when the underlings were given the keys to the kingdom, they could step in and make a difference.

Or not. Most likely not. But it was nice to pretend. As I packed, I harbored this insane secret hope that Jamie would waltz back into Cubicle Land, pick me up into his strong arms and carry me away to some fantasy place. Instead, an intern informed me that he had called in sick. Probably went up to LA to visit Jen. Even though it hurt to think it, for the baby's sake, I hoped he'd get back with her. Kids needed their fathers. Look what happened to Lulu when ours went AWOL for even a month.

I closed the box—two years of memories packed into a cardboard square—and allowed the guard to escort me from the building. (I was evidently too dangerous to be left alone for even a moment, heh, heh, heh!)

I placed the box in the passenger seat and turned the key in the ignition. The radio blared to life.

"And in other news, immigration officials nabbed two men they say were involved in a major drug-smuggling ring, operating from a secret underground tunnel in San Diego. Rocky Rodriguez, owner of Pacific Coast Cars and Felix Lopez, the son of convicted Mexican drug lord Roberto Lopez, will be arraigned this morning in federal court. News nine anchor Terrance Toller broke the story two days ago in a startling exclusive 'Terrance Tells All' piece that's sure to win him an Emmy or two."

I clicked off the radio. The story was everywhere. And Terrance got all the credit. That was one bummer about being behind the scenes. The general public had no idea that all Terrance did was read a script. So he not only got to keep his job, he got all the credit. He'd even been interviewed on *Newsline* and shockingly never once said he owed it all to his ace producer Maddy Madison.

I shook my head. This wasn't about me getting praise or promotion. It was about all the drugs the DEA had seized. Felix Lopez and Rocky Rodriguez going to jail. (Oh, what was News 9 to do without their advertising revenue?) It was about Immigration imploding the tunnel with dynamite. There'd even been reports on how the news story had probably saved the

US from a major terrorism threat. Homeland Security had reportedly called super anchor Terrance and thanked him personally.

Bottom line? I'd made the difference I wanted to make. I'd saved lives. Like my sister's. And countless other Americans. That was all that mattered.

But still, at the same time, it sucked the big one. I should have been fielding calls from the networks. Instead, I'd been scouring the Internet for TV stations hiring field producers. Problem was, my job was so specialized and the field was completely overcrowded, it'd probably take months—even years—to find a job like I'd had. After all, who would want some dumb local news hack who made a career of ridiculous "Products That Kill" stories and ended her last job by getting fired?

Answer: No one.

I had to face facts. There were certain things in life

I'd never have:

1) A job at *Newsline*
2) Jamie Hayes as a husband
3) A genuine non-counterfeit Kate Spade purse (Like with alcoholic beverages, you couldn't buy one with food stamps, which is what I'd be relegated to if I didn't get a job soon.)

My cell phone rang. I hesitated to answer the "private" number. Now unemployed, I didn't want to rack up minutes on a wrong number. But after the third ring, curiosity got the better of me. I pulled over to the side of the road to answer, practicing my best cell phone safety. After all, no job meant no health insurance.

"Hello?"

"Yes, is Madeline Madison there, please?" a woman asked.

Oh great. It was a telemarketer call. That was worse than a wrong number and used up way more minutes. "Sorry, I don't think you want to talk to me," I told the woman. "I'm unemployed. I can't buy whatever it is you're selling."

The voice on the other end chuckled. "I'm not selling anything."

"Well then, I don't want to take your survey. And I already know who I'm voting for. And …" What else was it that telemarketers always wanted? "… and the Visa payment is in the mail." I crossed my fingers on the last one.

"I'm very happy to hear that," the voice said, sounding even more amused. "It sounds like you've got it all under control. But about that unemployment thing …"

"Ah-ha! And I don't need to make money from home!" She thought she could sneak that one by me. Yeah, right. I knew she wasn't a legitimate employer type because since I'd only been officially fired less than an hour, I hadn't applied anywhere yet.

"That's good, because this opportunity would require you to show up at work."

I was getting impatient. I had places to go, people to see. Okay, actually my afternoon was completely wide open and I planned to veg and watch soap operas. But still!

"Listen, it's been real, but if you don't tell me who you are and what you want, I've gotta go."

"All right then," the voice said. "I'm Sara, an executive producer from *Newsline.* We know you were behind the Mexican drug tunnel story and we're wondering if you'd consider coming to work for us."

*

"Omigod, omigod! Jodi, you have to meet me for drinks. Right now!" I screamed into my cell phone. "This very second!"

"Earth to Maddy, you may be unemployed and carefree, but I'm still at work, remember?" Jodi reminded me over the cellular airwaves. "I've got to finish writing 'Celebrity C-sections.'"

"Celebrity C-sections?" I stifled a giggle.

"Yeah, you know. 'Madonna had one. Posh Spice, too. Now you, too, can get your stomach sliced open instead of being forced to give birth the old-fashioned way.' I have to get it finished for my edit tomorrow. We could meet up after work...."

Agh. That was totally unacceptable. I couldn't possibly wait 'til the end of the day to start celebrating my good news.

"Can't you tell them you're feeling sick?" I begged. "I hear there's a nasty flu going around. Surely you can catch it within the next five minutes. For your best friend in the whole wide world?"

"Well ..." I could hear the weakness in her voice and pounced.

"I'll buy the margaritas."

"Fine. One hour. At the border. But I'm bringing my logs and you're helping me write the script at the bar."

Woo-hoo! I knew I could count on Jodi to embrace her inner slacker! "See you there." I hit "end" and pulled back onto the road. Before I headed down to Mexico, I had some shopping to do.

*

The sun beat down on us as we sat at a little outside table in our favorite Tijuana square. The rotund, mustached waiter had delivered our mango margaritas moments ago, and I held mine up in a toast.

"To new beginnings," I said.

Jodi clinked her glass against mine. "Aren't you sad at all about losing your job at News Nine?" she asked after taking a sip. "You seem rather jubilant, all things considered."

I shrugged. "A little, I guess. I mean, it was a fun place to work. I spent two years of my life there. And obviously the circumstances of my departure were a bit on the sketchy side...."

"Don't get me wrong," Jodi said. "I'm really proud of you. What you did was amazing. Brave. Diane Dickson would have been proud."

I grinned. "She *is* proud."

"Huh?"

I laughed at Jodi's confused look. I couldn't blame her. She probably thought I'd lost my mind. It was too much fun not to leave her hanging for a few more minutes.

"I got you something," I reached under the table and pulled my new purchase out of its bag.

Jodi's eyes widened. "Oh, my God," she cried, reaching over the table for the Prada purse I held up. "I've never seen this style as a counterfeit." She turned the purse around, studying the seams, then opened it up to examine the lining. I had to laugh. She was such a fake purse professional. She looked up at me. "I can't find one thing wrong with this," she exclaimed. "It's like you found the perfect knockoff. I thought they were an urban myth. Where did you get it?"

"Nordstrom's."

Her eyes widened. "They sell counterfeit purses in Nordstrom's now?"

"No." I shook my head. "They sell genuines."

"But then …" Jodi stared at the purse, up at me and then down at the purse again. "You don't mean this is …"

"Yup."

"Oh, my God!" she screeched. "This is real?" She wiped her hands on her pants. "I hope I didn't get margarita stickiness on it." She cradled the purse carefully, as if it were a heavenly object.

"Merry Christmas. Happy Birthday. Whatever's closer."

"But you can't afford—I mean, you're unemployed. I couldn't possibly accept …"

"Oh, didn't I tell you?" I asked casually. "I got a new job."

"You did? That's so great! Where is it? Is it in TV? When do you start?"

I held up my hands, laughing at her enthusiasm. "One question at a time. Yes, it's in TV. I start in two weeks. It's in Los Angeles." I paused for a moment to enjoy her shocked face. "You're looking at the newest assistant producer at *Newsline*'s LA bureau."

"No freaking way." Jodi stared at me in joyous disbelief.

She knew more than anyone how long I'd dreamed of this opportunity. "But … how?"

I shrugged. "They found out I was the brains behind the drug tunnel story. They knew all about me sneaking it on the air and everything. Said they admired my tenacity for the truth."

"Who told them?"

"That's actually the best part!" I exclaimed. "Terrance."

"Terrance?" Jodi stared at me in disbelief. "As in narcissistic ninny Terrance Toller?"

"Yup. Remember how he appeared on *Newsline* last week? Well, they offered him a job. And he said he would only take it if they hired me as his producer."

"I would have never in a million years have thought Terrance would stick up for you."

"You know, he's actually a good guy underneath that shallow exterior he portrays," I informed her. "With insecurities and fears just like the rest of us. Fighting to survive in the cruel world of TV news."

"So interesting," Jodi mused. "But enough about Terrance. How about you! A job at *Newsline*—your ultimate dream come true."

"I know, right? A new job, a really nice salary, moving expenses and everything. And I wanted to give you the purse because without you calling me on the carpet when I was going to sell out for that lousy News Nine executive producer job, I'd probably be stuck in 'Products That Kill' hell for the rest of my life."

"Well, I accept it then." Jodi said, pulling the purse to her lips and kissing it. "Thank you. And congrats. Of course, I'll miss you tons."

I rolled my eyes. "I'm going to LA. Not Mars. I'm two and a half hours away."

"Four with traffic."

"Still, we'll see each other all time. Every weekend."

"I know." Jodi rose from her chair and walked around the table to give me a huge hug. "Congratulations, sweetie. You deserve it."

"Thanks, doll," I said returning the hug.

After a moment of best friend camaraderie, Jodi pulled away.

"While we're here, do you want to go check out the fake purses?" She frowned at the amused look I shot her. "You know, just to compare them to the real thing," she rationalized, tucking her new acquisition under her arms.

I started to giggle. No matter how things changed in life, there were some things you could always count on. "Okay, fine," I said. "Besides, I want to thank Miguel. After all, if it weren't for him, none of this would have happened."

"Totally. And he should be happy, too. After all, thanks to you, his brother's killers are in jail." Jodi's eyes took on a mischievous gleam. "He should give you a friends-and-family discount from now on."

"Oh yeah," I agreed as we headed toward the shop. "And then I can finally get that Kate Spade purse with the sewn-on label."

Hi, Sis,

How's it hanging? This rehab place blows. Totally boring. If I have to do one more arts and crafts project I'm going to kick someone's ass, big time. I mean, talk about incentive to get off drugs—just making sure I never have to come back to this hellhole would be a good enough reason for me. But hey, at least I'm getting well. I've even stopped puking three times a day.

So, they tell me during sessions that the ninth step to recovery is to say you're sorry to all those people you hurt with your addiction. Well, I'm actually only on step two, but you know me—I hate to go in order. So here you are, the official Lulu/Maddy apology Top 10:

1. I'm sorry I stole from you.
2. I'm sorry I trashed your apartment.
3. I'm sorry I made you worry about me.
4. I'm sorry I let Drummer use your toothbrush to clean his hash pipe out. (Though he did rinse it out afterward, I swear!)
5. I'm sorry I borrowed your DKNY top and lost it and then told you that someone broke into your apartment and stole it.
6. I'm sorry I broke that window to make "The Great DKNY Robbery" more believable to the cops.
7. I'm sorry about that time I told your high school boyfriend that you still had a Hanson poster hanging on your bedroom wall. (Though for the record I never thought he'd dump you over that and tell the whole school!)
8. I'm sorry for the time I drew on your face with permanent marker during your pre–senior prom nap. (But honestly, it really did look like a cool henna tattoo.)
9. Oh and remember that time mom accused you of being preggo? Well, that pregnancy test actually belonged to my friend Dora, but she didn't want her mother to kill her (they're very Catholic!) so we told Mom it was from you. Since you were so much older, we really didn't think Mom would freak as much as she did!
10. Hmm, can't think of a tenth thing, but I'm sure I'll think of more in the next few weeks. After all, there's not much else to do here.

Your loving sister,
Lu

CHAPTER TWENTY-ONE

Two weeks later Lulu was released from rehab and Dad threw a party to celebrate her recovery and my new job. Cindi decorated the yard with brightly colored balloons and streamers and Dad fired up the grill. Lulu and her friends hung out by the back wall, chattering about college applications and boys (not necessarily in that order) while Jodi and I hung out on the swings, sipping homemade margaritas. Cindi waddled over (she was getting quite big) with a heaping tray of cookies and coerced us to eat more than our share. She really was growing on me, now that I'd taken the time to get to know her a little better. She was smart and funny and sweet; it was no wonder my dad was crazy about her. Sure, it was still weird to consider someone younger than me as my stepmom, but they so obviously adored each other, it was hard to object.

"Hey, where's the party?" The back door swung open and, to my surprise, Mom stepped through. She was wearing a bright yellow sundress and looked tanned and healthy. Lulu bounced off the wall and ran to hug her. I waited until they were done, then gave her a squeeze myself. Dad greeted her cheerfully and even Cindi shook her hand hello. I could tell Mom still wasn't quite sure about the whole Cindi situation, but she was doing her best to remain pleasant for the family's sake.

We ate at the picnic table, chattering throughout the meal about the future. I told everyone about my new job and my new apartment in LA. Lulu chattered about rehab and all the celebrities she'd met there. And, under Mom's own urging, Cindi shyly gave us an update on the baby. It was a girl and they were going to call her Sarah, after Cindi's grandmother.

It was weird, for sure. But it was also kind of nice. After dinner Mom took me aside, leading me into the house. We sat down on the sofa.

"So you're okay with all of this?" I asked. "I mean, all of us hanging out together?"

"It's not my favorite thing in the world to see your dad with someone else," Mom admitted. "But he seems really happy. And I'm glad about that. The two of us were miserable for so long."

"What about you, though? Are you happy?"

"You know what, Maddy? I am. I really am." She smiled. "In the last month I've had more adventures than I've had in a lifetime. I've traveled the world. Tried new things. Met new people. And that never would have happened if your dad didn't leave." She shook her head. "Believe me, I'm still angry as hell over what he did. But at the same time, in a strange way, I'm grateful. My life is good now. I'm stronger and more self-reliant and I'm starting to live for me for the first time ever. And that never would have happened if I stayed in my loveless marriage."

"I'm glad you're having fun, Mom," I said, giving her a hug.

"But enough about me," she said. "What about you? You've gotten the job you always wanted, but for some reason you don't seem happy."

She always had been perceptive. "You're right," I admitted.

"Why is that?"

"Well, right around the time you left, this new guy came to work at News Nine …" I started from the beginning and told her the whole sordid tale, leaving out, of course, the one-night stand and accidental Ecstasy in the desert parts. There were some things you didn't ever share with your mother, even if she was suddenly all liberated and stuff.

I ended with Jen's pregnancy. "He says it won't change things between us, but I don't see how that could be the case."

"That's a tough one," my mother mused. "Does he want to be part of the child's life?"

"Yes. Unfortunately."

"*Not* unfortunately," Mom scolded. "Maddy, that's a good sign. He lives up to his responsibilities. Would you rather he be the type that runs away? A deadbeat dad?"

"I guess not."

"You know, Maddy. The world is changing. Families are being redefined. Look at us tonight, for goodness sake. And I believe if you find someone you truly love, you shouldn't let a little conflict get in the way."

"But this isn't like he has some mole on his left shoulder. It's eighteen years of responsibility."

"I'm not saying it will be easy. But worthwhile things hardly ever are," she said gently. "And oftentimes true love requires sacrifice. Do you really love him?"

"Oh yes," I said, my composure crumbling and tears bursting from my eyes. I'd been so strong for so long. Built up the wall and tried to tell myself I didn't care. But life without Jamie had a big empty hole in it, and it was slowly sucking the joy away. "I love him so much."

"And do you believe he loves you?"

I thought about it for a moment then nodded. No matter what happened physically between him and Jen on that last night they were together, I was sure of his feelings for me. "Yes."

My mom shrugged. "Then to me it seems pretty obvious what you should do."

And suddenly it seemed pretty obvious to me, too. "I've got to go, Mom," I said, rising to my feet. "I'll talk to you later."

She smiled. "Good luck, sweetie. Good luck!"

*

I broke every speed limit in San Diego driving to Jamie's apartment. When I got there, I couldn't find a parking spot and ended up double parking. I ran to the door and rang the bell, praying he'd be there. Praying he wasn't too mad at my ongoing stupidity and would listen to what I had to say.

"Maddy?"

The door opened and suddenly Jamie stood before me, dressed in low-slung dark blue jeans and tight white t-shirt. His beautiful green eyes looked hollow, circled in dark black, and it appeared he hadn't shaven in days. It gave him a rough, almost dangerous and unbearable sexy look that warmed something low in my belly.

"Jamie," I said. Now that I was here, I didn't know what to say.

"You haven't returned my calls," he said. The comment was matter of fact. Not judgmental. But I felt more than a squirm of guilt anyway.

"I've been … busy." How lame did that sound? How untrue. But what was I supposed to say?

"I've heard. Thank God your sister's okay." He shifted from foot to foot. "And I guess congratulations are in order, huh? On your new job."

"Thanks," I said, wondering who'd told him. Wondering what he thought about it. "How's the baby?" I asked.

He winced a little. "Jen and I went to the doctor today. They claim everything's in order."

"That's … good," I managed to say, feeling sick to my stomach all over again. As much as I loved him, it was still going to take some time to get used to the idea of him becoming, a dad. Just like with my own father's new baby.

"Yeah," he said simply, staring down at me without elaborating. I could see a million questions swirling behind his eyes, but knew he was afraid to push me. He raked a hand through his hair, and I remembered running my own fingers through those soft locks, breathing in the soapy scent of shampoo and aftershave.

"I can't take this anymore, Maddy," he said at last, his voice worn and hoarse. "I haven't slept in days. I've barely eaten. I feel sick all of the time. I've tried to stay away, give you space, but I'm at my wits' end."

I stared down at the ground. "I know. I've felt similar."

"What can I do to make you see I love you?" he asked, his tone more than a little frustrated. "I know this situation is awkward, but it doesn't have to be over between us. Why can't you see that? What we had was so special. Like nothing I've ever experienced before. And damn it, I'm not going to let you throw it all away."

"But what about Jen and the baby?" I asked, needing to be clear. "They'll need you."

"Yes. You're right." He nodded. "My baby will need a father. And Jen will likely need some financial and emotional support. I won't neglect my responsibility. I will love my child and be there for him or her no matter what. But that doesn't change anything between Jen and me. We haven't gotten back together."

"But you could," I protested. "Once the baby is born, you could." And that was the real reason, I suddenly realized, that I was resisting so much. I couldn't bear the idea that I could lose him at a moment's notice. That I could hand him my heart, only to have it crushed a few months down the road.

"No. That's impossible."

"Why?"

"Because I'm in love with someone else," he said simply, his words piercing at my heart. "Someone wonderful."

He looked down at me with love-filled eyes, and it took every ounce of Jedi mind control not to throw myself into his arms right then and there.

"This person you love," I said slowly. "What is she like?"

I could hear the smile in his voice, even as it sounded like he was holding back tears. "She's very smart for one thing. And she cares more about the truth than getting ahead. She's a loyal sister and daughter, even when she doesn't feel like it. She is a bit afraid of motorcycles but is brave enough to ride anyway. She loves to dance to eighties music and has all of Depeche Mode's bootlegs. And she's convinced John Hughes is a better director than Fredrico Fellini."

"Well, I'm sure this Fellini guy has his strong points, too, but you got to admit, Sixteen Candles is a tough act to follow."

Jamie laughed, dropping his hands to my waist and pulling me close. "This girl I love, she makes me laugh and she makes me cry. She's my muse. She encourages me to follow my dreams." He dropped his mouth to my ear. "I got a new agent," he whispered. "And he's very excited about the manuscript proposal I sent him."

"Oh my God!" I looked up at him, bursting with pride. "That's so awesome! Congratulations."

He looked down on me with loving eyes rimmed with tears. "I couldn't have done any of this without you, you know."

I dropped my eyes to the ground. I didn't know what to do. He took my chin in his hand and tilted my head to look back at him.

"I know I'm asking a lot," he said earnestly. "I know it'll be hard at times. But I will do anything to ensure that things work out between us. Anything."

"But …" My mind was blanking with all the practical reasons I knew I should be resisting more. "But I'm moving to LA. I can't stay here, you know."

"I'd never ask you to," Jamie said, sounding astonished that I'd think he would. "But I called some buddies at my old production company. They just won a contract with an LA-based reality show—'Who Wants to Marry a Movie Star.' It's at least six months of shooting work."

"And after that?"

"I'll find something else," he said sincerely. "I'll make it work—whatever it takes."

"But I don't want you to rearrange your whole life … because of me—"

"Don't you get it?" he asked, shaking his head. "I don't care. It's worth it. *You're* worth it."

My heart fluttered at his words. He thought I was worth it. No one had ever said those words to me before. No one ever made sacrifices like this for me before. And now it was my turn to make a sacrifice for him. To trust him. Believe him. Give him a chance.

"You mean that?" I asked, my one last question before accepting the idea that perhaps all my dreams really could come true.

"With all my heart." He pressed a hand to his chest to emphasize his point.

"Well …" I realized my whole body was trembling as I made my decision. "I guess we could … you know, give it a try."

His face lit into a bright smile and his whole body seemed to sag with relief at my words. Then, he threw his arms around me and pulled me close. I rejoiced in his familiar scent tickling my nose. I'd missed this. I'd missed him.

"You won't regret this," he murmured in my ear. "I won't let you down. I love you, Madeline Madison."

"I love you, too, Jamie Hayes."

And then he kissed me. And somehow, as he pressed his lips against mine, sending my pulse racing in the way that only he could do, I realized he could be right. This could actually work.

And hell, if not, I guess I could always pitch a "True Love That Kills" piece at the next *Newsline* story meeting.

It'd probably get great ratings.

ABOUT THE AUTHOR

Mari Mancusi used to wish she could become a vampire back in high school. But she ended up in another blood sucking profession—journalism—instead. Today she works as a freelance TV producer and author of books for teens and adults. When not writing, Mari enjoys traveling, cooking, goth clubbing, watching cheesy horror movies, and her favorite guilty pleasure—videogames. A graduate of Boston University and a two time Emmy Award winner, she lives in Austin, Texas with her husband Jacob, daughter Avalon, and their dog Mesquite.

Website: http://www.marimancusi.com

Facebook: http://www.facebook.com/bloodcovenvampires

Twitter: @marimancusi

Email: mari@marimancusi.com

OTHER BOOKS BY MARI MANCUSI

Skater Boy

Tomorrow Land

Alternity

First Kiss Club books
http://www.firstkissclub.com

Blood Coven Vampire novels
http://www.bloodcovenvampires.com/books.html

Coming fall 2013: *Scorched*